Death of a Prominent Citizen

WRI

ALSO BY CORA HARRISON
FROM CLIPPER LARGE PRINT

Death of a Novice
Murder at the Queen's Old Castle

Death of a Prominent Citizen

Cora Harrison

W F HOWES LTD

This large print edition published in 2021 by
W F Howes Ltd
Unit 5, St George's House, Rearsby Business Park,
Gaddesby Lane, Rearsby, Leicester LE7 4YH

1 3 5 7 9 10 8 6 4 2

First published in the United Kingdom in 2020
by SEVERN HOUSE PUBLISHERS LTD

A CIP catalogue record for this book is available
from the British Library

ISBN 978 1 00404 111 4

Typeset by Palimpsest Book Production Limited,
Falkirk, Stirlingshire

Printed and bound by
T J Books in the UK

MIX
Paper from
responsible sources
FSC
www.fsc.org   FSC® C013056

*This book is dedicated to my friend,
Cath Thompson and to my son, William Harrison.*

CHAPTER 1

The Reverend Mother shifted uneasily in her chair. The chair itself was not at fault. The committee dealing with slum clearance in Cork met in the luxurious surroundings of the Imperial Hotel on the South Mall of the city, and the chair, like everything else in the Imperial Hotel, was superbly comfortable. It was the typed figures before her that had caused unease. *On average twelve families live in each house;* she read the words without much surprise, but with a feeling of deep sadness.

It seemed extraordinary and deeply depressing. Years had gone by since Ireland had attained its freedom. And now over two hundred people were living along a city lane in thirteen houses that were declared to be, not only unfit for human habitation, but incapable of being rendered fit for human habitation. Four or five storeys high, relics of the long-gone Georgian age, these houses were sinking back into the marshy soil beneath them.

And then her eyes narrowed as her attention was caught by another sheet of paper. She picked up the page again. There must be some mistake.

'Sixty-one families,' she said aloud. 'Surely sixty-one families amount to more than two hundred people.'

'We count each family as three and one-third units, Reverend Mother,' said the bishop's secretary with an air of pride in his superior mathematical ability.

The Reverend Mother thought about the families in her school, thought about the children, those long lines of numerous brothers and sisters – *units*, she supposed that she should call them – all playing on the steps of those appalling houses, and their parents, more *units*, she supposed . . .

'In my experience an average family would number about twelve, not three and one-third,' she said sharply. 'So you could have up to seven hundred persons in those thirteen houses.' Her own figures appalled her, but she thought they were more accurate than those which had been produced for the committee to examine.

There was a murmur from those sitting around the table drawn up in front of a cosy fire. The Reverend Mother's position in the hierarchy of Cork, her forcible personality, her reputation for speaking her mind, made them reluctant to contradict her, but all looked deeply uncomfortable. Only one was brave enough to speak out.

'Dear Reverend Mother,' said Julie Clancy, 'God in his mercy tempers the wind to the shorn lamb. You forget that, although it may be true that a frightening amount of children are born to that class of people, many die in the early years.'

'To be replaced by others,' said the Reverend Mother, trying to put to the back of her mind the human suffering involved in these births and deaths.

She eyed Miss Clancy with dislike. What was the woman doing here? Representing the very wealthy Charlotte Hendrick, so she said. Lived with her, was a cousin upon her mother's side, served as some sort of companion and house-keeper to her. And was now sent along to this meeting where questions should have been asked of a prominent slum landlord about the appalling conditions in which Charlotte Hendrick's tenants lived. A perfunctory mention of illness, probably feigned. After all, Sister Mary Immaculate had seen the wealthy Mrs Hendrick emerging from Cork railway station in a taxicab only two days previously.

Much easier, she thought, for Charlotte to send a deputy who could plead ignorance. And Julie Clancy looked as though she were thoroughly enjoying herself, listening to an account of the living conditions of the poor of Cork. An unpleasant child, the Reverend Mother seemed to remember, looking back into the past days of over fifty years ago. One of those cousinly visits. Yes, there was something lurking at the back of her mind about Julie Clancy. Something that had never been quite resolved.

'In the meantime . . .' The new manager, Philip Monahan, was getting impatient. Not unsympathetic, decided the Reverend Mother, but wary of being sidetracked. 'In the meantime, I think we may all agree on voting the money for some new housing to be built for the unfortunate tenants of those houses which cannot be made fit for human inhabitation.'

'Why not make them fit? Could do a bit of repair work to the roof. Up to the tenants to keep the place in order. No point in renewing windows for people like that. They only break them again.' Mr Mulcahy was an accountant, but one of those people who had a view on every subject.

The owner of a building firm, sitting next to him, scowled. He was definitely on the side of building new houses, but he said nothing and allowed the accountant to narrate, with practised fluency, a little anecdote about out-of-work men standing around, and horror of horrors, smoking expensive cigarettes and ignoring a front door hanging from one hinge. The Reverend Mother thought briefly about explaining the addictive power of cigarettes and the emptiness of the lives of these people, but decided to save her breath.

'True, true.' Julie Clancy nodded sadly and the bishop, from his position as chair of the meeting, lifted his hands and sighed.

'And, of course, as Mrs Hendrick asked me to point out and I'm sure I need not remind the committee that the rent is minuscule. Minuscule.'

4

Julie was encouraged by the episcopal nod in her direction.

Modest, if paid by one family, thought the Reverend Mother, but a fair sum when paid by more than sixty families. Again she did the sum in her head. This landlord business was lucrative once you admitted the possibility of cramming each room as though it was possible to store human beings like logs of wood. She had heard of a place where families could only call one corner of the room their own and fitted their numerous children into that confined space.

'If only these people could be made to take responsibility for themselves and their children and not expect the taxpayer to step in.' The owner of a wine shop had the air of being personally aggrieved by this tale of poverty.

'Very much the point that Mrs Hendrick wished me to make,' put in Julie Clancy. She had taken a small notebook from her capacious handbag and was studying a closely written page – probably of instructions.

The Reverend Mother sighed again. These meetings went around and around in circles. Eventually it would end after a wasted morning. Resolutions would be passed, a good lunch would be served. Everyone would make a note of the next meeting in three months' time, shake hands and part.

Still the new manager had a determined air. She gave him an encouraging look. 'Perhaps Mr Monahan would remind us of his surveyor's report,' she suggested and was pleased when she saw the keen, eager look in his eyes.

'As I said, the houses are impossible to repair.' He raised one hand forbiddingly before the suggestion of some remedial work on the roofs could be suggested. 'The problem is, ladies and gentlemen, these houses were built two hundred years ago when the city of Cork was just a few houses on two islands – now North Main Street and South Main Street – surrounded by marshes. Most of this slum property that we are discussing . . .' He looked around him, enjoying, thought the Reverend Mother, the slight frisson of revulsion that the use of the word 'slum' had evoked. 'Most of the slum property which is of such concern to us now was then, as the city expanded, just built on this marshy ground. And now, two hundred years later, the foundations have slipped. I have to tell you all, and I would like it put on record, that I am deeply worried that some fatality will occur, sooner or later. And in the meantime, these houses are damp, very damp, full of mildew and crumbling plaster and infested with . . .' He stopped and gave an apologetic look at Julie Clancy who had drawn in her breath and was shuddering with horror.

'Rats,' said the Reverend Mother firmly. 'Rats is the word that you are looking for, Mr Monahan. The houses of the poor *are* infested; in fact, they are quite overrun with rats. I have a rat fund which I use to buy rat poison for the unfortunate women who have to live in such conditions.' She noted the bishop's secretary's expression of distaste and remembered, too late, that he was due to audit her accounts in a week's time. On the whole she liked to hide such matters as the purchase of rat poison, and sweets for the children, under some vague heading, such as educational supplies. However, it was too late to withdraw now, so she raised her chin, sat very upright, slipped her hands into the wide sleeves of her habit and waited to see what the reaction of the other committee members would be and what homespun wisdom would be offered to the denizens of these crumbling houses.

Julie Clancy, however, was before them all. 'There is another matter which dear Mrs Hendrick asked me to mention,' she said, looking around the table. 'Of course,' she went on, 'it may be decided that the ratepayers and the taxpayers cannot be asked to fund this grandiose plan of giving brand new houses to those who improvidently made no provision for themselves, but just in case that the decision is taken to proceed with this scheme, Mrs Hendrick wanted to know what compensation will be paid to landlords whose tenants have been seduced by the offer of a new house. Alternatively, she suggests that the council should offer a fair price for the landlord's investment and purchase the properties.' Julie sat back and looked happily around the table.

The bishop was looking shocked, but perhaps the use of the word 'seduced' on the lips of a lady accounted for that. Most of the rest of the committee, certainly all who had slum property to let, were looking interested, several leaning forward eagerly. Years of neglecting their properties, years of trying to extract rent from people who had little to spare, years of perfunctory repairs and half-hearted attempts to shore up the crumbling buildings had drastically reduced the value of a property portfolio. If the suggestion from the very wealthy widow Mrs Charlotte Hendrick – that the houses be purchased by the city council – were to be adopted, then suddenly this slum property could double in value to them.

'The monies which the city possesses are, as it is, still not enough to build decent housing for people who have lived in these conditions of squalor and deprivation for most of their lives,' said Philip Monahan drily. 'If, my lord,' he went on, looking across the table at the bishop, 'such monies were used now for a different purpose, I'm afraid that I would have to resign from this scheme and, in justice to myself, and with a view to obtaining employment in another city council, I would have to make public the reasons for my resignation.'

Oh, well done! The Reverend Mother uttered the words silently. She did like a man who would take a gamble and stick to his principles. Aloud, she said, 'I'm sure that all members of the committee have complete confidence in Mr Monahan and are willing to be guided by his expertise and by his experience. You have, I understand, Mr Monahan, worked in Drogheda, Louth and in Kerry.'

'Indeed,' he said, and inclined his head in her direction. Sitting very upright, he was very at ease, fingering through the pages of the report on the slum conditions in the city of Cork.

There was silence for a moment and then all eyes went to the chairman, clad in his episcopal robes.

'Well,' said the bishop, adroitly glancing at the clock in order to remind all of the pleasurable part of this meeting, 'I think that we can leave all those matters in your capable hands, Mr Monahan, and we will meet again on the first Monday of next month when you will show us the report from a builder as to the exact cost of these new houses. As for the possible purchase of the properties that we have been discussing, well . . .' said the bishop, drawing out his gold watch from some concealed pocket and studying it with interest, '. . . well, that is a matter which will, also, have to be left for another day. Thank you, everyone, for your time and attention, and I now declare this meeting closed.'

And then, as all got to their feet and made their way towards the dining room, he said, 'Reverend Mother, could I delay you for a minute on a different matter? I've had a message from your cousin, Mrs Hendrick.'

'Certainly, my lord.' The Reverend Mother rose

from her seat and went towards him. What now? she asked herself impatiently.

Julie Clancy knew all about it; she could see that. Had been waiting eagerly for the minute. Not even diverted by the delicious smell of roast beef which was wafting through the opened door as the committee members hastened to eat their well-earned lunch. She was beside the bishop now, almost panting with eagerness, looking proudly at the page covered with Charlotte Hendrick's distinctive scrawl.

'I understand that Mrs Hendrick, like all responsible citizens, is desirous of making her will,' he began. 'You, Reverend Mother, have had, Miss Clancy informs me, a letter about this.'

'On changing her will, so I understand, my lord. On the death of her husband many years ago, Mrs Hendrick informed all of her cousins, and her cousins' offspring, that she had made a will dividing her estate into equal shares for her seven nearest relatives.' Until the recent letter the Reverend Mother had forgotten about the whole business. Charlotte Hendrick was a good seven years younger than she and probably took immense care of herself. It had seemed unlikely that the convent would ever benefit from this legacy. 'I believe that she now wishes to leave nothing to six out of the seven and to gift the remaining person with the whole estate. The one who can prove themselves the most worthy,' added the Reverend Mother, and was not sorry to hear a

10

sharp note in her voice. What an abominable business! Expecting elderly and middle-aged people to jump through a hoop for Charlotte Hendrick's amusement.

The bishop looked a bit annoyed by this terse summary of the wealthy widow's intentions. 'So I understand and I believe that you have refused the invitation to put forward a proposition,' he said sharply.

The Reverend Mother looked at him with surprise. 'My Lord,' she said, 'I did not feel that you would wish a nun in holy orders to stay overnight in a secular home and that was one of the conditions.'

'Well, well, there are always concessions if the matter warrants them,' he said testily. 'I think that you should accept your cousin's invitation and I know that you will make the case for your convent to have whatever sum of money that the dear lady will leave behind when she goes to her everlasting reward,' he finished piously and the Reverend Mother, inwardly seething with rage, bowed her head obediently. She watched as he followed the rest of the committee into the Imperial Hotel dining room. Julie, she noticed, lurked in the hall, waiting, no doubt, to have a 'little word' before the Reverend Mother left the luxurious precincts of the Imperial Hotel. It was, by now, accepted by the committee that the Reverend Mother's duties in her school did not permit her to stay for lunch, but why was Julie not heading towards the flesh pots? Probably her mistress told her to come straight home. What an unpleasant woman! And now, to crown all, she was worming herself into the bishop's good graces.

'I bet he knows to the last farthing how much Charlotte Hendrick is worth,' she muttered to herself as she glanced out of the window to verify that it was still raining.

'He may not be right. Property is not worth as much as it used to be before the war,' said a voice from behind her. 'Still, I understand Mrs Hendrick does a bit of moneylending, in addition. Charges a fine interest, so I'm told, lends her tenant the rent when they can't pay. They know her down the quays as "old Mrs Hundred-Percent", if you will forgive me mentioning this, Reverend Mother. I understand that she lends a shilling and then wants two shillings back.'

'My dear Mr Monahan, my cousin, like a good businesswoman, may make as much money as she can in the city of Cork, but in these uncertain times she has most of her fortune snuggly invested in lucrative shares in England or in a South African gold mine,' said the Reverend Mother. She spoke crisply and without turning around, conscious of a feeling of irritation within herself that she had betrayed her inner feelings about the bishop to this young man. How appalling, though, of Charlotte Hendrick to make money from the terrible poverty around her. So if a tenant got lucky and had a day's work unloading a ship on the docks, Charlotte would take most of his earnings. 'The East Rand Mine, in South Africa, I believe,' she said aloud.

'Good,' he said calmly. 'All the more for you, if she decides that your charities are a worthy cause. You wouldn't put in a good word for me and my council house scheme, would you? We could put up a statue if she wished. Tell her that. I know a man who can do them cheaply; does a great job, makes concrete look like the finest limestone,' he finished.

'I don't believe that I have much influence over my cousin,' said the Reverend Mother. 'And I'm not sure that she would be too interested in a statue. In any case, she is a good seven years younger than I and may well live for another fifteen or twenty years. I think that you might be better off to pursue your plans about funding housing through local taxation. Once the tax is established then you have a solid source of income.' She drew in a deep breath. She still felt shaken by the stark figures in his report. 'Cork's problems will not be solved by one legacy,' she finished.

'You're right and you're wrong,' he said thoughtfully. 'I purpose to explore all avenues. Even one family taken out of one of those places is a small victory. Once I make a start I can steamroller ahead.'

And with that, he left her abruptly. Fizzing with energy, she thought as she watched him burst through the doors of the Imperial, beating the

13

lethargic porter by a good few yards. A gust of damp air swept through the hallway before the porter managed to reach the door and shut it out. The Reverend Mother looked after Philip Monahan as he crossed the road. She envied him his youth and his energy, but not the herculean task that he had set himself. She fished out her watch and held it some distance from her eyes as she peered at the time. Old age, she thought sadly. Bit by bit, it would conquer her. The sharp vision of her youth had gone. The scent of flowers had dimmed as well and recently she had found herself asking children to repeat what they had said. A surge of impatience ran through her. She had so much more to accomplish. She took her umbrella briskly from the stand and declined the porter's offer to call her a taxi. A quick walk would do her good, would help to banish that feeling of near despair which had descended upon her as she had studied Mr Monahan's report. She had almost reached the hall door when the porter's eyes showed her that she was to be accosted.

'Oh, Reverend Mother, could I just have a quick word.'

No getting out of it. Julie Clancy must have been lurking, waiting for the brash young man to take himself off.

'Of course, Julie,' she said, endeavouring to sound cordial. She looked back. The fire had begun to go out in the room where the committee had met. It was beginning to look uninviting on this chilly, damp day of early February. Hopefully the interview would not last too long.

'Shall we come in here?' she said and firmly led the way to a seat beside the draughty window.

Julie followed. Her plump face had lost its usual ingratiating smile and the corners of her mouth were turned down.

'It's just that I wondered whether you might talk to Mrs Hendrick. She would listen to you. She has such a good opinion of you, Reverend Mother. The whole of Cork has. You might be able to influence her.'

'You're talking about this will, are you, Julie?' The Reverend Mother considered the woman in front of her. Been with Charlotte Hendrick for the past twenty years, she reckoned. 'Companion', she supposed, was the woman's title, not even something as respectable as a housekeeper or a secretary, no, more of a dogsbody or a whipping boy when the elderly and wealthy widow felt out of humour with the world. 'What's the matter?' the Reverend Mother asked more gently as she saw the woman's eyes fill with tears.

'I'm afraid of being destitute in my old age.' A sob escaped Julie and she turned towards the window, rubbing at the damp with a forefinger. The Reverend Mother winced at the desolate, high-pitched squeak from the glass, but she restrained an impulse to deflect the finger. She had begun to understand. 'I thought that I would be secure at least . . .'

'You had thought that she would leave you a competence?' *The competence of life, I will allow you,* the young King Henry V had said to Falstaff. Julie, more worthy than Falstaff, though less amusing, was to be left adrift in an unmerciful world. She had served an unpleasant and demanding woman through all of these years and now she risked poverty and even starvation. Julie must now be nearly sixty, overweight, asthmatic and lacking in intelligence. The Reverend Mother had always found her irritatingly unpleasant, but now she looked at her with pity. 'You don't think that she might leave you the house, perhaps?' she ventured. The house would, of course, be far too large for Julie to keep up, but it was a most beautiful Queen Anne house, kept in perfect order, and might be sold for quite a substantial sum.

Julie shook her head. 'No, she told me. The house, everything, will go to the one person, the one of her seven nearest relatives who she thinks will make the best use of her money, the one who is most worthy and most capable.'

'And you don't think that will be you, is that right?' A stupid question. Poor Julie would never stand out as the most worthy or the most capable. She was weeping openly now, gasping into a lace handkerchief and there was an ominous wheeze as she gulped for air.

'She promised. She always said that she would make no favourites. Her property was to be evenly divided between her seven living relations: you and your cousin, Lucy, from her father's side of the family. And from her mother's side of the family, me, my brother, Claude, and then my cousin Brenda and Brenda's niece, daughter of Brenda's brother who died a few years ago. And, of course, there is Professor Hendrick, her husband's nephew. He's a great favourite of hers. So that makes seven heirs.' Julie wheezed noisily and her plump chest rose and fell in her efforts to take air into her lungs.

The Reverend Mother went to the door. The lounging porter straightened his back and came to attend upon her.

'I don't think that I can stay for lunch,' she told him, 'but perhaps you could bring me some tea, and could you call a taxi please. Tell the man it's for Bachelor's Quay.'

She would have to pay for Julie's taxi from her own purse, but hopefully the tea would be paid for by the bishop out of whatever monies financed the expensive lunch that all were now enjoying.

The porter was back quickly with the tea, glad of a little occupation, she supposed as, for the sake of charity, she endeavoured to dismiss the idea that he had been listening at the door and was eager to hear the rest of the story. He poured the tea with a solicitous air and whispered to her that one of the committee, a Mr Bennett, had ordered a taxi which had arrived a bit early. The taxi was waiting outside the door of the hotel and the man, when he had finished a cup of tea, would take the

Reverend Mother and the lady to Bachelor's Quay and be back in plenty of time. No hurry, no worry! He just about stopped himself from giving her a wink, but she understood clearly that Mr Bennett would be the one who paid for the little trip to Bachelor's Quay and thanked him sedately and without compunction. After all, she told her conscience, Mr Bennett, while he had been luxuriating in tirades against the improvident poor, had repeatedly said that he would never grudge helping a hard-working person. Julie might be not too clever, but she was certainly hard-working in the service of her rich cousin.

The hot tea, she was glad to see, was doing Julie a lot of good, but as soon as the large, slightly protruding eyes started to fill with tears again, she decided that it was time to apply a little hope to the situation.

'Of course, Julie,' she said in her most bracing manner, 'it's possible that Mrs Hendrick will leave her entire fortune to you. Why don't you think of a scheme to make very good use of her money? I have an idea,' she went on hurriedly as, faced with the look of total blankness on Julie's face, she knew that she had to improvise quickly. 'What about turning the house at Bachelor's Quay into a retirement home for elderly gentlewomen?' she ventured. 'It is such a pretty place and has a lovely view of the river. And ten bedrooms, I seem to remember. You would charge a suitable sum, to each guest, of course, and that would mean that you could keep on the existing staff and manage the house in the same efficient way as you have always done.'

The Reverend Mother got to her feet, feeling she had come up with rather a good scheme and decided to ignore the look of slight panic on Julie's face. When it came to the time for all to outline their schemes for the amusement of a bored and wealthy widow, why then, she would assist Julie to put the idea across and could chime in with admiration and slip in a few extra suggestions. She would brief her cousin Lucy to assist her with that. Much easier than trying to impress matters upon Julie in her present mood of despondency. She ignored Julie's dismal prediction that Mrs Hendrick had not long to live, reminding her sharply that the woman was a good seven years younger than herself, and concentrating on bracing platitudes. While turning to check the weather from the mist-covered window, she noticed that Julie had removed from her handbag the report on the living conditions in slum properties in Cork and had slipped it under a blotter on the table. It, like all the other reports from the efficient Mr Monahan, was marked on the top with the name of the intended recipient and would probably be posted on by the Imperial Hotel. No doubt, Julie feared to face a volley of outraged fury if she handed it over to her cousin and employer. It was, however, none of her business so she ignored the action and glanced out of the window. The rain was still falling and the overflow from the gutters was starting to splay out across the road. Time for them to leave before the flood mounted on to the pavement.

'Mustn't keep your taxi waiting, must we?' She said the words loudly enough to bring the porter to the door. He ushered them out, whispered something to the taxi driver, no doubt an assurance that Mr Bennett was calmly sipping his sherry and swallowing his soup. The meeting, because of Mr Monahan's startling plan and insistence on discussing his survey, had lasted a good hour longer than usual. The taxi man might as well make the short journey to Bachelor's Quay as sit, twiddling his thumbs, outside the door of the Imperial Hotel. Certainly he sped off with an air of enjoyment and Julie, sitting primly in the back, would also enjoy the ride.

The Reverend Mother breathed a sigh of relief. Julie was off her hands and she would dispel her own annoyance at the bishop's interference into family matters with a brisk walk down the quays and across the bridges. I must phone Lucy, she thought, and the prospect of a gossip with her cousin was enough to cheer her. Lucy, like herself, was supposed to be a beneficiary of the original will and would, perhaps, be a guest at the Hendrick household this evening.

It should, thought the Reverend Mother, prove to be an evening crammed with embarrassment. She was not looking forward to it. On the other hand, she would enjoy her own contribution to

20

the evening. And it would do none of those people any harm to hear a few home truths about the poverty and desperation amongst those with whom she worked. She reflected over her fellow guests. Why, she wondered, didn't Julie Clancy confide in her brother Claude? And wasn't Claude Clancy the owner of Clancy's Bar in Academy Street? Surely he should be able to care for his sister if she were to be thrown out of her home on the death of Charlotte Hendrick.

CHAPTER 2

'**W**hat a good thing that you are going after all. Well done the bishop, for forcing you to go. You need a little break from that convent, and it's been lucky for me, too,' said Lucy as soon as the Reverend Mother took her place in the back of the luxurious car and placed her feet upon the stone hot water bottle. 'You'll never guess the fuss Rupert made about taking the car out on a day like this,' she went on. 'The car, mind you, never mind about his wife. Didn't want *his* car to go out in case of floods. Once he heard that it would mean that I would have to leave you in the lurch, I told him that you would probably have to walk through flooded streets, w*ell*, he had to be quiet then and just mutter to himself. Didn't want me to go, in the first place, of course. Been irritable about it all the week.'

'I suppose the quays might flood,' said the Reverend Mother resignedly. She should have thought of that. Two days of non-stop rain and a high tide; all it needed now was for that south-easterly wind to strengthen and to blow that high tide up the river channel and the city would be flooded. It would, she thought regretfully, have given her a good excuse not to attend this stupid affair. 'I hadn't realized,' she said aloud. 'Why didn't you phone me, Lucy? I've been busy and didn't think about the weather.'

Her afternoon had been taken up with consoling and making arrangements for a family of children who had, on their return home from school, found that their mother had died of a haemorrhage while trying to give birth to the tenth member of the family. The children, already bereft of their father, had come running back to her with the tragic tale. She banished the scene from her mind. She had long learned that to dwell too much on such matters made her less effectual in dealing with them. She had made the best possible arrange-ments for the orphaned children and now would turn her mind to other matters.

'I suppose Rupert is not too keen on you putting in a bid for Charlotte Hendrick's fortune, is he?' she asked with a half-smile and imagined the outrage of the man who was the foremost lawyer in the city and certainly not short of money in any way.

'Men are so stupid; it takes a mother to make provision for her family. There's my poor Charlotte – I even went to the trouble of naming her after the unpleasant woman – well, she could do with a nice little present. Not a great match for her, poor sweet, but she would have her own way. In fact, I'd love to do something for all of my poor girls.' Lucy sighed sadly over the fate of her daughters, all of whom had made good marriages to wealthy or reasonably well-off men.

'Nonsense,' said the Reverend Mother. 'You just want to see what is going on and no doubt you'll get a few good stories out of it.'

'I don't really suppose that I can prove I am the most worthy to have her money,' said Lucy with an irrepressible giggle, 'but it will be fun to hear what everyone will say. And now that you are going too, well, we can have a good gossip before we go to sleep. I've told Julie to put us in one of those lovely old rooms at the front of the house. I must say it for Charlotte, she has the place beautifully decorated and incredibly comfortable. It will be like the old days, won't it? Do you remember the time we went to that dance at the Clancys, only months before Charlotte's mother died, and James Hendrick was there, flirting with everyone? We stayed awake half the night talking about him. Neither of us cared for him, but he was supposed to be very rich. Whosoever would have thought that little Charlotte would marry him? Marry a Protestant!'

'He had money, lots and lots of money,' murmured the Reverend Mother. 'Shares in a gold mine in Africa, I understand. Charlotte would have been almost twenty years younger than James Hendrick,' she continued. 'Her mother was dead and her father had taken to the drink. I suppose she reasoned just like that French king – Henri IV,

24

wasn't it, who said that Paris was worth a mass. She's certainly been living in the lap of luxury ever since she married James Hendrick.'

'That's what I like about you nuns,' said Lucy affectionately. 'You are all so thoroughly mercenary. I'm surprised that the bishop had to force you to come. I thought that you'd be dying to get your hands on her fortune.'

'Waste of time,' said the Reverend Mother briefly. 'I know what's going to happen. She's going to leave it all to her late husband's nephew. She should leave it to poor Julie, of course. After all, she's had that unfortunate woman at her beck and call for the last twenty years.'

'Ah, but she hates her,' said Lucy shrewdly. 'That happens, doesn't it? Charlotte treats her badly and then justifies it by convincing herself that Julie is a person to dislike. And, of course, Julie responds by slipping in sly little gibes and pretending that she didn't mean them. They hate each other, really. No, she'd probably love the idea of disappointing Julie.'

The Reverend Mother was silent, but only for a moment. She could say things to Lucy that she would not dream of allowing anyone else in the world to overhear. The window between them and the chauffeur was securely shut. 'Not a very likable person, though, was she? Julie Clancy, I mean. I was thinking about her as a child. There was something, wasn't there? Of course she was about ten years younger than we, wasn't she?'

'You're thinking of that time that she tried to murder her baby brother, aren't you?' Lucy gave a chuckle. 'Took the brake off his pram, didn't she? Luckily the pram ended up in a hedge and didn't crash against the stone wall and tip the baby into the road. Brenda saw her and told everyone. Julie's mother was furious because Brenda kept on saying: "She did it a'purpose, she did, she did, I sawed her!" Do you remember that? We went off to play tennis and left them to it. It rumbled on for the whole afternoon. Do you remember Charlotte making a big fuss of the baby – it was Claude, of course, wasn't it? And of course the more she fussed over Claude, the more poor old Julie was in disgrace. We never liked any of those Clancy children much, did we? Funny! Anyway, why are you so convinced that Nicholas will inherit, not Julie or Brenda or Claude or even you or I?'

'I saw Dr Scher before I came out. He always knows all the gossip and, of course, the university is a great gossip shop. Dr Scher gives a lecture there about pathology once a week and comes away every time with all the news,' said the Reverend Mother. 'He told me that Charlotte is very excited about Nicholas writing a book about Vikings and their impact on Cork. Apparently Hendrick is a Viking name, according to him, though I thought the story we had been told was that it was Dutch or something like that. Charlotte thinks that Nicholas's book will bring

26

great fame to the name in the city. She's already financing a trip to Scandinavia for him and under-writing the costs of producing a book. Oh, and apparently he's discovered that where her house is built was a Viking harbour.'

'I see how it is now,' said Lucy sharply. 'All those years she has been saying that she will leave her fortune divided equally between us all, but now she has to have an excuse to change that and leave everything to dear Nicholas Hendrick. She's going to hold a sort of competition so that no one can accuse her of being unfair. Still, it will be entertaining, won't it?' she said more cheerfully. 'And I'm so glad that you've come. We can have lots of fun discussing everything. I'll have to round up Julie as soon as we arrive and make sure that she has done what I told her to do and put us both into one of those big bedrooms at the top of the house overlooking the river. I rang her earlier to tell her and she was making a silly fuss about it, saying Charlotte had already allocated all of the rooms, and had put us into two of those little bedrooms, with a shared bathroom, on the second floor. I'd much prefer one of those big rooms on the top floor and I told her so. Told her that we would share. It's such a lovely old Queen Anne house, isn't it? Really modernized well, but without spoiling it in any way. Charlotte has had all of the old dressing rooms turned into bathrooms; did you hear that? Cost her a fortune, but she was determined to do it. She told me that she had an unexpected dividend from one of those South African mines and she wanted to get the house done up before her South African friends came to visit. We'll have such fun.'

And I am going to waste an evening, thought the Reverend Mother resignedly. Still, she had done her best for the stricken family. As always, the neighbours, despite their own poverty, had been moved to generosity and the children, in pairs, had been shared out among the families. The Reverend Mother had raided her stores for sweets for the children and packets of tea for the adults and the whole tragic affair had become shrouded, for the children, in a mist of bewilderment and unreality. Dr Scher and she had looked at each other when all had departed and with one accord had avoided discussing the matter; she telling him about her wealthy cousin and her splendid house and he chiming in with news from the university about Professor Nicholas Hendrick, whom he deemed as a fanatic about the Viking past of Cork city and relating the excitement, even among his own medical students, about the building of a replica Viking house on Merchant's Quay on this very evening.

'Well,' she said aloud to Lucy, 'I suppose it will be an interesting evening. You'll talk about your daughters and their pressing need for money. I'll talk about women who die in childbirth because they can't afford a few shillings for a doctor.

28

Professor Nicholas Hendrick will talk about the cost of trips to Scandinavia to track down some Vikings. And what will Claude Clancy talk about? I'd imagine that he'll keep quiet about that boy of his, Michael Joseph, and his links with the Republicans, but I suppose we'll hear a lot about the need for a really luxurious club premises to enhance the reputation of Cork city and glorify the name of Clancy. And, of course, there's Brenda O'Mahony and her orphaned niece Florence, Florence Clancy, isn't it?' The Reverend Mother didn't feel that she should mention her earlier conversation with Julie so she moved away from discussing the Clancys. 'Is your Rupert, Charlotte Hendrick's lawyer?' she enquired.

'Cer-tain-ly not!' said Lucy, spacing out the syllables with a fair imitation of her husband. 'Can you imagine Rupe? Always refused to have anything to do with it in the past when she was supposed to be leaving me one seventh of her fortune and he certainly wouldn't want to have anything to do with the present affair. Even refused to hazard a guess as to the solicitor who is to turn up tomorrow morning, make her will and then inform us all about it – what fun; just as though the woman was dead! – wish I knew who the solicitor will be, but everything is shrouded in mystery. Although, I would lay a substantial bet that Rupe knows who it is. He knows everything that goes on in the legal world of Cork. Well, here we are. No flooding, so far, thank goodness. Isn't that house pretty! I love the old wheel up at the top of the house! Oh, by the way, make sure that you admire Julie's arrangement of dried flowers on the hall table. It's the same one she has done for years but you must admire it. She spends hours doing those things.'

The Hendrick house was a very pretty one. A solid, tall block of a house, built of red brick in the reign of Queen Anne, almost like a doll's house from the outside, with its regular pattern of windows in clusters of three on each storey and its central door. The house, however, was not flat like a doll's house, but a solid cube-shaped building that spanned the space between Bachelor's Quay and the two lanes that connected it to Grattan Street at the back. A tall, sharply pointed gable stood up against the slant of the slate roof on each of the four sides of the house and framed a window that gave light to the spiral staircase in the centre of the house. On the Bachelor's Quay side, just below the gable, on the top storey of the house, the central window was framed by a pair of antique oil lamps, and a large pulley wheel was just above it, preserving the memory of a time when, two hundred years ago, the house was the lynchpin of a flourishing export and import industry.

'I must say it for Charlotte. She does keep the place in perfect order,' said Lucy as they waited for the chauffeur to get out their bags and ring the front door. She peered through the window of the car at a young man kneeling precariously on a windowsill on the top storey of the tall house.

30

'He's oiling it,' she announced. 'Look at that wheel, spinning around. And the brackets for the rope. All newly painted. Look at the way the wheel is turning in the wind. And a brand-new rope, I'd warrant. It looks perfect, though I don't suppose it is ever used much these days. It's Charlotte's pride and joy, though.'

The Reverend Mother leaned across her cousin and looked up at the pulley wheel fastened to a gable at the top of the house. She had a faint memory, as a child, of walking on the quays with her father and watching a bedhead being winched up by that pulley wheel. The young man, she noticed, was checking the rope, passing it through his hand, now standing nonchalantly on the windowsill. Testing it, doubtless, before coiling it on to the wheel.

'They say that the houses on the canal in Amsterdam have all got pulley wheels like this up on the top of their houses,' said Lucy. 'A friend of Rupert's was telling us about them. Some of them are five storeys high, apparently. The Dutch used to import goods from America a couple of hundred years ago, or so these people seemed to think. The boats would come into the canals and the goods would be winched up to the storerooms of the houses.'

'Do you remember hearing that the Dutchman who built the house used to import bricks and silk, oh and flax, also, into Cork,' said the Reverend Mother. She looked up at the wheel. Yes, in perfect order. Looked as though it were ready to hoist up the baskets of silk or flax unloaded from the ships from Amsterdam. She continued to watch as the young man, turning slowly, tied the short end of the rope to a bracket above the window and wound the rest of it around the wheel. The oil lamps looked in perfect order, also. Charlotte Hendrick certainly paid tribute to her dead husband's connections with the past. The whole house bore signs of being impeccably cared for.

The Reverend Mother got out of the car leaving Lucy to give her chauffeur instructions to be sure to say there was no flood on the quays when he went to pick up his master from Pall Mall. She stood for a moment, looking down the river and feeling the south-easterly wind blow her veil back from her face. It was only at moments like these that one realized how very bad was the stench on the Cork quays, normally. Today the wind blew straight from the sea at Cork harbour and there was an unusual freshness and even, perhaps, a tinge of salt in the air. She looked down at the smooth, wide expanse of the river, now welling up almost to the level of Bachelor's Quay, and down towards Merchant's Quay. A more likely place for a harbour, she thought, than Professor Nicholas Hendrick's belief that the harbour was as far up as Bachelor's Quay, beside the Hendrick house. Though he might be correct that Vikings lived on this spot. Perhaps this present Queen Anne house, already ancient, might have been built on the foundations of yet more ancient houses. Professor Hendrick would, she guessed, be eager to prove his theory, but archaeology to suit a private purpose was an expensive business. She sighed a little when she thought of the products of those rents, extorted from poverty-stricken dwellers in the Hendrick tenements, and dividends from gold mines in Africa, being spent on investigating the past like that, when the present was full of such horrors as she had witnessed this afternoon.

At that moment a taxi arrived and parked behind Lucy's car. The young man on the windowsill came rapidly, hand over hand, down the rope to pavement level, lithely jumping the last six feet or so and landing on the pavement with a soft thud.

'Nice car,' he said to Lucy's chauffeur in a casual, sure-of-himself manner. He smiled winningly at Lucy and then at the Reverend Mother. 'I'm Mrs Hendrick's chauffeur,' he added. 'My name is Anthony. Anthony Buckley.'

'Goodness,' said Lucy, while her own chauffeur gazed disapprovingly at the young man. 'You gave us all a fright. I hope that rope is safe.'

'It's a new one. I always test it first thing, and then I take it off and test it again every few months; no test like putting my own weight on it,' said the young man casually, but his eyes were not on them, but on the newly arrived taxi behind. He spoke the last words over his shoulder as he rushed over to open the door of the taxi.

'Good evening, Mrs O'Mahony; good evening,

Miss Clancy,' he said while offering a hand to the elderly woman who struggled out of the back seat. His eyes, however, noticed the Reverend Mother, were not on Brenda O'Mahony, but on the young, short-skirted girl who bounced out from the other door and stood smiling at him.

'Goodness, Florence, you have changed. And your lovely hair! You've had it all cut off. And marcel waved! Still, it suits you.' Lucy exchanged kisses with her cousin and with her cousin's niece while the Reverend Mother decided that a handshake was adequate from a member of the church. Florence, she noticed, was scarcely polite in her greetings and appeared to be far more interested in the performance of the young chauffeur than in meeting elderly relatives and stood beside him as he manipulated the rope, moving it up and down.

'Well, this is a fine to-do, isn't it?' Brenda O'Mahony spoke tentatively and with a wary eye on the front door, while the Reverend Mother tried to remember when they had last met. Vague memories of family weddings came to her mind where she and Lucy had met their cousins, but she had little memory of Brenda since then.

'Oh, bother, I've forgotten my keys', said the young man loudly as he searched his pockets in a theatrical style. 'I usually test a new rope by tying a light weight to one end of the rope and making sure that it flies up. Works like a see-saw, one up and the other end down,' he explained

34

with a kindly air to the Reverend Mother, picking on her as the oldest person in the group.

'What about me?' asked Florence with an innocent air. 'I'm a lightweight. I only weigh seven stone.'

'Oh, Florence, darling!' Brenda was horrified. 'Overexcited!' she said in a stage whisper to Lucy. 'Florence just loves visiting dear cousin Charlotte,' she informed the Reverend Mother. 'Here, Florence, take my keys!' she scrambled in her bag, produced a formidable bunch and then watched anxiously as the young chauffeur used a thin piece of cord in order to tie the bundle to the rope, just above the large knot, and then gave a firm yank to the other side of the rope.

'You won't lose them, will you?' Brenda showed signs of regretting her hasty offer as she watched anxiously as the bunch of keys shot up towards the wheel.

'No fear, the knot on the end of the rope will stop it going any further than the centre of that weather shield above the wheel. Watch! One knot goes up and the other knot comes down,' he repeated.

Brenda's keys had disappeared within the weather shield, but now as the young man manoeuvred the other end of the rope upwards, they reappeared and began to descend.

'Told you so! It's like a seesaw. One side of the rope up and then the other side down. That pulley wheel is strong enough even to be able to take up an iron bedstead.' He handed the keys back to Brenda, but his eyes were on Florence's admiring face.

'And even a brazen monkey,' said Lucy in a low voice into the Reverend Mother's ear, before taking matters into her capable hands. 'Come along, Florence,' she said aloud. 'I haven't seen you for ages. I'm dying to hear all of your news. Oh, here comes Nicholas!'

It was Professor Hendrick himself, followed by Julie, and welcoming all as though they were his personal guests. Very at home, thought the Reverend Mother and guessed that Dr Scher was right when he predicted that this would be the heir. He was casting poor Julie into the shade and she appeared as though she were merely a servant in the house, while he played the part of the son and heir. A bit like a Viking himself, she thought. Very tall, with a prominent brow. Nose and chin jutting forward. Blond and blue-eyed. A cultured voice. Talking to Lucy while directing the young chauffeur to take their bags from the car.

'Yes,' he was saying to Lucy. 'These are my four boys. Eric, Harald, Ingmar and Odin. Aunt Charlotte wanted some furniture moved in the library, so I brought the gang along. Boys! Come and meet some more members of the family.' All Viking names, thought the Reverend Mother. This was a man with an obsession, probably a mission in life. Spent his free hours digging for Viking remains in the small garden of his Aunt Charlotte's house, and in the nearby lanes, according to Dr Scher, who had added, 'I wonder what the unfortunates who live on either side of those lanes think about a rich man spending money grubbing in the dirty soil there.' Dr Scher had sounded contemptuous, but he was not, she thought at the time, a man to be interested in the past. Medicine and avoidance of disease was what drove an elderly man like him, to work as hard as anyone half his age. 'I've had a word with Nicholas on many an occasion,' he said. 'Nabbed him in the college grounds and gave him some good advice. "I hope you and your students all wear good leather gloves and wash afterwards when you go grubbing around in that old soil; there's anthrax and many other nasty diseases to be picked up there," I said to him one day when we met in college, in the *Aula Max*. And I told him to keep his students away from Cockpit Lane – "there's typhoid and goodness knows what else, there," I said to him. But will he listen to me? Of course he won't! He's a fanatic. He will do anything to trace the past. Myself I find that the present keeps me busy enough. But he wants to relive the days gone by and I'm just a practical man who finds that the present gives him enough problems to solve.'

A fanatic, thought the Reverend Mother as she came forward and greeted the professor and shook hands with his four tall sons. A fanatic and a man with a mission. She distrusted fanatics. They invariably swept all others aside and felt that all

37

actions were permitted if they were done in order to achieve a good end. A good-looking man and the father of four good-looking sons. Early to late teens, she thought. Fine boys. All looked like him.

'So where was this Viking harbour, then?' she asked good-humouredly and listened to his fluent reasoning. No real evidence, she thought. In her own profession she distrusted those who built an argument upon a theory rather than upon hard evidence – finding that such people were often made quite unscrupulous by their determination to prove their thesis to be correct. Nevertheless, she kept up a lively conversation with him and his boys to form a screen between them to drown out Julie's petulant complaints.

Julie, the Reverend Mother gathered from the flow of excuses, had already allocated herself and her cousin Lucy to adjoining small single rooms, on either side of a shared bathroom, on the Grattan Street side of the house, apparently on the instructions of Mrs Hendrick. Lucy, fluently and with many small anecdotes, had concocted girlhood memories so that she and her cousin could share the large room, more of a suite, really, according to Julie and which was overlooking the river on Bachelor's Quay. Based purely, as far as the Reverend Mother could remember, upon their attendance at one ball in the Hendrick house, this was, of course, a tissue of lies, but told with such a wealth of small details and of evocative memories that, in Lucy's hands, it became a masterpiece and the Reverend Mother was unsurprised when Julie, while warning that Mrs Hendrick had personally decided where each guest was to sleep, collapsed in the face of a stronger personality; a scullery boy was directed to take the cases up to the room of Lucy's choice and maids sent to light fires and make up the beds.

The Reverend Mother, while listening politely to Nicholas's lecture about the Vikings, awaited her opportunity to interrupt him. 'Well,' she said eventually, 'I wish you very good luck with your investigations and with the house building demonstration this evening. And now, I feel that I should go and inspect this marvellous room and admire the view which has been won for my sake by my cousin.'

He laughed a little at that. But in a second he had turned away and was directing his eldest son to bring some notes over to the university and giving instructions to the other boys about placing small pieces of sodden wood carefully into boxes in a shed. A man with a mission and with a vision, she thought and did not wonder that he had fired Charlotte with enthusiasm for his dream.

No sign of Charlotte. Odd that, she thought as she sought the guidance of a maid to escort her to the bedroom on the Bachelor's Quay side of the house. Mrs Hendrick was, apparently, occupied with her rent collector and they would not meet until just before the dinner hour. Still, there were plenty of staff on duty and Julie was, she supposed, in charge of all arrangements. Nicholas Hendrick, also, seemed to be making himself very much at home. He overtook her in the hallway and went straight into the library while she followed the parlour maid to the top floor.

'No doubt we will meet Charlotte at dinner,' she said to Lucy as she came into the room and then she saw that Lucy was not alone. There was a man with her, and his face was familiar.

'You know Claude, Claude Clancy, don't you, Reverend Mother?' Lucy with her usual adroitness came to her rescue.

'Of course,' said the Reverend Mother instantly. She could not remember whether they had met in the flesh since adulthood, but there was no doubt that his face was very familiar to her from newspaper photographs. Claude Clancy ran a club, a most fashionable club, situated on the Grand Parade and the favourite, according to the *Cork Examiner* newspaper, of the wealthy and fashion-conscious citizens of Cork. Overweight and a bit puffy around the eyes was her immediate verdict, but she supposed that it went with his job. Had a troublesome son. What was it that Lucy had told her about young Michael Joseph?

'I hope that we have not turned you out of your room?' she enquired. This was, as she could see from a quick look around, a beautiful room. An immense four-poster bed, and two smaller beds, each in their own little cubicle, each screened by expensive silk curtaining. A velvet-covered couch and a pair of matching chairs were drawn up in front of the centre window – a wonderful place to enjoy the spectacular sight of the river, the bridges and the northern reaches of the city. Two doors, discretely closed, but leading, no doubt, to these converted dressing rooms of which Lucy had spoken. Everything in the room spoke of taste, of money and of unceasing housewifely efforts.

'No, no, I'm over there on the other side of the house from you. On the Grattan Street side of the house. Nicholas and I share a bathroom. Not at all such a nice room as this, but I don't grudge it to you, Lucy, nor, you, Reverend Mother, of course.'

'Tell the Reverend Mother what you were telling me, Claude. About the Dutchman and his cubes.'

'I'm sure that she knows that story.'

Claude wanted to talk about the will, she guessed, but there was, after all, nothing to be said so she decided to follow Lucy's lead. 'No, not at all,' she said, though she had a vague memory of hearing something about it. 'Nothing about "cubes" – it was all about tulip bulbs when I heard the story.'

'Well, this Dutchman made his money from tulip bulbs and he decided that what Ireland needed was some decent bricks, not the rather soggy, crumbly efforts that the natives were producing, so this Dutchman, having made a fortune on selling tulip bulbs, bought up a shipload of bricks, set sail and then he landed in Cork, in the early days of Queen Anne. Sailed up the river

41

and stopped his ship on Bachelor's Quay and looked about for someone to help to unload his bricks which he purposed to sell at the market on the Coal Quay. As it was the hungry season, the time in May when most country people had eaten up their store of potatoes and the new ones had not come yet, there were lots of strong men hanging around, just like nowadays, looking for a job of unloading the ships. And, to cut a long story short, our friend the Dutchman found himself across the road from the ship on an empty piece of land giving a lesson on how to put bricks together and how quickly one could build with them.'

'And the story is,' interrupted Lucy, 'that they worked so well that they made a hollow cube, thirty feet long, thirty feet wide and thirty feet high. He even providentially showed them how to leave spaces for windows and a door.'

'And so many people turned up to watch and wanted to have a go that the Dutchman set another team to work on a second cube. And by the end of the day, they had built what is now the ground floor of this house – four cubes altogether, forming four lengths. Each cube was a large room.' Claude took his part in the story.

'And then, of course,' said Lucy, 'he thought of making a magnificent house for himself, living in Cork and importing bricks for the natives and so the first, second and a third storey were built with those large gable windows on each of the four sides of the roof giving light to the stairs. Most of the cubes on the upper stories are divided into two rooms and a bathroom, now, but the ones on the top storey overlooking Bachelor's Quay are the original size. We have this one,' continued Lucy with a note of satisfaction in her voice, 'and Cousin Charlotte has the one in the middle which used to be the old storeroom, made for the dry storage of the Amsterdam silks, so I heard. I've seen an old picture of Cork and it was full of brick-built buildings then. The Georgian, limestone buildings came later.'

'Still got the pulley wheel above the central window of Cousin Charlotte's bedroom,' put in Claude.

'We've been watching it working,' said Lucy. 'Why don't we go in and have a look at the room. I haven't seen the place for ages. Come on, Claude, you can escort us. Cousin Charlotte won't mind. She's busy with her rent collector.'

'Do we dare?' Claude looked slightly scared. Money has a great power over people, reflected the Reverend Mother. She was on Lucy's side. She wanted to see the room. Not too polite, perhaps, to go into your hostess's bedroom, but, on the other hand, the hostess was not being too polite herself when she failed to greet her guests.

'Yes, I'd like to see it,' she said sedately.

'Well, she did tell me that she would be occupied with the rent collector until dinner time,' said Claude. 'I'll blame you, Lucy.'

Nevertheless, he led the way, talking loudly and cheerfully relating the story of the baths being winched up, one by one in a rope cradle from the pulley wheel when the dressing rooms were converted into bathrooms.

Charlotte's room, the central room on the Bachelor's Quay side of the house, was even more splendid than the one which Lucy had chosen. It had just one bed, set in the middle of the left-hand wall, and opposite it the wardrobes and chest of drawers, but there was a splendid expanse of polished oak-boarded floor and the eye was immediately drawn towards the tall window and the view beyond.

'Look, Reverend Mother!' Claude crossed the room, opened a door in the wall and displayed a wonderfully luxurious bathroom. 'That bath is made from elm, a good hundred years old. It has to be repainted every year of course, but it holds the heat wonderfully. I have one in my bathroom, just like it. Nicholas and I share a bathroom, a bit sliced off from each room. There were six bathrooms put into the house a few years ago. Just imagine six heavy wooden baths being winched up by that wheel.'

'How very interesting!' said the Reverend Mother. 'We've just watched the chauffeur trying out the rope. Apparently Mrs Hendrick likes to make sure that it is kept in perfect order and now I can see why.' She walked back, threw open the window and reached up to touch one end of the rope. She was firmly determined to keep the conversation centred on the house and its history and to avoid any discussion about the wretched will. Otherwise ill feeling would arise and the overnight stay would be even more unpleasant than she had already visualized. 'I suppose when you were a small boy you were fascinated by things like that winch and pulley,' she added, closing the window again.

He brushed the matter aside, had something else to talk about; had already turned his mind to more important matters. He cast a perfunctory glance around and then firmly led the way back into the first room and perched himself on the end of one bed.

'This business tonight,' he said, 'what do you make of that? What's going to happen, do you think? Seems a very strange sort of affair, doesn't it?' He was sharing his views between Lucy and the Reverend Mother. His voice was light-hearted and amused, but his eyes were deeply anxious. The Reverend Mother began to wonder what was wrong with this Claude. He had, she thought, a note of desperation in his voice. She began to feel interested in him. Money, had said her friend, Dr Scher, is a strange thing. It enrichens and it poisons. And sometimes it does both in different order.

'I think that you could have stayed away, Claude,' complained Lucy. 'The whole of Cork knows that business of yours is worth a fortune.'

'You mean that it takes a fortune to run.'

The Reverend Mother left them to it and walked across to the window, looking down on to the river. Recently Dr Scher, when he had come to visit an elderly nun in the convent, had brought with him an old map that he had picked up in an auction house. Slightly more than four hundred years old, during the fifth year of the reign of Henry VIII, she seemed to remember. It showed Cork, the north branch of the river and the south branch. She had thought of it earlier today while listening to Philip Monahan's horrific survey of the slum tenements. There were, indeed, some buildings marked on the two islands which were now named North Main Street and South Main Street but the rest of the flat land where the city was now built was marked as marsh, and the main streets of the present city, including Patrick Street and the South Mall were mere streams or river channels. In the seventeenth and eighteenth century the streams and channels, all except for the north and the south channels, had been tidied into culverts and the culverts had been roofed over to become streets. But every so often the river took back the land. And, of course, quite often Bachelor's Quay below them was covered over with water which lapped against the foundations of the house.

However, this site on top of which the Hendrick house had been built was a solid one. Probably a stray clump of sandstone rock in the midst of the marsh formed its base. Whatever was its origin, it had stood up against the river floods. Whoever had built it, had taken the precaution to raise it a foot above the ground and built it upon a very solid foundation. Perhaps it was indeed a remnant of the Viking era and deep down below this present house had been a Viking house, perhaps a leader's house. The tradition would have remained and when the English had taken over Cork in the time of King John, why then, perhaps, that would have been another house. And when that had crumbled away, the foundations would have remained. A prime site near to the river, but raised well above it. Even now it was well above the present road, and not subject to flooding. Interesting to be an archaeologist, she thought and imagined tracing through the remnants of the past.

And then she thought back again to the meeting this morning and to Philip Monahan's assessment of those terraces of Georgian houses built upon the marshland and most of them now occupied by ten to twelve families. Those houses, these slum dwellings, cynically used to make the maximum amount of money by people like her wealthy cousin, Charlotte Hendrick, should never have been built and should now be abandoned.

God is not mocked. The words came to her mind and she shivered slightly and said a quick prayer that if there was to be flooding tonight, it should pass without any loss of life or any damage or further destruction of the crumbling living places of the very poor.

'And, of course, one cannot add a new wing without vast expense.' Claude was going on about his business and doing his best to convert Lucy to an understanding of how much he needed money in order to save his business. 'But, you understand, without expansion, one contracts. And that is fatal when running a business.'

'You are so right.' Lucy sighed as though she had been running businesses and making money for all of her life, instead of marrying a very prosperous solicitor when she was still in her teens. 'Really,' she went on with a quick glance over her shoulder to ensure that no servant was present, 'really one did rely on getting one's share of this money. Not quite fair, is it? Not at all what we have all expected, is it, Claude?'

'I think that we all need to get together. Perhaps tackle her. Tell her how much we had relied upon her.' Claude lowered his voice. 'You know how it was, don't you? One counted on getting a substantial sum. We all knew that cousin Charlotte was a rich woman. I must say, that I've heard on the grapevine that she is worth . . .' He lowered his voice even more and whispered again.

The Reverend Mother's eyebrows shot up. That sum was, indeed, even when divided into seven shares, money worth having.

'Of course,' continued Claude, 'one would welcome the whole sum, but speaking for myself I was quite satisfied with getting what had always been promised.'

'Me too,' said Lucy eagerly. 'Though, of course, one would not exactly turn down the whole sum . . .'

'True, true.' There was a wistful note in Claude's voice. 'But on the other hand . . .' There followed a long silence. The Reverend Mother listened with amusement. What was going to come next?

But when Claude spoke again it was of the flood and he spent some time congratulating himself on buying a business that was situated on the third storey of a building on the Grand Parade. 'Be enough to give Cousin Charlotte a heart attack to watch the water lapping from the windowsills,' he said. There was, thought the Reverend Mother, an odd note in his voice and to her surprise, Lucy, always so quick to comment, did not reply. It seemed as though both were contemplating possible occurrences, or, indeed, a certain fatality tied up with this predicted flood.

There was a strange silence in the room for the next few seconds. She was about to make another comment on the flood herself, when Claude spoke.

'She must be well into her sixties now,' he said with a note of speculation in his voice.

'Goodness, I suppose that she might,' said Lucy with an air of astonishment and the Reverend Mother smiled to herself at that note of incredulity. She knew Lucy's age as well as she knew her own; they had been brought up together after the death of both their mothers from tuberculosis and both, she could swear, had pushed Charlotte, the eldest of the Clancy cousins, in the pram. Lucy, like she, would be well above seventy. But she had to admit that few would now know how near in age they were. The services of an expert hairdresser who had tinted her cousin's hair to a delicate ash blond did much. And the help of expensive face powder and other cosmetics, a lively manner and well-chosen clothes, ensured that Lucy looked a good ten or even fifteen years younger than her birth certificate would show.

'Health not good, is it?' Claude was obviously brooding on his rich relative. 'Didn't think she looked too lively the last time that I saw her,' he continued.

'Well, you know, at that age,' said Lucy, finishing her sentence with a little shrug of her elegant shoulders.

'A shock, anything can bring on a heart attack.' Claude went to the window and looked down. 'Goodness, the river is flowing very fast. And that high tide won't go down until late tonight. Dear Cousin Charlotte must be getting quite worried. I think that I'll go and see whether she has finished with the rent collector. Perhaps I'll just tap on the door and see if there is anything that she wants me to do. I'll just check whether she is in any way troubled.'

'She won't. Won't be troubled, I mean,' said the Reverend Mother drily when the door closed behind Claude. 'Charlotte Hendrick has lived in this house for over forty years and she knows well what happens in the case of a flood. I'd say myself

50

that this place won't have a problem. Did you notice how well the house is built up above the level of the road? Dutch man or not, this house was built by someone who understood the problems of flooding in Cork. And it will only annoy her to be asked whether she wants anything done so I shouldn't bother, if I were you, Lucy.' She went on with unpacking the small suitcase that she had brought.

'As if I would be so stupid,' said Lucy, tossing her head. 'And I'm beginning to regret coming. I don't think that someone like Charlotte will be interested in my girls. She probably is totally deficient in the maternal instinct. I think that I won't bother making a submission. I'll help you with yours if you wish. The two of us together should give that wretched Nicholas Hendrick a run for his money. And as for Claude Clancy, I don't think that he has a chance and I think that he knows it. Why should Charlotte Hendrick care about a little club at the top of a building in the Grand Parade? I don't suppose that Charlotte has been in a club during her entire life. In fact, I don't believe that any one of us has a chance against Nicholas. Now let's unpack and enjoy ourselves. We could go downstairs, I suppose, but I'd say that we'd be cosier here having a gossip. We'll see enough of the others at dinner time. To be honest, I don't think that I'm too keen on any of the Clancy family and as for Nicholas Hendrick, well, he's far too pleased with himself for my taste.'

51

'Lucy, what was the husband, Charlotte's husband, Mr Hendrick, like?' asked the Reverend Mother, succumbing to the desire to gossip which always came over her when she met her cousin. She put her washbag into the bathroom, touching the bath. Yes, definitely wood, not porcelain. Painted with white paint, but still holding the warmth of wood. One of those baths, she thought wistfully, where one could lie for half an hour and read a book – not something that she would ever get the time to do during her busy life. And the idea of not sharing a bathroom with a dozen other nuns was an impossibility. Banishing the notion of wasting half an hour on a bath, she went back into the room to join Lucy on the couch looking out on the splendid view of the river. A log fire was burning brightly in the tiled fireplace and she sank into the cushions with a sigh of relief. Her bones ached in this weather and a little luxury was welcome. 'Do you know, Lucy, I just can't visualize him,' she said. 'I've seen Charlotte over the years, of course, mainly at family funerals, but I can't recollect the appearance of the husband at all. Did he look like a Viking, like the nephew?'

'Viking,' snorted Lucy. 'All nonsense, this Viking business. Just something that Nicholas dreamed up when he studied archaeology. Rupert says that he reckons that the family was originally from South Africa, Boers, you know, and that the name should be spelt with "ik" on the end, not "ck". And he says that the family have always got their money from South African gold mines, so that proves it, doesn't it?'

'The nephew looks Viking, though,' pointed out the Reverend Mother. 'He's got that nose, that profile. Looks splendid.'

'Nonsense!' Lucy was vigorous in her scorn. 'Charlotte's husband was a thickset little man, no more like a Viking than I am myself. Very Dutch-looking, I'd say. The nephew, Nicholas, gets his looks from his mother. English. A horsey type from the Home Counties. Big, very tall, a bit raw-boned, but you know that sort of look, though I don't like them in a woman, well, they suit a man. Nicholas has her height and her bone structure. An only child. I do believe that Charlotte's husband paid for him to be educated in England. That's where he gets the accent. And, of course, dear Charlotte thinks that he sounds very posh and she worships him.'

The Reverend Mother thought about snobbery, thought about the inequality of wealth, the idiocy of the rich in shipping their children across the channel in order, in many examples, to get an inferior education, though it might be adorned by an English accent.

She sighed to herself. There were times – very secret times, and thoughts which she kept well hidden behind the starched breastplate of her habit – when the Reverend Mother almost doubted the existence of God. If there was a God, why did He allow such terrible suffering, such dreadful imbalance between the lives of the rich and the lives of the poor? Perhaps there was no God. Perhaps the world was ruled by some malevolent being. The thought probably was a sin, a sin that should be confessed, but every time that she thought of revealing her doubts to another human being, she repressed the thought impatiently. As things were, she had a certain influence in the city of Cork, she had achieved something in educating the children of the poor and doing her best to ameliorate the terrible conditions in which they and their parents lived. It would leak out – the sanctity of confession, she thought cynically, would crumble in the face of curiosity from the bishop or the bishop's secretary – yes, it would leak out that she had eccentric views. A hint would be dropped in front of the bishop. She would lose her influence, lose the moral and intellectual ascendency which, privately she admitted, she held over his lordship. She needed to keep her own counsel. And so she banished the thought from her mind and turned her energies towards something that she should and could, perhaps, accomplish.

'So, poor Julie,' she said briskly. 'I'm a bit worried about her. She's afraid of being destitute. She was quite upset this morning after the meeting. Charlotte should do something for her, Lucy. You must admit. She's been at Charlotte's beck and call for so many years.'

'If it turns out that Charlotte is going to leave everything to Nicholas Hendrick, well then Julie will be in a bad way. I don't see him being sorry for her,' said Lucy. 'He's not the type,' she added.

'And if she leaves everything to you, Lucy?' Unlikely, thought the Reverend Mother, but she watched her cousin's reaction with interest. Mouth suddenly opening. An offer to house Julie? And then closing again as reality hit. What, in fact, could be done with Julie Clancy, dogsbody for at least thirty years?

'Goodness,' said Lucy. 'Well, to be frank, I wouldn't want her around the house. She'd give me the creeps. Reminds me of Uriah Heep in *David Copperfield*. She's always so "'umble". I suppose that we'd pension her off. Rupert would work something out. Find her a little house by the sea, or in town if she'd prefer it. Oh, bother, I think she'd probably get quite depressed. She would keep calling in and complaining, pretending to do little jobs for me. No, I don't want the responsibility of her. Could she be a nun, or something?'

The Reverend Mother smiled with amusement. No, she thought, certainly not, but aloud she said, 'Perhaps you don't want Charlotte Hendrick's money and property after all, Lucy? It would bring a lot of responsibility with it. It's not just poor Julie. Charlotte has hundreds of tenants living in terrible conditions. You'd have to do something about all of them, also. You couldn't leave them in mouldering, rat-infested houses with sometimes four families in a single room. You couldn't turn your back on that, could you? Not if you were responsible, not if you were the owner of these places. Come on, admit! It wouldn't be in you.'

'Rupert would look after all of that,' said Lucy firmly. 'You don't understand, Dottie. You want the money for other people, but the rest of us want it for ourselves and that is a very different matter. You'd need millions and millions to do anything about the poor areas of Cork. You'd be better off keeping your mind off them. I do. I think my duty is to my own family. I'd do anything to make sure that my girls are happy and secure and have all the nice things in life. And, of course, I want things for myself. I'd like to go on a cruise; visit India; have a mink fur coat; all sorts of things. I could sit down and write a list as long as your arm and I'd still think of more things that I need.'

The Reverend Mother looked at her with interest. She had always imagined that her cousin had everything possible that she needed, but it looked as though she were wrong. She thought over the other relations, Julie, who really did have nothing, but would probably, like Lucy, want luxuries in her life. And then there was Julie's younger brother, Claude. An anxious look in his eye. That club of his not doing well? It was possible. Cork – the whole country – was in the grip of a recession. Freedom from Britain had not been the solution to its many social ills. In fact, it had swapped a military war for an economic war. Claude definitely was worried about money. And he had a son, she had heard, who was causing problems. Would probably like to get him out of Cork, get him away from bad influences. Perhaps he could equip him to seek his fortune in South Africa, but that, of course, would take money.

And the archaeologist and his family. Nicholas Hendrick would want money to fund research into Viking Cork. He was already writing a book about it, but he would need to hire archaeologists; workers; people to do the digging. He would want to set up digs in various parts of Cork. Even perhaps purchase property where he suspected that Viking remains were concealed below the foundations. And there were his four sons. He would want a university education for them. Would want to establish them up in life; arrange marriages; buy houses. The list would be endless.

'What about Brenda O'Mahony and young Florence, Lucy?' she said. 'Do you know them at all? They are both due to inherit, aren't they? Florence will have her father's share, of course.'

'Don't know too much about them,' said Lucy. 'But Brenda won't be too pleased if Charlotte changes her will. I seem to remember that Brenda's husband lost a lot of money in a shop that he used to own in Fermoy. The Republicans sacked it some years ago. Can't remember why, though I've a feeling that he used to sell wine to the soldiers' barracks in Fermoy, so it may have been that. The daughter, no, adopted niece, yes, of course, she's poor Jack's daughter – you remember,

57

he died of stomach cancer, poor fellow. Well, she's a bit of a bluestocking – supposed to be very clever. Someone told me that, but I don't think I know too much about her. Seems a bit of a handful; Brenda will have trouble with her if she's not careful.'

Should be an interesting evening, thought the Reverend Mother. All of these people, desperate for money, all trying to eat and drink as though it were a normal social occasion.

And Lucy and herself.

I, she thought, could spend a million if anyone cared to make me a present of it. That is, of course, she amended her thoughts, if the bishop were to allow me to keep it.

'Dinner,' she said aloud, 'should be an interesting meal. Everyone will be eyeing up the opposition. What do you think, Lucy?'

'Should be a good one, anyway,' said Lucy in animated tones. 'What do you suppose that we'll get for dinner? She is supposed to have a top class cook. Someone told me that. And it's such a treat to have a meal that one has not ordered oneself.'

The Reverend Mother gave her a quizzical look. Lucy's expression and tone of voice had completely changed. Almost as though she had dropped a veil to cloak her words of a few minutes earlier. Now she was back to her usual lively, animated self. Probably the best way to approach the evening. Lucy would be at her top form in a social setting and Charlotte, surely, would be enough of a hostess to treat the affairs of the evening in a fairly light-hearted fashion.

Nevertheless, the Reverend Mother wished that high tide had been six hours earlier and that the quays had flooded from Merchant's Quay down to Bachelor's Quay, not enough to endanger houses or people, but just enough to prevent this affair from taking place. She had an uneasy feeling about the evening.

CHAPTER 3

D anger was in the air. Merchant's Quay and Merchant's Place were fast turning into a riotous assembly and what was worse, the IRA looked to be involved. Eileen MacSweeney, now a hardworking university student but an erstwhile member of that illicit organization, gazed around the wet quays apprehensively. There was a huge crowd. Dockers with coal-blackened faces, unemployed men in ragged clothes and unshaven faces, women enveloped in shawls, barefooted children, lots of university students, some still dressed as Vikings, but amongst the crowd were some familiar figures, dressed in belted raincoats with slouch hats pulled well down over one side of the face.

And these figures moved here and there, fomenting anger, egging on desperate men, urging them to tell the world of their troubles. From time to time, she saw them take out some coins and hand them to some of the men who were shouting the loudest. Money for drink, she guessed and knew that the IRA were there in order to stir up trouble.

That wretched loudhailer belonged to the rowing

club at the university. She couldn't walk away from it. If only she had not allowed Mickey Joe Clancy to leave it in her charge.

But, of course, all of the trouble had started with him. Eileen wished heartily that her love of motorbikes had not tempted her into coming down the quays with Mickey Joe Clancy. She should have known better, should have guessed that he would get her into trouble. Her own elderly motorbike was laid up in the garage for repairs and she had been seduced by the prospect of a ride on the back of his brand new bike given to him by his wealthy father, the owner of a club in the Grand Parade – the price for a job that he had to do for his pa, or so he said.

'It will be great gas, Eileen!' He kept repeating. And, of course, Mickey Joe Clancy, son of Claude Clancy, the well-known owner of Clancy's Bar on the Grand Parade, was, with his head of blazing red hair, his non-stop jokes and his fizzing exuberance, great gas himself. Clever fellow, too. Was in her history class at the college. She liked going out with him, liked meeting his student pals. Felt that in some way it got her away from her past history and made her more of a typical carefree university student. But tonight she had badly wanted to see Ivor Novello in *The Rat* at The Pavilion Cinema. He, of course, had other ideas and had talked her into this.

This business of building a Viking House on Merchant's Quay had seemed initially like a fun, university-student prank. The drama society, dressed up as Vikings, had arrived on the quay in dinghies disguised as Viking ships and then built, in the centre of Merchant's Quay Square, a real, authentic Viking house from trunks of hazel tree saplings that had been cleared from the lower grounds of the university and towed down the river earlier that day. Fifty or sixty students straining every nerve. Lifting the slender tree trunks, hammering, everything prepared beforehand. Every piece of wood cut to size, every hole drilled. Netting for the roof and then bales of hay to simulate a thatched roof. A mock battle. Professor Hendrick had made a speech into a loudhailer, thanked everyone for coming, said a few words about the Vikings and then had disappeared.

Suddenly the mood had changed. The rain stopped and although the river lapped at the edge of the quay, the crowd had swelled. Funds had been collected for a barrel of beer for the builders of the house, but all of the public houses around were doing a roaring trade. The dock labourers had finished unloading the coal from the Welsh ship, had been paid, and were now spending their wages on pints of good Cork Murphy's or Beamish Stout. Mickey Joe had joined some of those ominous men in belted gabardine raincoats, faces well-hidden behind the slouch hats. She should have guessed, she thought. Mickey Joe Clancy, for all of his tousled hair charm, was a wild boy; she knew that and she guessed that unknown to his father he might actually be part of one of the IRA secret cells, the ones they relied upon for information. He'd had a grin on his face when he had left her. His guilty, small-boy expression. She didn't trust him.

And she thought it was asking for trouble, this business of getting drunken and desperate men to inspect the Viking House, built in half an hour, with its warm thatched roof and clean wooden walls, and then to bring them up to the loudhailer to describe their own living conditions. The crowd sighed and groaned and shouted in anger at the descriptions of terrible over-crowding, of crumbling walls, filth from sewers rising through the floorboards and of rats attacking babies.

She stared apprehensively at the angry crowd and cursed herself for giving in to him.

Time they stopped this and had the dinghy race which was supposed to be the culmination of the evening's affairs. The students dressed as Vikings were going back into their boats. The tide was rising and the wind blowing up the river from the Atlantic was getting stronger. There would be a risk that the racing dinghies would be smashed to pieces against the quay walls if they were not moved quickly back to their own quiet backwater in the university lower grounds. There seemed to be some arguing going on about whether they would be able to have a race as they had planned.

Eileen went across to the edge of the river, holding on to the safety chain in case a rogue wave came down the river from the harbour. There was already a young man there, balancing hazardously on the stone wall. 'Make up your minds,' he was shouting. 'Now or never. You've got ten minutes. Leave it any longer and the high tide will come roaring up the river and smash those boats to smithereens.'

Not a student himself, thought Eileen. The accent was all wrong. Cork was a very class-conscious place and even the few students who had scholarships soon learned to modify their way of speaking.

'You know about tides, then, do you?' she asked him.

'I work up the quays there, upriver.' He jerked his head in the direction of North Main Street. 'Work as a chauffeur. Rich old lady on Bachelor's Quay. Where do you come from? And what's a gorgeous girl like you doing out on the quays on your own. I'll walk you home if you like,' he offered.

'I'll tell you what you can do, like a good boy,' said Eileen. 'You can stand here and when those jokers make up their mind to start this race, you can come across and tell me and then I'll announce it over the loudhailer.'

'And going home?' Not one to give up, this chauffeur. Slicking back his hair and trying to look like the bees' knees.

'Sorry, handsome, you're out of luck,' she said kindly. 'I've got my own boyfriend here and he's got a motorbike to take me home. A brand-new

64

one, too. Next time you have the Rolls Royce, though, I might take a ride.'

He didn't like that. His face darkened. One of the bad-tempered lot.

'Just as well,' he said shrugging his shoulders. 'I'll have you know that my mistress is having a party tonight and there's a real gorgeous girl there, a young cousin of my mistress. Got hair like a film star, real blonde and all them marcel waves.' He gave Eileen's smooth dark hair a contemptuous look and then swaggered off, saying over his shoulder, 'And she's dead mad about me, I'll have you know.'

More fool her, thought Eileen, but she spotted Mickey Joe coming in her direction. He stopped to speak with the chauffeur, she noticed. Seemed to know each other well. Mickey Joe said a word in his ear and the chauffeur nodded and went off.

'Know him, do you?' she asked when Mickey Joe came up to her.

'Seen him a few times. He works for a relation of mine, an old woman called Mrs Hendrick, a sort of cousin of my father, lives on Bachelor's Quay,' he said carelessly. Then shouted to the students in the boats: 'The river is coming up too fast, lads; you'll have to get the boats back to the lower grounds of the university before they're smashed to pieces.'

'I'll get back to the loudhailer, then,' said Eileen. She might as well see the evening through. It had occurred to her that she could make a good, dramatic article about the evening for the *Cork Examiner*. And her articles for the *Cork Examiner* were an important source of income for her these days. It would be a purely factual account, she planned. She would have to be careful. She would start by painting a dramatic scene of the water-washed quays; the gaslights; the Viking costumes; the boats; the blackened faces of the dock workers; the beshawled women and the barefoot children. And then she would move on to their stories. All very low-key and factual. No emotion. Just let the readers judge for themselves.

She was about to look for the next speaker when she was tapped on the shoulder.

'Who's organizing this affair?' said a voice in her ear.

Eileen knew him instantly, had seen his photograph on the *Cork Examiner* when he had first got the job of City Manager. Perhaps she could get a few words from him.

'Not me, Mr Monahan,' she said instantly. 'One of the college boyos landed me with looking after the boating club loudhailer. I'm waiting for him to come back. What do you think of it all?'

'It's sheer stupidity.' He sounded impatient. 'These sort of shows never do an ounce of good, just provide opportunities to crack down on the unfortunates. What good did 1916 do? Got a whole lot of clever people shot, people who could use a pen, could fight for change. And what happened? They burned down a few buildings, got

66

sympathy for the landlords and demonized the tenants. The newspapers will be full of this tomorrow and fat landlords will write letters to the papers about disgraceful behaviour and then the powers-that-be will think they are justified in treating poor people as if they were mad dogs. This sort of thing just encourages that attitude.'

'You think that you can do better.' All of a sudden, Eileen felt furious. 'They are trying to do something. What have you done, anyway? Gone to meetings. I've seen your picture in the *Examiner*, sitting on committees. So what should people who feel strongly do? Sit back. Do nothing? Has anyone ever been successful?'

He shrugged his shoulders when she said that and then he smiled a little. 'I suppose you are one of Professor Hendrick's history students, are you? What's your name?'

'Eileen,' she said. Something about him irritated her. He had a contemptuous air. She began to forget her earlier apprehensions. After all, they were giving a voice to people who were normally silent.

'Well, you know your history, Eileen, I hope. Most of these protests just end up making things worse for people who are already in a very bad condition. These speeches, these marches, may make a difference after many long years go by, but your man up there' – he nodded towards the man bellowing into the loudhailer – 'well, he'll be worse off. If his landlord gets wind of what he's saying

67

here tonight, he'll have him out on the street tomorrow morning. And he'll probably blacklist him for dock work so the result of all this shouting tonight will probably be that he, his wife and his children will be worse off than they ever were and that baby will probably die of hunger and cold.'

Eileen stood very still. 'Is there nothing to be done, then?' she said and heard her voice tremble. 'It seems a terrible thing to do nothing when there is such terrible suffering around us.' She stared at him angrily and then relented. He's drunk she told herself, but something within her acknowledged that he might have right on his side. She herself had left school at the age of fifteen to go off and join the IRA. The battle had been won. Ireland, after a few years, had regained its freedom from Britain after eight hundred years, though at the expense of a partitioned country where the northern six counties had remained under British rule. But then it had lapsed into a vicious civil war between pro-treaty and anti-treaty factions and thousands had been killed. Had it worked out? Were the people any better off? She feared that she knew the answer to that question.

'Does it ever work out?' she asked and to her annoyance, heard her voice tremble.

He laughed. 'I suppose the French Revolution was successful eventually. Wouldn't want to see it happen here in Ireland, though, would you? Have a guillotine out here in Merchant's Square, would that work? Line up the landlords and the property owners, chop off their heads. Would you and the other students have the guts to do something like that? You could sit over there and do your knitting while the heads of the landlords rolled into baskets. That would be fun, wouldn't it? And of course, we mustn't forget the female of the species – more deadly than the male, so they say. There's a woman landlord up there in Bachelor's Quay who owns scores of terrible houses and screws the rent out of poor tenants until she has them wrung dry and then dumps them on the rubbish heap. Should we cut off her head as well?' He eyed her with a smile on his face and then, without waiting for an answer, said, more gently, 'Well, I'd better be off. Live over in Glenville Place. Come and see me some time and I'll tell you all about the French Revolution. I'll be safe going down the quays, won't I, do you think? Not full tide until midnight, so they tell me.'

And then in a loud, but quite tuneful voice, he went off down towards the quay side, singing a song in the French language. 'The Marseillaise', she thought. She remembered hearing it sung at the French club at college and she had memorized the words:

> Allons enfants de la Patrie
> Le jour de gloire est arrivé
> Contre nous de la tyrannie
> L'étendard sanglant est levé

Drunk, she said to herself. Dead drunk. Not worth thinking about. But his song had stirred her blood and his good advice was lost. She had to do something, she told herself. Surely protest must bear fruit eventually. Merchant's Square, to the back of the quay, was full of people, well-dressed people as well as the poor. Do everyone some good to hear about the conditions that some of these unfortunates were living in. Ironic to think that a thousand years ago, the Vikings might have been more comfortable. She pictured Philip Monahan striding along the quays: Merchant's Quay, Coal Quay, Kyrl's Quay and Bachelor's Quay until he reached Glenville Place singing a song of revolution, while he preached patience and obedience to municipal laws. She half wished that she was going with him along those quays and engaging in a discussion about the French Revolution with him.

She would like, she thought, to get away from Merchant's Square. She had a horrible feeling that something bad might happen.

CHAPTER 4

'A bad night out on the quays, tonight,' said Lucy lightly as she peered through the curtains of the window of the dining room. 'Do you remember that book, was it *The Last Days of Pompeii* and the opening lines: "It was a dark and stormy night; the rain fell in torrents, except at occasional intervals, when it was checked by a violent gust of wind which swept up the streets . . ."'

'I think it was another one of his books,' said the Reverend Mother, joining her, 'and not all that appropriate,' she added. The rain fell, but it was a silvery, misty rain and the river that had slopped over its banks and spread in ripples across the road reflected the gaslight in shimmering streaks of silver. But there was an odd feeling of menace. From the quays there were echoes of shouts and yells that penetrated the glass of the windows and she had an uneasy feeling that all was not well in the city on this wet night. The river was rising very rapidly. It was only eight o'clock now and high tide would not come for another few hours. That south-easterly wind that she had felt earlier on was a forbearer of floods when it combined with the autumnal high tides. All Cork people knew that and usually the floods were a signal for all to get indoors and to go as high as they could within the buildings before high tide arrived.

But not tonight.

Judging by the sounds, there were crowds out on the quays. Voices were raised to the highest pitch; angry shouts could be heard and from time to time she could hear the sound of artificially enlarged voices shouting out messages. Silently and carefully she slid down one of the sash windows and now, although she could not distinguish the individual words, she could hear a voice. Someone with a loudhailer was whipping up anger amongst the dwellers of the tenements and the sound was swept up the quays by the wind. The accent was not that of a college student, but a rough, angry voice, probably one of the men who lived by the docks and gained an irregular livelihood by unloading ships and unblocking sewage-filled drains. A worrying sound.

'What's going on out there?' Claude Clancy was by her side.

'Trouble,' she said, but she slid up the window again, bolted it and redrew the heavy velvet curtains. For once she hoped for heavy rain and an increasing flood. The sooner all were off the streets, the better for everyone.

'Julie! Get the shutters put up,' snapped Charlotte. Her tone was that of someone with a recalcitrant dog and Julie scuttled off obediently.

During the meal, the Reverend Mother studied her cousin Charlotte carefully, though surreptitiously. Charlotte had lost weight, did not look well; did not look at all as though she were enjoying herself. A bad idea, this summoning of relatives, this competitive business of setting one member of a family against another. Charlotte ate virtually nothing, and yet the food was superlative. The Reverend Mother wondered momentarily about what happened to the leftovers but decided that it was none of her business.

'Coffee in the library, Julie,' said Charlotte. She took a small bottle from her handbag, slipped a tablet from it into her mouth and rose to her feet. The Reverend Mother wondered again why the woman had gone to the trouble of this public performance. Surely no one doubted her right to leave her money to whomsoever she pleased. A letter to all after she had changed her will might have been a kind thought, just in case some had relied on the money, but there had been little need for all of this fuss, particularly if Dr Scher was correct and the woman had already made up her mind to leave her entire fortune to her husband's nephew, the Viking-like Nicholas Hendrick.

The coffee was Turkish and accompanied by Turkish cigarettes and an expensive-looking brandy. The Reverend Mother cheerfully and loudly refused the coffee and asked for a cup of tea in lieu. She caught a look of envy on Julie's face and immediately demanded her company in sharing a pot and requested the maid to bring two cups. Everyone else meekly took the strong, pungent coffee, though it was hardly to the taste of Brenda O'Mahony, she thought. Her niece, however, praised the coffee vociferously and asked for some of the very pale brandy to go with it and then daringly copied Nicholas and Claude in smoking one of the Turkish cigarettes. The Reverend Mother watched with interest. Florence had been a silent, shy child the last time that she had met her, but now she was assertive and loud-voiced. A bluestocking, Lucy had said.

'How old is she now?' She murmured the words to Lucy and took care not to look towards Florence as she uttered them.

'Should be almost eighteen. She's a couple of years younger than my Charlotte,' said Lucy eyeing the girl with disfavour. 'A bit young to be smoking and drinking brandy, isn't she? Wouldn't like any of my girls to do that in public, especially before they were married.'

'I don't suppose that it's any more intoxicating before marriage, than after marriage,' observed the Reverend Mother. Florence had embarked upon an animated conversation with Nicholas Hendrick. Certainly a self-confident young lady. She loudly and emphatically contradicted Nicholas in some observation that he had made about the influence of Vikings on housebuilding and was now embarking upon a lecture to him about the dangers of having a theory before undertaking sufficient research.

'Hmm,' said the professor after patiently enduring for a few minutes. 'Now we mustn't hog all of the conversation, young lady, must we? What does everyone else think of the matter? Which comes first, the chicken or the egg?'

This simple question resulted in a dead silence. Florence, in receipt of a frown from her adoptive mother and an even heavier frown from her rich relation, lapsed into red-cheeked embarrassment. There was a sharp knock on the hall door. The sound of a familiar male voice. Philip Monahan, thought the Reverend Mother, and remembered the notes for the meeting that Julie had tucked into the leather blotter on the desk in the Imperial Hotel. He must have decided to bring them round himself. A murmur of words from a girl. She wouldn't want to disturb her mistress at dinner. The man's voice again: 'I understand. And don't worry, I'll do my best for Bernadette, Philomena,' and then the maid's voice again. The Reverend Mother frowned. Where had she heard these two names, Bernadette and Philomena, before?

Charlotte put down her untouched coffee cup and turned to her relatives. 'Now, let's get down to the business of the evening. I've decided, as I told you all in my letter, that my fortune, such as it is, would be best kept in one piece. I would like to feel that my husband's money was used to make a substantial difference in a worthy cause. Florence, my dear, tell me what an eighteen-year-old girl like yourself would do if I were to leave you all of my money?'

Not very fair on the youngest member present to be made to go first, thought the Reverend Mother, and then pricked her ears. There was a sound of heavy footsteps on the stairs outside the door and then the hall door slammed shut – perhaps a manservant, but would a manservant tread the marble stairs and the hall boards with such heavy assurance? Or had Philip Monahan only just left? She frowned a little. None of my business, she told herself, and settled herself to lend as much noticeable interest and approbation to Florence's plans as she could display. Florence wanted money for education. She spoke passionately about her desire to travel. Her wish to learn Russian as she felt the language might be of great importance in the future. First she would go to Paris and take a master's degree in French and then, the dream of her life, she would go to Moscow, study there, become fluent in Russian and then write a book about the Russian art treasures and become rich and famous. A glance at Charlotte's stony face made her hesitate, trip over her words, muddle and repeat herself, and soon she was close to tears.

'I'd give anything to go to the Hermitage Museum in St Petersburg,' she said breathlessly. 'I want to see—'

And then there was a sudden interruption. A resoundingly loud bang like a heavy stick hitting wood came from the shuttered window nearest to the Reverend Mother. Both she and Lucy started with alarm and Charlotte smiled sourly.

'Some hooligan,' she said curtly. 'Carry on, Florence. There's no problem, no need for alarm. You told Buckley to put up the ground-floor shutters on all the windows, didn't you, Julie.' Her tone held a warning note and Julie responded instantly, almost like a well-trained dog.

'Yes, of course, Cousin Charlotte.'

Another loud bang, this time on the window behind Claude and Nicholas. The rioters had gone around to the Grattan Street side of the house. Claude jumped, noticed the Reverend Mother, but Nicholas stayed very still and then, rather ostentatiously, lifted his coffee cup in a nonchalant fashion and drank from it. There was nevertheless an uneasy look in his eyes and others stiffened. The house was now surrounded by angry rioters.

'I say,' said Claude rather nervously. 'Those shutters. Old house and all that. They're good and thick, good strong wood, they'd be renewed from time to time. What?'

No one answered his comment but all seemed to listen anxiously, all awaiting the next blow.

Julie's eyes went to that curtained window and there was such a look of apprehension and tension in her face that Reverend Mother felt great sympathy suddenly for her. Charlotte, she thought, was very bad for Julie and the relationship was a disastrous one. No sooner was that thought in her head, than a third bang came from another one of the outside windows, this time from the one behind the sofa where she and Lucy sat.

There was a crash and a splintering of wood. The shutter had given way.

'That's a stone, and a big one, too,' said Nicholas.

The Reverend Mother replied as calmly as she could. 'I think you are right.'

'Should I send for the police?' asked Julie nervously and then twisted her hands together as no one answered her question, but all looked towards Charlotte who said nothing.

'That might be a good idea,' said the Reverend Mother, endeavouring to make her voice sound calm.

Charlotte smiled sourly. 'Don't worry, Reverend Mother. Just some trouble on the quays. Nothing to concern any of us. Julie – see to the shutter. Send Buckley out. Carry on, Florence. You haven't convinced me yet.'

Not the most encouraging of sentences and the Reverend Mother was not surprised when Florence began to stumble over her words as she endeavoured to continue.

Beneath the muddled sequences of thoughts that had, possibly, spent too long churning around in her mind, the girl had an aim and it was interesting one, and probably far more worthwhile than her contemporaries', such as Lucy's daughters who appeared to be fixated on the idea of dances, clothes and then good marriages. The Reverend Mother did her best to encourage Florence, but, between the occasional thuds of stones upon the shutters, the intermittent hammering on the door knocker and the lack of interest from the audience, it was obvious that her words, like Florence's own, were falling upon deaf ears.

There was no sound of hammering, though, the Reverend Mother noticed. Perhaps the chauffeur had declined to risk his life among the rioters. Julie had slunk back, opening the door a crack and sidling in, taking her seat near to the door. All eyes went to her and then slid away.

'I think that it all sounds a most ridiculous waste of money,' said Charlotte Hendrick eventually, interrupting poor Florence in a slightly muddled description of the medieval icons to be seen in some obscure monastery.

Florence flushed a dark shade of red and sat back in her chair. Her chance of a fortune to fund her education seemed to have abruptly disappeared. Claude said, 'See one Russian icon and you see them all!' Julie looked suddenly more cheerful, whether at the cessation of the blows, or because she now rated her chances a little more highly. Nicholas Hendrick leaned back in his chair with a complacent expression on his face. Brenda said, 'Thank you, darling, all very interesting, I'm sure, though I'm an old-fashioned type and I think, my pet, you'd be much happier in the end if you forgot about Russia and Paris. Why not just spend a few years at the college here in Cork? I'm sure that cousin Charlotte would like you to do something like that.'

'Lots of handsome young men at the university

here,' said Lucy encouragingly and Florence gave her a weak scowl, while Julie chimed in with some anecdote about the daughter of a friend who had 'caught' – and Florence cast her eyes to the ceiling at the verb – a young man who was studying medicine and now they had a lovely house in Tivoli, or was it . . .?

Julie stopped abruptly. The noise was back. Not stones, now, but chanting. There was a roar of voices from outside on the quay. Nothing could be distinguished but the one word 'Hendrick' and at that all suddenly felt silent. Nicholas was on his feet instantly, declaring his intention of calling the police and then going up to the first storey of the house in order to see what was happening. There was a strained silence for a moment or two after he left, but then, Julie, at Charlotte's barked instruction, shut the door after him and a murmur of low-voiced remarks began to fill the silence until Nicholas returned and shrugged his shoulders at the assembled company.

'Police are on their way. The river is flooding,' he said. 'Couldn't see anyone. Don't suppose that we'll have any more trouble. I'd say that it is knee-deep on the quays by now. The brave heroes will be off to their kennels. I've had a word with one of the maids. The shutters are all in place and there is a torrent of water going down Grattan Street.'

At this moment there was another onslaught of stones against the hall door, heavier ones this time, judged the Reverend Mother. Nicholas jumped to his feet and went back out of the door. Charlotte looked pointedly at Claude, but he ignored her, cleared his throat and took some piece of paper from an inside pocket.

'Well then, Claude!' said Charlotte abruptly, seeming bored with the whole discussion. 'Let's hear what you would do with a substantial sum of money. Not purchase any Russian icons, I would guess.'

'What me? I'll be dashed if I would waste a penny on them.' Claude launched into a confident presentation of his ideas for expanding his business and making his club the most south-after place of entertainment by the wealthy of Cork. The Reverend Mother half-listened, but her thoughts were on what was happening outside on the quays. The cries of angry men, the stones against the window shutters. She bit her lip. So, so stupid. It would all make their lives worse.

Her mind went to Philip Monahan as Charlotte harangued Claude on the fallacies in his plans. Monahan's was the only way. He had organized the law to dissolve the corrupt Cork City Council and was now endeavouring to raise funds in order to move the poor of the city on to more salubrious and higher land outside the 'flat of the city', as Cork people named it. The Reverend Mother wondered briefly whether he would ever manage to achieve that uphill struggle before turning her attention back to what was happening within the room. Brenda's pathetic attempt at getting money to restore her husband's wine business in the town of Fermoy had been sneered at; Julie's plan to turn the house into a boarding house for retired ladies had been laughed to scorn; and Lucy had made a half-hearted attempt to interest Charlotte Hendrick in the plight of the newly married who did not have enough money to finance an expensive way of life. After these had been dismissed, she found herself declining to make a case. She and her school would manage in the way that they had been managing for years, getting money from here, there and everywhere. Her powers of begging, of shaming officialdom, of tapping resources open to her because of her position in Cork, of her family name and her own reputation would not be lessened while she was still alive and sentient. Philip Monahan's scheme was the bolder and the more radical. Knock down the terrible tenements, rehouse the unfortunate inhabitants in new buildings, in clean, fresh air outside the disease-laden fogs and fever-carrying smells of the city.

'I think, Mrs Hendrick,' she said levelly, 'that a large portion of your money should be used to support Mr Monahan's scheme to build new houses for these unfortunate people.' And then she sat back and waited for an explosion.

Oddly it did not come. Charlotte Hendrick also sat back. Her lips were a little tighter than usual, her eyes narrowed as they looked across at her elderly cousin, but she made no response whatsoever. The

Reverend Mother waited calmly, noticing that the sound of the river seemed to have entered the house as though someone had opened a door or a window on to Bachelor's Quay. She fancied that she heard the slap of water against the side of the house. There was less light coming through the crack in the shutters and the curtains now appeared not green, but inky black. A gas lamp had been smashed, she guessed. The noise was getting worse. The mob was angered by the strong defences of the house. Charlotte rose to her feet.

'Let's go upstairs to the drawing room,' she said and led the way without a glance at her guests. There was a thunderous slamming of metal against the wood of the hall door as they mounted the stairs, but Charlotte didn't even turn her head as she ushered them into the drawing room and pointed out seats.

And then, at last, came the sound of a police siren. There was visible relief on all their faces. The Reverend Mother wondered whether unarmed police would be able to control the riot. Pent-up feelings had been released and might now be difficult to contain.

'Nicholas,' said Charlotte and now her face cleared and she turned on her husband's nephew an expression that seemed almost benevolent. 'Now, Nicholas, perhaps you would explain how you would like to squander your uncle's hard-earned money.'

The words were sharp, but they were delivered in

an affectionate, slightly teasing manner. In, thought the Reverend Mother, an aunt-like manner. A typical aunt/nephew relationship with a man who had been, as a boy, a frequent visitor to the house. Nicholas, encouraged by the friendly tone, raised his voice over the noise from outside and gave an inspiring lecture on the Viking connection to the city of Cork. The noise began to die down, the rioters retreating from the police and moving back downstream towards Merchant's Quay and so Nicholas was able to hold the floor without interruption, though the threat may have only retreated and could return.

The Reverend Mother looked around the room and noted the expressions on faces that pretended to listen. Depression, a sense of failure, resentment perhaps; these were to be expected, but the predominant appearance on the faces around her was of humiliation. Dr Scher had told her that it was well-known that the widow's money, in its entirety, was to be willed to Professor Nicholas Hendrick. If Dr Scher had known that, the story was probably all around this city filled with gossips. Each one of the mendicants here, all looking for an inheritance, had probably heard that. Had heard it, forced it to the back of the mind, but now in the face of this fluency from the nephew and this obvious pride and benevolence from the wealthy widow, the story had been proved to be true. Not to put too fine a point upon it, thought the Reverend Mother, they had all been taken for suckers and now humiliation was written on each face. Surprising how Charlotte

84

Hendrick appeared to be unaware of their feelings and almost seemed to be expecting everyone present to join in with her admiration of her talented nephew, whose bony face now glowed with satisfaction and anticipation.

How foolish they all were. Providing an evening of amusement for a wealthy woman suffering from boredom. As soon as Nicholas sat back with a smile of satisfaction on his face, the Reverend Mother hauled up her watch from the depths of her pocket, bringing, to her slight embarrassment, a very sticky wrapped sweet with it. She hastily replaced the sweet, kept there for emergencies, and consulted her watch with an air of gravity.

'I fear I must leave you now,' she announced. 'I keep early hours and still have my office to recite.' And with that, she got to her feet.

'Goodness,' said Lucy, seizing upon the opportunity, 'is that the time? Yes, I wish you all good night.'

In a few moments they managed to get out of the room to be followed by the others. As they mounted the last set of stairs, the Reverend Mother could hear Brenda calling Florence in ever more irritated tones. She frowned. Florence had slid from the room just before the end of Nicholas's dissertation. Where was she? None of her business, but perhaps Lucy was right. Florence was a bit of a monkey. She hoped that the girl had not gone to seek out that young chauffeur in his private quarters on the Grattan Street side of the house.

'No kissing, no goodnight wishes from our hostess – well, none that meant anything, just ringing the bell for the maid,' said Lucy when they reached their room and were warming their hands by the minuscule coal fire that burned tentatively in a fire basket set into the marble fireplace.

'Some more coal, please, my dear, and two drinks,' she said to the servant and then went over to the window. 'Goodness! Come and see. The river has spread across the quay. It will be lapping at the first-floor windows soon,' she said.

'I doubt it,' said the Reverend Mother indifferently. The house, she thought, had been built on a raised block of sandstone, the foundation line of bricks imbedded into the rock. It had withstood the rigours of floods for over two hundred years. 'Once the tide turns, the flood will subside. Think of the Vikings,' she added with a trace of malice.

'I do not,' said Lucy with emphasis, 'want to think about the Vikings, not ever again. I've heard enough about Vikings to last me for the rest of my life.'

'Don't be such a bad loser,' said the Reverend Mother. Rather dubiously, she was feeling the sheets.

Lucy opened her mouth to reply and then shut it quickly again as the maid came into the room with a tray bearing a pot of tea, small milk jug and a basin of sugar lumps. 'Ann will be up in a minute with the coal, ma'am,' she said. 'Is there anything else that I can get you, ma'am?'

'A couple of hot water bottles would be lovely,' said Lucy. 'I suppose that it must be the river, but the sheets feel a bit damp.'

'You are embarrassing that girl; I don't know how you can do it,' observed the Reverend Mother as the door closed behind the maid.

'Never mind. I'll give her and the other girl a good tip when I leave.'

'And there will be Ann with the coal scuttle, also,' remarked the Reverend Mother, but when the girl appeared, she was a little surprised. Surely she knew that face.

'Are you Ann?' she asked hesitantly.

'Yes, Reverend Mother. Do you remember me? I used to go to your school. I left early.'

That very round face with those two very round eyes. Recollection came back. 'But you used to be called Philomena, isn't that right?'

'That's right, Reverend Mother,' said the girl. 'But when I started work here the missus thought Philomena was too fancy, so I was changed to Ann.'

'I see,' said the Reverend Mother. The power of the rich, she thought. Even a name bestowed at the baptismal font can be changed at a whim. And then another thought came to her. 'But Mr Monahan called you Philomena, isn't that right? I noticed the name.'

'That's right, Reverend Mother, he knows my sister. You remember Bernadette, don't you, Reverend Mother?'

The Reverend Mother nodded and smiled. Yes, she remembered Bernadette. Another fancy name. Pregnant before her thirteenth birthday, that was the memory that she had of Bernadette. A man in a pub, she seemed to remember. Bought the girl some food and supplied her with Murphy's Stout.

'Mr Monahan is trying to get the landlord to do something about her place. She's got four little ones now and the place is falling down around their ears,' said Philomena and gave a hasty and guilty glance around before deftly building up the fire with half a scuttle full of coals. 'I'll be off then,' she said nervously once the flames were shooting up and she backed herself out of the room.

'Good fellow, that Mr Monahan,' said Lucy. 'Nice of him to trouble himself about the sister of that girl. I don't think that dear cousin Charlotte will think much of his re-housing scheme, from what you tell me of his ideas.'

'I don't want to waste another moment on Charlotte Hendrick,' said the Reverend Mother. 'Lucy, I'm worried about Julie. What a life for her! She seems genuinely frightened of the future. Did you see her face when Charlotte laughed at the idea of her managing a business?'

The Reverend Mother awoke abruptly in the middle of the night. The rain must be over; moonlight shone through a crack in the heavy velvet curtains. Something had roused her. She was sure of that. She was a good sleeper and the moonlight would not have bothered her. The sound of slow, even breathing from across the room told her that Lucy still slept.

But she had definitely heard something. Now that she was awake she was quite sure of that. It had been a noise of a door shutting or perhaps a window. There had been a definite and quite loud click from somewhere beyond the wall of the room. Moving carefully and quietly, and taking care not to disturb her cousin, she pushed her feet into her slippers and put a dressing gown over her nightclothes and checked the bathroom. No, the window was firmly closed and locked. And yet she had certainly heard something that was like the click of a window.

Then she sat on the edge of the bed and wondered what to do next. Any unusual sound or movement in her convent would be her responsibility, but here in the house of her cousin, she had no business to investigate anything.

And yet she was uneasy. Now that she was fully awake she realized that the noise had come from the room next door, from the bedroom occupied by her cousin Charlotte, the place where the bags of flax seed and baskets of Amsterdam silk had been stored a couple of centuries ago. The window had certainly not been open in that room when she and Lucy had looked in earlier that afternoon, and she would be surprised if it had been opened later on, given the mist and the rain when all had retired to bed.

But that sound had surely come from there.

Could Charlotte be ill? The evening may have been more of a strain upon her than it appeared at the time. The Reverend Mother hesitated for a moment and then decided that no harm could be done by a quick check.

The room she shared with Lucy was illuminated faintly through the thick curtains by the moon. Its light was enough to show that a bedside candle stood on the small table beside her. Moving quietly, she struck a match and taking the handle securely between finger and thumb she cautiously made her way across the thick carpet and went to the door. The passageway outside was lit by a single gas lamp, but the Reverend Mother held on to her candle and made her way down to the entrance to her cousin's bedroom. She put her hand on the doorknob and twisted it carefully, anxious not to attract attention from Claude or Nicholas, who slept on the opposite side of the central staircase. She would, she thought, just open the door soundlessly, peep in and then withdraw if all seemed well.

The door was stiffer than she had remembered it had been when Lucy had opened it earlier. She twisted again, but then realized that the door had been locked. One more try convinced her; there was no doubt about it, no possibility that the door was merely stiff. It was definitely locked and no key was in the keyhole. There was no sound now. All seemed to be well. She stood for a while looking around her at the dimly lit passages and stairways. There were lights on in the storey below, on the Grattan Street side, where the other guests were housed but all was still and silent on this top floor. There was, she realized, a definite draught coming from under the door and it puzzled her. The window of Charlotte's room must be wide open, but why on a bad night like this?

Well, there was no point in rousing a household over an open window in the bedroom of her hostess. Feeling still rather mystified, she made her way back into her own room, replaced her candle, replenished their fire with some fresh coal and then went back into her bed, taking her pocket watch from the bedside table. Already past midnight. Tomorrow, no, today, there would be breakfast to endure and then, doubtless, some unpleasant moments when Charlotte revealed that she was leaving her entire fortune to Professor Nicholas Hendrick, but after that she would be free to go home to her convent. Lucy, she imagined, would be as relieved as herself to make her farewells. And Charlotte, once she had dropped her bombshell, would not want to detain her guests. The woman, she thought, as she pulled the blankets and thick eiderdown up around her shoulders, had not looked at all well.

CHAPTER 5

The bells from Shandon had sounded the eleventh hour when Eileen decided that she was definitely going home. But as she looked around for Mickey Joe, she was tapped sharply on the shoulder. She turned around indignantly, but it was not one of the poor tenants, nor one of the students. A tall, heavily built man. Well-dressed. Large moustache and bald head.

'Out of my way, young lady, I need to use that machine,' he said and gave her a push that made her stumble and almost fall as she stepped back. He squared his shoulders, sucked in a breath and pushed his mouth right up close to the loudhailer, almost touching it. Eileen watched him. If he hadn't pushed her she would have shown him where to stand and how to speak, but now she was determined not to say a word. Let him find out the hard way!

And so she walked away and stood at a distance, watching him with amusement. The crowd had thickened here on Merchant's Square, back from the river. The floods were greater further up the quays, towards Cork harbour, she guessed. But

92

the wind had begun to rise and the fog was being blown away. The mist had ceased and the moon had come out from behind the clouds. Eileen thought about walking home but decided to wait until this fellow had finished with the loudhailer and she could hand it over to someone; Mickey Joe Clancy, hopefully, though he seemed to have disappeared.

'Are any of my tenants here?' The man bellowed like a bull in an effort to be heard. 'Listen to me, everyone, I say! Are any of my tenants here?' He stopped and looked around, but none of the crowd were paying attention. The loudhailer had lost its novelty value and his words were blurred, in any case. The poor of Cork were beginning to enjoy themselves. Several sing-song sessions had begun. Women, as well as men, crowded the road outside the public house and children raced around, shrieking loudly, excited by the wind, while others tried to catch the eels that bubbled out of drains. They weren't interested in straining their ears to interpret the distorted sounds that boomed in the background. He might as well save his voice and go home, thought Eileen, but the landlord kept going. His face, she noticed, was an even deeper shade of purple and his eyes were protruding from beneath his bushy eyebrows.

'Listen to me, everyone. Listen to me. If any of my tenants are here . . . You just listen to me, my men, or it will be the worse for you,' he yelled into the mouthpiece, the words distorted and the sound hitting against the tall stone tenements on the quay and blending in with the songs and yells. Standing quite close to him, Eileen could hear the words as he uttered them, but even a few yards away no one else seemed to be listening to the unpleasant booming sound.

'This is your landlord speaking,' he shouted. 'Listen to me, you men! Listen to me, you drunken sots! You've all been paid for unloading that ship. Don't think that I don't know that! And if you have squandered that money, money that you owe to me, on drinking, well I'll have no mercy on you . . . Do you hear me, my men! Get out of that public house immediately or you might find yourselves and your families out on the street tomorrow morning. Just you make sure that you don't spend the money that is due to me. Just you keep your money for your rent. My agent will be around to you in the morning.' He screamed the words into the loudhailer, but they went unheeded as far as Eileen could see. No one could properly hear. He was just background noise.

The riotous singing went on from the public house. From time to time, someone stumbled out, went around the back of the building and then went straight into the bar again. Fairly drunk, the majority of them in there, thought Eileen. The men would have been paid about half-a-crown to unload the ship and most of that money was being spent on barrels of stout. They took no notice of the landlord who was now trying to call out the names of the streets and the lanes where he owned tenements, these four- and five-story-high crumbling houses where families tried to exist in conditions of terrible damp and squalor. The man was standing back a little now from the mouth of the loudhailer and some of the names that he screamed out could be identified: Pike's Lane, Hoare's Street, Ballard's Lane . . .

But there were no anxious exits from the public house. More men were going in there. Empty barrels were wheeled out and a cart arrived from Beamish & Crawford with new supplies of crates of the stronger glass-bottled beers. The singing went on, becoming more and more raucous. And then an enormous bottle was carried in to raucous cheers.

Purple-faced with fury, the landlord of the tenements gazed around him, glared at Eileen. She responded with a shrug of her shoulders. None of her business. She moved away a little to distance herself from him. Hopefully he would soon go home and so should she. By now she had plenty of material for a good article for the *Cork Examiner* and she wanted to type it out before she got too tired. Let Mickey Joe look after the loudhailer. It wasn't her responsibility, after all. She didn't ask to be given that job. Nevertheless, she scrambled up on to the windowsill of a derelict house and strained her eyes to see if she could pick him out from amongst the crowd.

To her surprise, in the distance, she noticed that

the chauffeur, Anthony Buckley, was back again and this time, he had a girl with him. Yes, he was telling the truth. That girl had posh clothes and her blond hair was crimped in one of those marcel waves.

Oh, well, she didn't care. She was about to turn away when she noticed he was carrying a rope coiled up and draped over one shoulder. He seemed to be looking for someone and as she watched, she saw that he was approached by Mickey Joe. There had been an arrangement between them; that was obvious. The rope was handed over and then the chauffeur and the girl turned and went back in the direction that he had come. Mickey Joe, also, disappeared – to her annoyance, as she wanted to hand over the loud-hailer and also to point out to him that the purple-faced landlord was now charging off in the direction of the public house on the quay. Fights were beginning to break out. Time that the organizers started to take measures to calm things down a little. There would be bad trouble, she thought, if that fellow went in there, into the pub and started shouting his threats in the face of the crowd swallowing their porter. By the sounds of things, most of the people inside and the people standing in the doorway, were, all of them, dead drunk. She watched apprehensively. The men's faces were still blackened from the sacks of coal which they had unloaded. It lent them a strange and a sinister look. The furious landlord pressed on. He was expecting them to get out of the way, to melt at his approach. But they didn't. He yelled something. Waved his stick and a few men stood back, but only by a few steps. Now there was a narrow pathway opened up, flanked by the coal-stained faces. They were allowing him to go forward, but their silence in the face of his shouts was ominous and from her perch Eileen noticed that as he got nearer to the door, the gap behind him closed and the men formed a solid barrier behind him.

The man's stick came into play again as he was faced by the tense crowd at the doorway. She could see how he waved it above the heads. Half drunk, or very drunk, himself, thought Eileen. Stupid man! He thought that he was faced with the usual scared, subservient tenants that he encountered on the roadside, queueing up for work on the docks, or avoiding the rent collector. He didn't know that they were drunk not just with Beamish, but with a feeling that he was in their power.

'Will you get out of my way, you sods,' he was yelling. His voice, now that he no longer had the loudhailer to distort it, sounded clearly across the quay. Eileen climbed down from the stone slab and started to go across, then stopped herself. There was a low murmur of anger, a dangerous sign and she knew enough to keep clear. She stood back and looked around. No sign of Professor Hendrick; he had long disappeared. No sign, either, of Mickey Joe, or of any of the students. The boats and the students were gone. The quay was now jammed with men, big strong dock workers, many of them originally from the country, well-made and muscular. They were mostly drunk and in no mood to listen. There was going to be trouble. Eileen knew enough to tell her that she should go home now while she could, but something stopped her. This, she thought, was going to be a big, big story, far bigger than the one that she had already rehearsed in her mind. There was going to be a confrontation between a landlord and his tenants. Already, as she listened intently, she began to rehearse some breathless sentences in her mind. But, also, she could not keep from her mind the feeling that she bore some responsibility for what might be about to happen. She had been in the forefront of the effort to work up the tenants, to make them cry the crimes of the landlords to the skies, she had given them power by showing them how to use the loudhailer. She had been partially responsible for that low murmur of the anger and hate which came like a growl from a pack of wild dogs. She looked around frantically, trying to see any of the organizers, to see someone who might help, but none were anywhere near to the public house. And that stupid man was still roaring and shouting at the crowd.

'Get out of my way, you men.' They were drunk, but he also was drunk. Definitely drunk and lacking in all caution. Screaming out his words. 'My name is Mr O'Sullivan. And I'm telling you that any tenant of mine who is wasting money on drink will be out on the road tomorrow if he can't pay his rent. And don't give me any sob stuff about wives and children, either. You should think of that before you waste money on drink. Do you hear me, men?'

And with that, he plunged into the public house waving his stick and clearing a passage through the drinking men.

There was an odd sort of silence on the quay after he had disappeared. Eileen could see how men looked at each other. Some women gathered up children with shrill shouts and moved away into the shelter of the lanes. A few men moved away, also, but most came forward, quite slowly, but advancing. And then stood in clusters. They were all silent, tense and listening, but there was an ominous roar from within the public house: a deep sound that issued from the open door and the open windows of the overcrowded building.

And then a terrible scream rose above all other sounds. Not an ordinary scream. This was a strange, gargled sound, a sound like a wounded bull, almost a howl but with that shrill note of intense fear underlying the shriek for help.

Some people emerged from the lanes, came as if that scream had summoned them, as if some force had pulled them back; as if, against their will, they had been drawn back to the scene. They stood well back, though, and waited. The howls came again and again. And over and above them was the sharp sound of breaking glass.

The solidly massed crowd that jammed the entrance to the public house parted, then stood back almost deferentially, drawing back to allow the tenement landlord to come out. The man was streaming with blood. His face, his scalp, the loose skin on his neck had been sliced with the broken bottles, but more ominously, there was a large glass splinter, almost the size of a dagger, protruding from his stomach, and oddly, he held it in place with one of his hands. His face was dazed and he stumbled badly, only saved from falling by the sheer numbers that pressed together on either side of him, leaving a bare width of a few feet clear and allowing him to emerge.

'Hang him; string him up!' There was a low growl from the men that emerged from the public house. They had formed themselves into a solid wedge of people behind and on both sides of the bleeding, howling man.

Eileen felt her teeth begin to chatter. Someone from behind her flung a stone with deadly accuracy at a gaslight on the quayside and then others followed. One by one the lights started to go out until only one gas lamp and a glimmer from the public house lit up the scene.

'Hang him! Hang him! Hang him! Hang him!' The shouts had begun to turn into a chant. Those who wore iron-tipped boots beat the rhythm against the stone flags of the quayside and others with sticks drummed it out against the chains. Someone laughed, very loudly. A different feeling was emerging from the crowd around him. These men had been drinking all through the evening. Intoxicated and filled with aggression. But on the outskirts of the crowd, there was a ripple of movement away from the drunken mob. The women were the first to move, nervously gathering up the children, but they were followed by some of the men. People were beginning to sidle away into the dark shadows.

And then something was flung through the air and it landed with a thud just beside the remaining gaslight. Eileen could see it plainly. It was the coiled-up rope, the rope that the chauffeur had brought. It spurred the men into action. A low mutter, getting louder by the minute. 'Hang the bastard!' Ominously, the words echoed from the tall derelict houses that lined Merchant's Square, doubling the effect. 'Bastard! Bastard! Bastard!' The words began as an angry hiss, but then exploded into a roar. Eileen felt herself freeze with horror. It couldn't be happening. She would have to do something. From behind her a cracked adolescent voice said, 'Jaysus! Holy Mackerel!' She looked around frantically. About fourteen, she thought, hair beginning to sprout from his chin. A very deep voice. Just what she needed.

'Quick,' she said to him. 'Quick, shout into the loudhailer. Tell them the Peelers are coming. Tell them that they'll all end up in jail. Say it! "The Peelers are coming! Scarper!" Go on, roar it out!'

He was beside her in an instant. She pushed him

into position and switched on the loudhailer. His voice boomed out, load, hoarse, cracked and menacing and it was echoing around the quay.

'The Peelers are coming!'

The words were taken up; were repeated by those around them; shouted out in tones of warning; even those across the river seemed to hear them and thronged to the quayside. The gas lamps were all lit up over there and Eileen could see how the crowds coming back from evening benediction at the Dominican Church were gathering along the river's edge and pointing across the wide expanse of the River Lee.

And then came the loud, ear-piercing, deafening wail of a police car's siren. A new acquisition and people were not used to it. Several women clapped their hands to their ears, but they did not hesitate, didn't wait to see. They just went back towards the lanes. No sober person would risk being caught on the scene. She could hear the words 'Union Quay Barracks' from the crowd. Tuckey Street, Barrack Street and the other police barracks would be sending men, also. The wisest thing was to be gone as soon as possible.

Eileen's heart skipped a beat. She was known to the police. There had been a time when her face was on a poster in every police barracks in the city. She would not be forgotten. If they saw her in the middle of this crowd that was whipping up a fever of hate against the landlords, they would likely arrest her. She could not afford any break in her

102

studies now. She needed to get that degree and she had taken a vow to keep away from trouble and to drop all political activity for the next few years. She looked around frantically and then made a quick decision to abandon the loudhailer.

'You've got a great voice. Keep it up, keep warning them,' she said encouragingly to the young lad and then she took to her heels, running in the opposite direction. No point in looking for Mickey Joe. Let him look after himself. When she reached Fish Street, she turned without hesitation into it. There was a network of narrow lanes in that area, dark and so restricted in width that there was not the slightest possibility that the police car could follow her there. After a few minutes she slowed to a walk. The river was flooding. That could be seen even in here. The drains were spewing their foul-smelling contents out on to the road and she walked with care, hoping that she could avoid the rats, relieved that she was wearing her knee-high boots and had not bothered to change into something fancier for the evening out with Mickey Joe.

Resolutely she endeavoured to avert her mind from that bleeding, howling figure that had stumbled out from the public house.

But one question kept intruding itself into her mind as she waded through the flooded lanes.

Why had the chauffeur given that rope to Mickey Joe?

The implication was clear, terrible and

unbearable. She couldn't avoid it. Mickey Joe was prepared to commit murder and the chauffeur was his accomplice. She knew where that rope had come from. She had often passed the splendid house on Bachelor's Quay where he worked and seen the rope that hung down from the pulley wheel high on the wall overlooking the river.

Only one thing was unsure. Would the rope be used to hang the man before the police arrived on the scene?

The siren of the police car had ceased, but the roars and the shouts and shrieks still continued. The boy that she had left with the loudhailer had ceased to cry out. Nothing but the angry roar of the crowd. She did not know what was happening.

Eileen slowed to walking pace and then stopped. It was no good telling herself that what was happening on the quays was none of her business. The image of that bleeding face and that shard of broken glass protruding from the blood-soaked clothes could not be banished. She had been there. She had allowed the man to shout that inflammatory stuff into the loudhailer, had been part, earlier on, of stirring up the bad feeling against landlords. She would have to go back and see what had happened to the guards. Resolutely she turned and began to run, forcing herself to go as fast as she could, not allowing herself time to think or time for her courage to evaporate. There was an ominous rumble of sound from the quays. She could just about distinguish the words. 'String him up! String him up!' Why weren't the guards on the scene by now? Had they turned and fled in the face of that immense crowd of angry people?

When she burst out from the narrow entrance to the lane she could see what had happened. The last tide barrier must have broken and now the river had spilled out in waves across the street and was lapping against the doors of the tall tenements at the side of the quay. The police car had made no further progress. She could see it dimly in the distance, the large red letters G A R D A on its radiator were just about visible, but its wheels and its two headlamps were beneath the flood water. Neither lights nor siren would be working now. They would have been better off with the rowing club's loudhailer, she thought, but there was no sound from that either. Either the boy had got frightened and abandoned it, or someone had seized it and thrown it into the river. For a moment she faltered. It would be so much easier to dive back into the narrow lane and to make her way home, but then another of those terrible screams rose above the chanting of the crowd. It was from the injured landlord. She recognized the voice, hoarse with fear. No aggression, now. No false posh accent, no scolding. Nothing in that voice but fear. The fear of an animal who scents death.

Eileen pushed onwards, feeling the flood waters rise up around her boots. Hard to make progress with the weight of the water. Another scream. But just the beginning of one. It was cut off mid-breath. A choking sound. She visualized that purple face, those heavy jowls and as clearly as though she had seen it, the noose around that fat neck.

The chanting and shouting died down. Seemed as though suddenly cut off. There was an odd silence. A voice rose up. A policeman. A familiar voice. Patrick, she thought. The words were indistinguishable. Muffled by the sound of the water beating against the walls. Eileen caught an odd word here and there. 'Disperse' – stupid word to use – half the people there wouldn't know what it meant. And then something about 'homes'.

'Go to your homes!' That was definitely Patrick and for a moment Eileen admired his courage. There would be only three or four of them from Barrack Street. And they would have no firearms. Nothing but their cudgels and the knowledge that anyone arrested would be handcuffed and dragged off for a night in a cell. But then, downstream from St Patrick's Bridge, there was a roar of engines, a sound of klaxons, a few shots fired in the air over the river. The soldiers were coming, coming down from Collins Barracks on the hill. Their lorries built with enormous wheels, keeping them high up off the ground and above the flood. In a minute they would be across the bridge and would be coming up Merchant's Quay.

There was a frantic movement of people in the background of Merchant's Square. Eileen found herself engulfed in a swarm of people who were moving back, retreating from the quays. The men were sobering up now, she guessed. Very little noise, no more shouting, just a solid wave of bodies moving to the lanes, almost shepherded by a solid press of uniformed police from barracks all over the city. The police cells would be full that night. She couldn't afford to be amongst them, to be hauled up before a magistrate in some court tomorrow morning.

Eileen neatly sidestepped the crowd, ducking into a deep recess between the end of one terrace of houses and the beginning of another. The gas lamp here was still working, and it threw a bright circle of light on the flooded pavement and roadway in front of the house's hall door. However, once she had retreated a few steps further back into the lanes behind the quays, she found herself in darkness. She kept one hand on the rough stone at the side of the end house and edged her way along the cobbled surface, listening to the rough shouts of policemen who were now gaining in confidence as the rioters became more subdued.

Luck wasn't with her, however. She had only taken about twenty paces back when her foot met a wall. She ran her hand over it. Not a rough wall, but a smooth one, built of cut stone. Another set of houses had been built here, back-to-back with the houses on the quayside. Cautiously she moved along but there was no exit. The lane had come to a dead end. She would just have to wait until the crowd moved away and the *Garda Síochána* had taken their prisoners back to the cells in any of the eighteen barracks scattered around the city of Cork.

Eileen felt deeply sorry for these poor men. They had a hard life and they lived in terrible buildings and then one day they get some work, had an hour of happiness and oblivion and this happens. Nothing she could do, but anger welled up within her as she stood silently waiting for the quayside to empty.

She could hear the voices of the policemen and she recognized one voice in particular. It came from a police car crawling past on the pavement. She heard its siren. Not blaring out to intimidate, but issuing a series of small, short warning signals. It was moving cautiously, progressing almost foot by foot, a constable in front of it, signalling with his torch. The water now was barely lapping around the lower half of the four wheels. Patrick, she thought, with a grin. There was something about the extreme care of the manoeuvre which was so characteristic of him.

For a moment she wished that she was with him, that she could appeal to him to get her out of this mess, but that was stupid. The last person she wanted to see was Patrick Cashman. Inspector Patrick Cashman. He knew everything about her past and would be unlikely to believe that she just got caught up in this riot by accident. No, she would have to wait it out. She felt tears welling up in her eyes and wished that she was at home with her mother, sitting by the new range that she had bought with her earnings from the *Cork Examiner* and her mother telling her, as usual, that she was the cleverest, the best, the most wonderful girl in the world.

But was she clever? Or just very, very stupid to have got herself involved in this affair. That man, that landlord, had looked on the point of death. Perhaps he was dead now. Hanged by the neck from a gas lamppost.

Eileen didn't think that she could stand it any longer. She had to get home. The shouting had mostly died down. The soldiers were gathered around the public house where the riot had exploded into terrible violence. Men were being arrested and taken back to police barracks all over the city. It should be safe to move. The bells from Shandon rang out, once again. Twelve peals now: midnight. Her mother would be getting worried. She had to take a chance on it. Luckily she was wearing a dark coat and she was used to the dark. 'Cat's eyes' her mother used to say fondly when she was a child.

So, keeping a hand on the wall and moving slowly and cautiously she went towards the quay. The noise was dying down. A few sharp police whistles in the distance, towards Patrick Street on the south but less noise on her own side of town. Those lucky enough not to be arrested had slunk away to their own tenements. The students had disappeared and the public house which had been at the centre of the dark deed now showed no light, save for the glint of a candle in an attic bedroom.

By this time she was able to walk freely. Nevertheless, she thought that she would not go down the North and South Main Streets just in case the police were still around. It would be safer to go home through St Mary's of the Isle. Bachelor's Quay, she noticed, was well lit by the lamps across the river and the pavement was clear of flood water. She went as quickly as she could, but just before she turned the corner into Grattan Street, passing by the huge house belonging to the wealthy Mrs Hendrick on the corner, her eye was caught by a movement on the wall by her side.

She knew the house well. As a child going to market in the Coal Quay with her mother she had been fascinated by the wheel and by the rope that was coiled around it and kept fastened on to a pair of brackets. Once she had even seen an enormous bath in a rope cradle being winched up the wall. Now as she looked up she could see that a window had been left open – strange on such a wet and foggy night – but that was not all. The rope with its iron winch was not coiled around the wheel, but hung loose, almost reaching pavement level as though ready to pull a weight up to the top of the house.

CHAPTER 6

'Now, Dottie, I've ordered early-morning tea and biscuits, so just you stay in bed and enjoy a little comfort for a change.' For a moment, the Reverend Mother, still half-asleep, was taken aback. Ever since, over twenty years ago, she had moved to the position of superior in her convent she had enjoyed the luxury of an unshared bedroom and the sound of her cousin's voice brought her back to a time almost sixty years ago when she and Lucy, both mother-less children, almost sisters, had shared a bedroom at home, at school and then later during the many invitations to weekends and balls and other parties in the widely scattered country houses of County Cork. No one, except her cousin Lucy, ever called her 'Dottie' or even 'Dorothy' these days. She was 'Reverend Mother' to most of the denizens of Cork city.

'You startled me; I must have slept in.' The Reverend Mother lay still for a moment. 'I was awake for a while in the night,' she went on sleepily. 'I heard a noise, heard a banging noise. It seemed to be coming from our bathroom, I supposed at the time. The door was open to our bathroom and I thought a window might have been left open.'

'And of course you had to get up and close it like a responsible Reverend Mother,' teased Lucy. 'If it had been me, well, I would just have pulled the covers over my head and gone to sleep, but I don't suppose that you did.'

'I did get up, but the bathroom window was shut. The noise had not come from there. And our bedroom window was shut also. I thought then that it might have been next door to us. Somebody knocking on the wall or something. I put on a dressing gown,' said the Reverend Mother slowly. 'And I went out into the corridor, but the door to Charlotte's room, well, it was closed and although I knocked quietly, just enough for someone awake to hear, but not loudly enough to wake a sleeper, there was no answer. I tried the handle of the door and it was locked.'

'And so you sensibly went back to bed. And shut the bathroom door, I hope.'

'It was shut already. I had shut it myself after I had finished in there. But there was definitely a draught coming from under Charlotte's door as though there were a window open in there. I wondered, though. It didn't seem like a night for a window to be opened.' The Reverend Mother lay very still for a moment, trying to remember exactly what had struck her as strange the night before. Somehow she had an uneasy feeling, but perhaps that could have been traced to the unpleasant events of the evening before. She thought back to the faces as they listened to Nicholas's fluent exposition of how he would use the money of his wealthy aunt, if he were lucky enough to inherit.

There had been disappointment on those faces – yes, disappointment, but anger also. Her mind pictured them all. Florence, flushed, and even slightly tearful, feeling mortified perhaps, as she listened to Nicholas, that she had not been equally eloquent about her dreams before slipping out of the room as if she could bear no more. Brenda beside her, poker-faced as always, but a strange gleam from her eyes. Claude, biting his nails, restlessly clenching and unclenching his hands, Lucy, even Lucy, had been tight-lipped and wearing an expression of dislike.

As for Julie, well, there had been something about the expression on Julie's face that had made the Reverend Mother feel deeply uncomfortable. Lucy's words 'they hate each other' came back to her and she bowed her head. She had never been someone who dodged the truth and her memory of Julie's face last night had shown to her the stark truth of her cousin's observation. There had been hate upon that face as she listened to Charlotte Hendrick's scornful verdict on her idea to use her cousin's fortune to run a boarding house. Money is the root of all evil, she repeated to herself and sighed heavily. If only the wretched stuff were not of such vital importance. Perhaps in the biblical story of Eve, that apple was really a symbol of worldly riches, an occasion of sin, as the catechism put it.

'I'll be glad to get home,' said Lucy decisively. 'This has been a waste of time. I'm sure that she will give everything to Nicholas.'

'Yes,' said the Reverend Mother. 'I shall be glad to be home.' The convent, she thought, was a pleasant place to live. On the whole, everyone there worked for a common good, worked to care for and to educate the children of the poor. She was, she thought, so much happier than Charlotte Hendrick who thought only about the power and the virtues of money. Soon, she thought, she would get up, dress and make her excuses to her hostess. Lucy, she reckoned, would not want to stay too long, either.

But breakfast in bed would be a wonderful treat.

And then she sat up in bed. 'Did you hear something, Lucy?'

'I thought I heard a scream.' Lucy put down her powder compact and got to her feet, but had not got to the door before there was a sudden frantic battering on it. The Reverend Mother swung her legs over the edge of her bed, pulled on her dressing gown and seized her clothes. She would dress in the bathroom. Lucy could deal with the matter for the moment, but she had an odd instinct that something serious had happened. That had been a piercing, almost frightening scream. As she dressed rapidly, she could hear that the scream was followed by loud sobs.

'Julie! What's the matter? Come in. Don't wake the house. Come in, Julie. What's wrong? What has happened? Sit on that chair there. Ah, here comes Ann with the tea trolley. Bring it in here, will you? Thank you, Ann. Just put it on that table there. Miss Clancy is not feeling well.'

The Reverend Mother calmly pinned the folds of her wimple and then adjusted her coif, but her mind was active. There had been, she thought, a tension in that dining room last night and it would not be surprising if something had resulted. Or was it perhaps a burglary in the night. She hoped that Charlotte had not collapsed.

'Don't let the girl go into that room! Don't let her! It would frighten her to death!' Julie, from what the Reverend Mother could hear from behind the bathroom door, was about to descend into a full-blown fit of hysterics. Lucy could deal with that, though. Despite Lucy's fragile and delicate appearance, she was, her cousin knew, both practical and resourceful. The Reverend Mother arranged her habit, buckled her belt, automatically checking on her bunch of keys, pinned her veil to her wimple, gave a hasty glance in the mirror and then sailed forth, noting with one rapid glance that the hysterical Julie was now gulping down tea and that Philomena (renamed Ann) was obediently awaiting orders.

The Reverend Mother wasted no time. 'You've

been in Mrs Hendrick's room, Julie, is that right?'

Julie was sobbing into her hands, and did not reply.

'And you, Ann,' asked the Reverend Mother. 'Did you go into Mrs Hendrick's room?'

'Miss Clancy opened the door for me, Reverend Mother,' said the girl. 'It's never locked usually, but it was locked this morning. I couldn't bring in the tea. Miss Clancy opened the door with her own key and then she screamed and came out. She told me not to go in. That's right, isn't it, Miss Clancy?' The girl hesitated a little and looked over towards Julie as if seeking corroboration. 'I didn't see nothing,' she said, but her face was white and she looked scared and the Reverend Mother guessed that it was unlikely that the girl had not looked into the room. 'Miss Clancy saw something; she screamed, didn't you, Miss Clancy?'

Julie sobbed in reply and said something inarticulate, but the Reverend Mother had heard enough. 'Stay here with Mrs Murphy and Miss Clancy,' she said to the girl and with a steady step she went to the door. Julie, she thought, rather uncharitably, might be better without too much of an audience.

A well-designed house. The passageways and stairs were well-lit from the four good-sized gabled windows set into the roof at right angles to each other, facing the four points of the compass. There even seemed to be some rays of early morning

116

sunshine coming from the eastern side. The Reverend Mother went swiftly down the corridor and found without surprise that Julie had left the door to the main bedroom wide open, with the key still in the outside lock. She went in, stood for a moment, looking around. Such a beautiful room! A large room; a replica of the one which she and Lucy shared, but with far less furniture. A storeroom in the days when the house was first built and the pulley wheel had been fastened to the wall outside. On coming into the room in normal times, the eye would be immediately drawn to the spectacular view of the river. The heavy velvet curtains were drawn now, but not completely. The window had been opened behind them and there was an open space of a couple of feet between the curtains as they blew gently in the breeze, letting in the cold, morning air and light.

The Reverend Mother's eyes were not as good as they had been in her youth, but even so, even from the back of the room, she could see that there was a body on the floor – and it had to be a body that was slumped there; the strange angle of the head and that ominous dark stain on the Turkish rug in front of the window all pointed to that. She stood for a moment by the door and then, shutting it firmly behind her, she crossed the room.

The place was freezing cold. Nobody in the bed. Easy to see that as the upper sheet, blankets and eiderdown had been folded back. Charlotte Hendrick lay in a heap upon the rug placed on the boards below the sill. Fully dressed. Head tilted backwards, exposing her neck, and the Reverend Mother's eyes went to it immediately. Blood everywhere. A pool of it coalescent upon the floor, staining the shoulder of her dark blue dress, a wide slash on her neck. The Reverend Mother bent over the body, and touched a hand. Stone cold. Not cooling but already cold. Gently she lifted the hand and then allowed it to fall back. No stiffening as yet. She signed the forehead with the sign of the cross and prayed aloud: 'Tibi, Domine . . .'

The words of the prayer came automatically as she commended the soul of 'our sister' to the mercy of God and prayed for her to be freed from all evil. The convent, founded almost a hundred years ago, had seen many deaths of elderly nuns recently and these had, indeed, been sisters to her, all had been closer to her than the woman, her cousin, who lay there. Nevertheless, there was something very different about this death. The Reverend Mother finished her prayer, signed herself and then the corpse with the sign of the cross, got to her feet, gazed speculatively at the window, but did not touch it. The door beside the bed, though, was a different matter. She went towards it, remembering the fact that it was one of three doors in the room. A door to the bathroom. The window in here was closed and everything was in perfect order except that a sponge bag, missing its string, had been left on the wash table, no doubt to be removed by Julie or one of the maids. There was a strong smell of expensive talcum powder in the room and the Reverend Mother looked sadly around at the little room, at the Jacquard towels, the Hermès soap and the exclusive Dr Teal bath salts. Charlotte had all that money could buy. But had she been happy in the possession of such wealth?

After another quick glance around, the Reverend Mother shut the door again and then opened the door to the dressing room. The window here was shut also and all was in perfect order, though it bore the look of a room not often used, clothes hanging on a rail, many of them looking years out of date, but all well-cared-for. The clothes that Charlotte wore currently were probably in the large oaken wardrobe that took up a good six foot of space against the wall opposite the bed.

And then, with one last glance around, the Reverend Mother locked the door to Charlotte's room. She cast a glance down towards the door to the room which she and Lucy had shared, but it was shut and no sound came from it.

So Lucy had managed to calm Julie. She, as well as everyone else, would have to be told what had happened, but first she had another duty. She went down the circular staircase and into the library. There was no one there, and all of the chairs were in the same position as the evening before, even the coffee and teacups were still on the tray in front of the fire. The room had not been touched. Perhaps the servants were waiting for directions from Julie. The Reverend Mother did not hesitate, but crossed the floor, went into the small office beside the library, lifted the telephone, gave the number to the lady in the telephone exchange, speaking in a curt tone which precluded any attempt at friendly greetings and gossip. The phone was answered instantly.

'I need to speak to Inspector Patrick Cashman, immediately!' she said sharply to the garrulous elderly constable who was in charge of the office at the police barracks. She had not long to wait before there was a click of a switch and a few seconds later, a familiar voice.

'Good morning, Reverend Mother.'

'Good morning, Inspector.' Thank goodness, he was already in at work. A hard worker, Patrick. He had been a diligent and meticulously careful boy as a five-year-old pupil at her school and he had not changed. She needed to speak to him urgently, but she hesitated. There was a slightly echoing sound from the telephone which had prevented her from calling him Patrick. He, also, must have heard that sound. When he spoke again, it was not to her.

'Thank you, constable,' he said and then there was the sound of a receiver being replaced.

'Patrick,' said the Reverend Mother, endeavouring to make her voice calm and matter-of-fact, 'I'm staying at my cousin, Mrs Hendrick's house, on

Bachelor's Quay and I'm afraid that I need you . . .'
She broke off there. The sound of a footstep in the
hall outside. Instantly she put the telephone receiver
on the desk and went to the door and locked it
without hesitation. When she went back to the
phone, she turned her back to the door and held
the mouthpiece very close to her lips and spoke very
quietly.

'I'm afraid something serious has happened here,
Patrick.'

'Anything to do with the trouble on the quays
last night?'

'Not that, Patrick,' she said. 'The trouble is here,
within the house. The owner of the house, Mrs
Hendrick, has been killed, murdered, I would
think. Her throat has been cut. She is definitely
dead, I would say, but, of course, you will bring
Dr Scher with you, won't you? I've locked the
door to the bedroom where the body is lying.'

'I'll be there in under ten minutes.' He discon-
nected immediately. Almost before the last word,
which sounded very faintly in her ear. Minutes. It
had to be minutes, not hours. That was an impossibility. Ten minutes would be good. She put down
the receiver herself and found, to her surprise that
her legs were trembling. She looked longingly
at the soft, cushioned easy chair beside the fire,
but that was impossible. She needed to get back
up to Lucy. Help her to manage Julie. And the
girl Philomena. Patrick, she guessed, would prefer
to tell the news to the household himself.

121

CHAPTER 7

Patrick put down the phone and thought for a moment. With anyone else, he would have gone straight to the house, assessed the situation and then phoned the police doctor if he found it necessary to do so, but the Reverend Mother was one hundred per cent reliable so once again he picked up the phone.

'Sorry to disturb you so early in the morning, Dr Scher,' he said formally when the phone was answered by a sleepy voice.

'Don't suppose you got much sleep yourself, last night, Patrick, did you? How is everything now?'

'Quiet,' said Patrick. 'All is quiet now. How is that man?' He asked the question, but guessed at the answer.

'Dead. Loss of blood. Trauma.'

Laconic, but a certain degree of emotion behind it. Didn't like losing a patient. Or perhaps it was the thought of what would now follow. It will mean a hanging, thought Patrick. Judge, jury, lawyers, rate-paying general public, they will all want a life for a life. He averted his mind from the vivid mental picture of the headlines in the *Cork*

Examiner, headlines screeching out for vengeance. A scapegoat would be sought, he thought grimly and resolved that he would go by the oath that he had sworn when he had first become a *Garda Síochána*, a guardian of the peace. He repeated the words mentally. *I will faithfully discharge the duties of a member of the* Garda Síochána *with fairness, integrity, regard for human rights, diligence and impartiality, upholding the Constitution and the laws and according equal respect to all people.*

Not an easy oath to keep with all the pressures upon him from superiors, from newspapers, from wealthy citizens who felt they paid the salaries of the policemen. To be *diligent* came easily to him, but to be *impartial* and to *accord equal respect* to all people could sometimes be a struggle between his conscience and between pressure put upon him by superior officers and political parties. Still, he had managed well so far. Had been made an inspector and had secret hopes that one day he might become a superintendent. With a slight feeling of shame, Patrick hastily averted his mind from his own future to the bleak and terrible present.

'I've just had a phone call from the Reverend Mother. She was staying the night on Bachelor's Quay with a friend, no, a cousin.' Patrick looked back at his notes, annoyed with himself for making a mistake. 'The woman is dead. Murdered. Her throat has been cut. Found in her bedroom.'

'A cousin?'

'That's right. A Mrs Hendrick. Lives in that big house on Bachelor's Quay, the Sherriff's house, they call it. The one with the wheel above the middle window on the top storey. Owns a lot of property around the quays. Lots of those lanes by North Main Street and Devonshire Street, and . . .' Patrick stopped himself. All of this was of no interest to Dr Scher, though his own mind was actively pursuing a link between the deaths of two landlords. 'Do you want me to get the body moved to the barracks, or would you like to see it first at the house.'

'See it there first. Could give you a time of death if I see it *in situ*. A lot depends on how warm the woman keeps her bedroom. Bachelor's Quay, you said. Meet you there in twenty minutes or so. I'll just grab a cup of tea and some toast.'

And the doctor replaced the phone. Would he be able to eat toast? wondered Patrick. He himself had merely taken a cup of tea. That sickening scene on the quays last night was still very fresh in his eyes. And Dr Scher had had to deal with the consequences of it. He tried to force his mind away from it and to focus on the Reverend Mother's astonishing news, but it was difficult to banish the images from his memory. There would be no mercy in the courts. He knew that. Provocation would not be considered to be an excuse. Resolutely, he shut the folder on his desk and locked it within his drawer. This new murder would now have to be given attention. The

Reverend Mother had said 'murder' and he had never known her to make a mistake.

They had rounded up the ringleaders from last night. One or two minor characters still to be questioned, but Joe could handle that. Inspector Patrick Cashman, himself, would be expected to take immediate charge of the murder of an eminent person like Mrs Hendrick of Bachelor's Quay.

The matters were doubtless connected. This woman, Mrs Hendrick, was a well-known land-lord. The dead man, also, had been a landlord; both had been an owner of streets filled with tumbledown tenements where the unfortunate denizens eked out a life of starvation and disease, punctuated with crime and drunkenness. That atrocity outside the public house on Merchant's Quay, that had been the start of it all. But how on earth had these men got into that solid and well-staffed house on Bachelor's Quay? And what was the Reverend Mother doing there on that night of all nights?

Patrick took down his coat and his cap from the hook behind the door and made his way out towards the entrance to the *Garda Síochána* Barracks.

Guardians of the Peace, he thought bitterly. Which clever fellow up in Dublin had thought of chris-tening the police force of the newly freed Ireland with that optimistic name and then turned it into Gaelic, for good measure. Wasn't working too well, whoever had dreamed it up. Not too much peace.

At that moment, the phone rang from behind the door into the superintendent's office.

Patrick hesitated for a moment. The superintendent was a member of the old Royal Irish Constabulary who had been lucky enough to retain his job when the new nationalist civic guards were formed. He had a leisurely attitude to his duties and the chances were that he had not yet arrived at work. Patrick had his hand on the doorknob, just about to enter and take the call when the ringing tone ceased and he heard the man's voice, booming through the door.

'Dreadful, dreadful, what an outrage!'

Patrick moved away. Someone ringing up about last night. He would leave his superior to deal with this call and all other calls. In fact, the calls would probably be coming in all the morning as outraged citizens phoned to complain that they felt unsafe in their beds. Nothing to do with him. But he had barely reached the door to the front office when the superintendent's door was thrown open and his name was called.

'Dreadful news! Dreadful news.' The superintendent was puffing with outrage. 'You won't believe this, Patrick, but a prominent citizen has been murdered in her bed by one of these scoundrels! My God! What an outrage! In her own bed!'

'In her bed,' repeated Patrick. It would have to be the same murder as the Reverend Mother had just reported to him. He would not, of course, betray that he knew anything about the matter.

Luckily, at the moment, the superintendent was just looking for an audience for his outrage.

'Yes, Mrs Hendrick. Mrs Charlotte Hendrick. Her cousin, Miss Julie Clancy, rang up to speak to me. In a terrible state, poor woman. Could hardly get the words out. The blackguards! A window open and a rope reaching down to the pavement. Of course, they were out to murder the landlords, one and all of them. That's what last night's affair was all about. Unfortunate woman. She inherited a lot of property from her husband, you know, Patrick. Poor man! He'd turn in his grave if he knew what had happened to his unfortunate wife. Very good man. A great supporter of our church.'

This, thought Patrick, is getting worse and worse. The superintendent was going to take a deep and personal interest in this murder. He would require daily, if not hourly, updates on the progress and would be insistent that the blame was pinned upon someone soon. His mind flipped rapidly through the faces of the men now locked in cells. Drunk, all of them, last night. Buoyed up with the last shreds of self-righteousness. This morning they would be sick and sorry. But it would do them little good at this stage. Later on he would have to give evidence before the magistrate who would undoubtedly commit the ringleaders to stand trial. He had most of them, he thought.

And there would have to be a hanging, perhaps more than one. Two landlords dead. And one of them an elderly widow sleeping peacefully in her bed.

He took out his notebook and wrote some words in order to satisfy the superintendent. 'Mrs Charlotte Hendrick,' he said aloud. 'Bachelor's Quay, that's right, sir, isn't it? I'll go straight away and phone Dr Scher to examine the body.' And then he left immediately before he could be inundated by any instructions or admonitions.

Tommy, the constable on duty, was as old as Patrick's father would be if he were still alive. Though whether Patrick's father was still alive, was something that no one in Cork knew as the man had skipped off to England when Patrick was a year old. Nevertheless, the fact remained that Tommy was just a constable and Patrick, due to hard work, and almost sleepless nights, had passed all of the police examinations and was now an inspector. Patrick was wary of Tommy. His first duty was always to report everything to the super-intendent and he had no loyalty or even respect for anyone else in the barracks, although he was always correct in outward formalities. Tommy was a hangover from the days when the English ran the police service and a Protestant lad like Tommy, despite a total lack of brains, could easily get a job, but was unlikely to be able to move up the promotion ladder.

'Taking the car, are you, Inspector?' asked Tommy now, his tone a reproach. The superintendent, another hangover from the days when Ireland was a colony of Britain, was ensconced within his room and probably had no notion of going out, but Tommy liked to feel that the *Garda* Ford car, standing there, beautifully polished and cleaned under his supervision after the night's work, should remain ready for the superintendent's use if he wished to go out.

'Yes, I am,' said Patrick and left hastily, before any queries could be embarked upon. The superintendent and Tommy were very close and it was not a good idea to antagonize the elderly man. He had barely reached the car when an ancient motorcycle drew up beside him, spluttering noisily.

'Any comment on last night's disturbance on the quays, Inspector?'

Patrick looked wary. Eileen MacSweeney, though a good four or five years younger than himself, was a neighbour and playmate of his youth. When that young lady started calling him 'Inspector', he became cautious. That meant that she was in the role of part-time reporter for the *Cork Examiner* and that any word he spoke might stare at him from the headlines of a newspaper. Those articles of hers about the slum conditions in Cork might have been well meant, but already they were causing a lot of trouble – like last night's disturbance. It gave him no satisfaction to throw desperate, drunken men into cells and to be reliant on hoping that some self-satisfied, well-fed and well-housed judge would have some mercy on them. But, of course, there could be no mercy for the ringleaders. Not with that terrible death. His mind went to the scene on the quays, the blood dripping on to the wet pavements, the terrible groans . . . He shied away from that picture again. Attack, he decided, was the best form of defence.

'You're getting into bad company, Eileen,' he said severely. 'Philip Monahan is all right. I respect what he is trying to do, but people like your latest friend, Mickey Joe Clancy, well, you'd be best off to keep away from him and his gang of ruffians.'

'He's a patriot.' Eileen's face had flushed.

'He's a university student and a troublemaker,' said Patrick. 'I wish he'd concentrate on his studies and stop stirring up trouble. That Viking business was one thing, but he and his friends stirred up trouble afterwards and don't you deny it. And now, if you'll excuse me, Eileen, I have important business to see to.'

Those last words were a mistake, he thought, as he indicated with an arm through the window and pulled out into the early-morning traffic. Important business to her meant news that she could sell to the *Cork Examiner*. Nothing that he could do about it, now. She was behind him as he went down Barrack Street and when he crossed into South Main Street, he could see from his mirror that she was still on his tail. It was early, but there was a fair number of donkeys and carts making for the Coal Quay markets and, cautious driver that he was, he had to slow right down to ensure that he did not risk injuring any of the children running behind the carts. He went right over and across Old George Street, now ridiculously and patriotically renamed Washington Street in honour of George Washington, rather than George Street after King George of England, and thus not offending Republican susceptibilities. He had hoped that she might turn towards Patrick Street and the offices of the *Cork Examiner*, but no such luck. She stuck doggedly to him and even when he took a shortcut through Devonshire Street, she was on his tail. He kept a sharp lookout here. This place had been another centre of trouble last night, but now all seemed calm. The usual hopeless-looking women, wrapped in shawls, standing on doorsteps, most of them with the downy head of a feeding baby at their neck and their eyes gazing unseeing across the street. None of these would have taken part in the troubles last night. Most would have been with their children in the over-crowded rooms. Nevertheless, he felt a certain unease at passing them in this labelled police car and a spurt of anger against Eileen MacSweeney rose within him. If he had not wanted to shake her off, he would have approached Bachelor's Quay from the respectable Western Road, home to the clerks and shopkeepers of the city.

That Philip Monahan had right on his side. He had to admit that. These terrible slums needed to be torn down and their inhabitants found decent places to live. It had to be done sensibly, though, quietly and within the law. No sense in stirring people up to riot and putting the lives of landlords in danger.

When Patrick arrived, he parked the *Garda Síochána* motor car by the pavement in Grattan Street, as there was still some flooding on Bachelor's Quay. He had a quick look around, but there was no sign of Eileen. Somewhere, in Devonshire Street perhaps, he must have shaken her off. With a feeling of thankfulness, he got out, carefully removed the starting handle of the car, placing it in the special bag which he kept for it within the boot of his car and then mounted the steps to Mrs Hendrick's enormous house. Ten bedrooms in that house, someone had told him once, ten bedrooms for the gentry, not counting the beds for the maids and the manservants, who were housed above the stables next door. No horses, now, of course. Just a car, being washed by the chauffeur. He looked hard at the young man. Had seen him last night slinking back into the shadows when they had arrived at Lavitt's Quay.

The door was opened by a girl whose face he vaguely recognized. She bobbed politely and said, 'Come in, Inspector Cashman. The Reverend Mother is expecting you. She asked me to show you into the library and to tell you that she will be with you in a minute.'

So the Reverend Mother had taken charge. Despite the seriousness of the occasion, despite the horrors of last night, Patrick felt a slight amusement. He handed his hat to the maidservant and inspected the hall door. Well barred. Two large bolts, one at the top of the door and one at the bottom. And a heavy chain that plugged into an iron holder and would allow the door to be opened a crack. Any visitor after a reasonable hour could be interrogated as to his business before a door could be opened to admit him. The house was well protected. Patrick gave a last look at the substantial and quite undamaged oak panels on the door and then followed the servant into the library.

The room, he decided, looking around at the chairs untidily grouped and the indentations on the cushions, had only received superficial attention from the maidservants – perhaps a quick tidying and sweeping and a new fire lit. Surprising, he thought and he wondered whether the hand of the Reverend Mother was behind this omission. He sat down on a seat by the window and when the girl had gone, he looked thoughtfully around.

The room smelled heavily of some exotic cigarette smoke or perhaps cigar smoke. A very opulent-looking room. Old-fashioned, but very comfortable. Two sofas, covered in deep green velvet, still bearing the impress of bodies. Five large armchairs drawn up in a semicircle around a long, low, mahogany coffee table. Eight people had sat around this library after their dinner and then all had gone to bed. Eight people and a house full of servants. There looked as though there had been no disturbances so all had gone to bed, unaware of much of the violence more than half a mile away down the quays. The atrocity at Merchant's Quay had occurred around midnight. The man had still been alive when the police arrived and quite soon afterwards a detachment of the army had been on the scene. Shots had been fired. The ringleaders had been arrested. The crowd had been dispersed. Patrols had been set up in the surrounding streets. How had that woman been murdered during the night?

The Reverend Mother had left orders that he was to be shown into the library and she would have had some reason for that command. He had the utmost trust in her sharp brain and so he occupied his waiting time in looking around the room in more detail.

Eight people had sat around within this room. He seemed to see the imprint of their bodies upon the luxurious cushions. One chair dominating. Set in front of the others, slightly aside from the fire, but still occupying a dominating position. A sofa, or couch. Two had sat there. The cushions were slightly imprinted. Another sofa, slightly more imprinted. An upright chair. And another directly opposite. Two men, perhaps. And then a small, very upright, slightly more uncomfortable chair, set well back from the fire, possibly in the draught from the door leading into the hallway. Patrick took a chair by the window, looked around and wondered about the last evening of the woman who now lay dead above stairs.

He had not long to wait. Quite soon there was a footstep outside. A firm, decisive footstep, moving swiftly across the hallway and then the door was opened and she came in.

'Patrick,' said the Reverend Mother. 'How good of you to come so quickly. I'm afraid that something very serious has happened here. My cousin, Mrs Charlotte Hendrick, has been murdered, I fear. I found the body myself and I am quite certain that she is dead. And not by any natural causes or self-inflicted in any way.' The Reverend Mother took in a long breath and looked at the inspector in a way that showed she was absolutely sure of her facts. 'Yes, I'm afraid that she has been murdered, Patrick. Dr Scher, I'm sure, will confirm, but it does appear to me that someone took a knife and slit the woman's throat. When I looked at her, I could see the wound. The bleeding had stopped, but the incision was still quite noticeable and the blood, though clotted, was shed, I would say, not too many hours earlier. I felt for the pulse and it was not there. The body, at this hour of eight o'clock in the morning, was already cool. I have locked the door of the bedroom and here is the key.'

'Any signs of forced entry into the bedroom, Reverend Mother?' Patrick had his notebook out. He took the proffered key and placed it within a deep pocket.

'None,' said the Reverend Mother calmly. 'The bedroom door was found locked, though normally, apparently, my cousin did not lock her door. The maidservant, as was customary, had gone in to wake her mistress with a cup of tea and found the door locked and went for the spare key to Mrs Hendrick's cousin, Miss Julie Clancy, who acts as housekeeper. They entered the room together, saw the body and saw the blood.'

Patrick waited. His first instinct had been to connect this death with the atrocity on the quays last night, but now he began to wonder. Experience had taught him to trust the Reverend Mother and he was prepared to put the other matter to the back of his mind for the moment. She was looking around the room now, looking as though she was sorting matters in her own mind before summing them up for his benefit.

'Is there a possibility that someone in the house may have killed her?' he asked after a minute. With anyone else, he would not come out so openly with a question like that, but the Reverend Mother, he knew, was utterly trustworthy. He watched her turn the matter over in her mind and knew that she had much to tell him.

'Mrs Charlotte Hendrick was a very rich woman, Patrick,' she said after a minute. 'For many years she had kept her relatives dancing attendance in, not to put too fine a point on the matter, the expectation of a substantial legacy. She repeatedly said that she intended to divide her considerable fortune in seven equal shares between these relatives: myself; my cousin, Mrs Murphy; her husband's

136

nephew, Professor Hendrick; and her cousins on the other side of the family, the two Clancys: Miss Julie Clancy and Mr Claude Clancy, who is the owner of a club in the Grand Parade, I understand. And then there was Mrs Brenda O'Mahony and her adopted niece, Florence, also from the Clancy side of the family. That makes the seven close relatives.'

Patrick noted all this down in rapid shorthand and then waited.

'But then,' continued the Reverend Mother, 'we all received a letter saying that she had changed her mind and was now proposing to leave her fortune, an impressively large one, I understand, to the person who, in her judgement would make the best possible use of it. I understood from the letter that we, the seven nearest relatives, were to make a presentation on the evening of the invitation and that, on the following morning, her solicitor would come and a new will would be made. It was,' concluded the Reverend Mother, with a certain touch of disapproval in her voice, 'a rather unpleasant and divisive business and not one that, if the bishop had not expressed an opinion, indeed, a definite instruction, that I would have liked to take part in. However, given his lordship's wishes, I had no alternative but to attend in the company of my five cousins and Mrs Hendrick's husband's nephew, Professor Hendrick.' And with that she sat back and folded her hands within the wide sleeves of her habit. 'It was,' she added after a second's silence during which she glanced around the library, 'a somewhat unpleasant evening.'

'And quite dangerous,' said Patrick quietly. He raised his head from his notebook and looked around the room and pointed towards the chair that faced into the centre of the room.

'Mrs Hendrick sat there, just in front of you all?' He put it as a question but was not surprised when she nodded. The chair obviously was for the woman who would address the gathering. And the rest, where had they sat? Patrick looked enquiringly at the Reverend Mother.

'Her cousin, Miss Julie Clancy, a relation on Mrs Hendrick's side of the family who acted as companion and housekeeper to Mrs Hendrick, sat there,' she said, indicating thze small, very upright, slightly more uncomfortable chair, set in the draught from the door leading into the hallway. 'And Julie's brother, Mr Claude Clancy, sat on that chair facing the window and just opposite to Professor Hendrick. My cousin Mrs Murphy and I sat on this sofa here and Mrs Brenda O'Mahony, with her adopted niece, Florence, sat opposite us on the other sofa.'

Patrick nodded, did a quick sketch with a number beside each piece of furniture. Not important, probably, but somehow it gave him a feel for the atmosphere on the night before the death of the woman who had sat there, on that padded and very high upright chair, dominating the proceedings, looking down upon the seven relatives who had always hoped to inherit a share of her considerable wealth.

'And a feeling of failure might lend a certain urgency for the murder if someone felt that they did not do well in staking a claim to the fortune yesterday evening.' Patrick felt that he might have worded that statement a little more tactfully, since he was talking about the Reverend Mother's relatives, but she immediately gave him a nod of approval.

'Precisely,' she said. 'And, I must tell you, Patrick, that I would judge all, including myself, to have failed to make a positive impression. All, except for one, and that was Professor Hendrick who gave us a splendid talk on the Vikings in Cork a thousand years ago and made the case that he would use the money to uncover more facts about them and, if possible, to trace the Hendrick name back through the centuries and to prove that it was of Viking origin. I feel, and I would imagine that all of the other guests would agree with me, that if Mrs Hendrick had the opportunity to change her will this morning, that she would have left her entire, and very considerable fortune, to her husband's nephew.'

'And nothing to the others.'

'That was what she planned,' said the Reverend Mother quietly. Patrick could see that she was looking at him appraisingly, speculating, perhaps, whether to say more. Waiting to see how much he would guess for himself.

'She was a rich woman,' he said, feeling his way and when she bowed her head, he went on, still slightly tentative, but now wondering whether the murder of this wealthy woman, this wealthy landlord, was, despite his first thoughts, quite unconnected with the murder of the other landlord, last night on the quays. That had been a case of men drinking heavily after they had been paid for unloading a ship, then realizing that the money that should have been reserved to pay the rent, and perhaps to repay the interest on loans, had now been squandered. The alcohol had fuelled a storm of guilt and that guilt had then been released after a torrent of abuse from a landlord. The men knew that there would have been no mercy on them, and that they and their families would be thrown out on the streets. This combination of guilt and fear had built up to a storm of anger against the man who would do this to them and who then had the stupidity to enter the public house and to berate them for wasting their money.

But an elderly woman, a landlord also, of course, but sleeping peacefully in a house full of people – somehow he doubted that she would have become the target of that drunken gang. In any case, the ringleaders were still on the quays by the time that he and his men had arrived and a detachment of the army had come minutes later and cleared the quays of people. It was, of course, just about possible that someone, not one of the ringleaders, but someone with a different landlord, who was slinking home quietly through the back lanes, suddenly thought of Mrs Hendrick. However, he would bear in mind that this house, a solid, well-built, well-staffed house, would doubtless have been securely locked up last night and that it would have been difficult for someone to enter surreptitiously. He looked across at the Reverend Mother.

'She was a rich woman,' he went on, 'and so even one seventh of her estate would be worth . . .'

'Probably about five thousand pounds,' she said, and he could see a certain expression of jubilation cross her face as her eyes widened for a moment. It was smothered instantly, but he knew that, for one joyous moment, the Reverend Mother had seen in her mind's eye what she could do with five thousand pounds. And if she thought like that, well, the other relatives certainly had a strong motive to kill this old lady before she had a chance to change her will and to leave the entire sum to a favoured nephew.

'Something else that I should tell you, Patrick, is that I heard a noise, rather like a bang of a window, in the middle of the night. I stood outside in the corridor for a minute. I even put my hand upon the door leading to my cousin Charlotte's room, but it appeared to be locked. There was no more noise and I half-wondered whether I had dreamt the matter and so went back to bed.'

'But you didn't, didn't dream it.' Patrick did not even introduce a note of doubt or of interrogation into his voice. The Reverend Mother, in his experience, did not make mistakes. She did not reply, and he left the matter. He stared across the room, tapping his pencil against his teeth and turning the whole affair over in his mind. Seven people. He could eliminate the Reverend Mother, of course. And probably her cousin, Mrs Murphy, wife of the wealthiest solicitor in the city. He could not see why Mrs Murphy should need money and, come to that, could not see an elderly lady cutting the throat of another elderly lady. Not unless she were desperate for some reason or other. His eyes went back to the chairs and the sofas, set out in a semicircle, facing that dominant chair in the centre. Professor Hendrick, it seemed from the Reverend Mother's words, was likely to seize the jackpot and get the whole sum of money for himself. That ruled him out. He would, at least, wait for the will to be changed. But the fellow who owned Clancy's Club . . . well, he might be in need of money. He seemed to remember hearing some rumours. Patrick made a quick note to check on the bank account of Mr Claude Clancy. And Mrs Brenda O'Mahony . . . O'Mahony of Fermoy – was he her husband? He had gone bankrupt recently. Patrick scribbled another note and then lifted his head. The Reverend Mother was looking towards the door, also.

'Was that the doorbell, Patrick?'

'Probably Dr Scher.' Patrick hoped so. He didn't like the sound of this case at all. Too many highly connected and related people from the merchant princes part of Cork society. It would, he thought, be a bit of a nightmare sorting it out and he would welcome Dr Scher's assistance.

It didn't sound like Dr Scher, though. A very strong, powerful voice. Loud, resonant. Could hear every word.

'Mr O'Brien,' announced the voice. And then, slightly impatiently. 'I am Mrs Hendrick's solicitor. From the firm of O'Brien, Dunne & O'Brien. Mrs Hendrick asked me to call this morning. Could you fetch Miss Clancy, now, please, my good girl.'

The maid's voice, stammering slightly, just saying the words 'Mrs Hendrick' over and over again as though a gramophone needle had stuck. And then the solicitor's voice, again. Strong, imperative.

'Just fetch Miss Clancy, now and as quickly as possible, my good girl. I'll make my own way into the library. Bring Miss Clancy to me in there.'

And then the door from the hall to the library opened and a very tall, very lean man entered, carrying a small attaché case. He looked slightly startled when he saw the figures in there, and his eyes went immediately from the Reverend Mother to Inspector Patrick Cashman.

'Good morning, Mr O'Brien,' said the Reverend Mother. 'This is Mr O'Brien, Mrs Hendrick's solicitor, Inspector Cashman.' Very like his grandfather and his great-uncles, she thought. They, also, had that innate arrogance. She remembered them well.

'Good morning, Reverend Mother.' Mr O'Brien showed no sign of surprise in meeting her. He looked around the room as though expecting to see others and then gave a puzzled frown at the police inspector. 'Is something wrong?' he asked.

The Reverend Mother sat back, nodded to Patrick, and left him to deal with the question. He got to his feet, shook hands firmly with the solicitor, and made his way to the door, almost colliding into Julie Clancy as the door opened and she came rushing in.

'Oh,' she gasped. 'Oh, Inspector! Oh, Mr O'Brien! You're here already!'

'Excuse me, Mr O'Brien, I will be back in a minute. Now, if I could trouble you for a minute, Miss Clancy.' Patrick adroitly steered her away from the door and firmly closed it behind the two of them.

Gone to check with Julie about the presence of the solicitor and probably to view the body and hear what Dr Scher has to say before he makes any public announcement, guessed the Reverend Mother and knew a moment of fierce pride in the transformation of a ragged, dirty, small boy from the slums of Barrack Street into this assured and competent police inspector. He had done the manoeuvre with such adroitness and such self-possession. How much education can perform! And a steady job, of course, but that resulted from educational qualifications. And how appalling that despite the promises of the Republicans of 1916:

'all children of the nation to be cherished equally', how appalling to think that second-level and third-level education was still the preserve of those that could pay for it or for the tiny proportion who managed to gain scholarships.

'Well, at least it has stopped raining,' she said politely to the solicitor and suppressed a smile at the thought that, once again, the Cork habit of commenting on the weather had filled an awkward moment.

'Terrible weather, isn't it?' Thankfully he took up the thread of the conversation and the matter lasted them for the next few minutes. There was another knock on the front door which interrupted them on the subject of flooding and for a moment both paused and looked towards the door of the library. A murmur of voices, too low to be heard through the heavy wood of the baize-covered door, and then the sound of footsteps. The maid and another heavier, masculine tread. Not coming in here, going past the doors leading off the hallway and then up the stairs. Dr Scher, thought the Reverend Mother, going up to view the body. She did not share her insight with the solicitor who was looking quite puzzled, but immediately embarked upon a story of her childhood when the flooding of the River Lee had been so bad that it had swept away the main bridge of the city. Mr O'Brien capped that by a boyhood recollection of launching a dinghy from the steps leading up to his father's premises in South Mall. They had begun to run out of stories when footsteps were heard on the stairs again and then a hysterical sob.

Both the Reverend Mother and the solicitor gave up the pretence of talking and listened unashamedly. Hard to hear Dr Scher. Both he and the inspector had dealt with matters like that before. But Julie Clancy was beside herself and her voice wailed out, punctuated by a series of sobs. And then the doctor's voice, soothing, possibly a pill given. But the voice alone might have done the trick, because the hysterical sobbing seemed to tail out and in the silence that followed, the Reverend Mother heard the young voice belonging to the maidservant, Philomena, and then rapid footsteps running off to the kitchen and then back again. Hot milk, perhaps, surmised the Reverend Mother.

'Everyone has to be in the library waiting for the solicitor. And she said that she wasn't going to be there and to tell everyone that she wasn't well and was going to spend the day in bed. And I wasn't to allow anyone to come in and say goodbye . . .' Julie's voice wailed out and terminated in some more hysterical sobs.

'That's true, Reverend Mother,' said the solicitor in a low voice with a nod towards the door. 'Mrs Hendrick gave me strict instructions. I was to come here, read the will to the relatives, tell them that she wanted no conversation whatsoever about the matter. I gathered that I was to make sure that they left the house without any attempt to try to make contact with her. Do I understand that some accident, some fatality . . .?'

His voice tailed away and she, in her turn, nodded. It was obvious he guessed that something had happened, but she did not feel it was her place to discuss the matter. He had to await the official announcement, just like the rest of the visitors. Where were they? she wondered. Had all taken refuge in their bedrooms, and were waiting to be summoned? Or were they gossiping in low tones in the drawing room?

'I think I'll just go ahead and do what she instructed me to do,' he said after a minute's silence when, doubtless, he had mentally consulted some obscure law book about carrying out the instructions of dead clients.

'I see,' said the Reverend Mother. Now that his client was no longer in a position to redraft her will, she wondered what he was going to say. Of course, the original will would now, in all probability, be evoked, unless, of course, it had been destroyed in the presence of witnesses. What would happen then? She began to turn over in her mind those aspects of the family tree which she could remember. Were some more nearly related than others? None were near relatives. It was going to be interesting to see. And it kept the sin of covetousness at bay to speculate on relationships.

And then something about the scene that she had witnessed that morning in the dead woman's bedroom came to her mind. She thought about it carefully, putting her thoughts together about its significance. But she decided to reserve it for the moment. Patrick had enough on his hands just now.

It was, though, she decided, quite significant and she was sure that she had drawn the right conclusion.

CHAPTER 8

Eileen, idling the engine of her motorbike until Patrick got out of the police car, waited in Grattan Street around the corner from Bachelor's Quay. She smiled to herself as she saw him reach into the boot of the car, take out the starting handle and place it safely inside his attaché case. Good old Patrick, careful as ever! She suppressed a giggle when she saw he even had an empty gabardine bag, lined with newspaper, all ready to receive it and keep it from contaminating other articles. She kept her distance, though, until he had gone through the front door, waited an extra few minutes and then she slipped into the yard and opened the kitchen door. She was in luck. A familiar face.

'God, Phil,' she said enthusiastically. 'I hardly knew ye! Look at the style! And your hair is gorgeous!'

'Oh, Eileen! Come in. Could she have a cuppa, Mrs Barrett? She's a neighbour of mine from Barrack Street.'

'Thought I'd come round an' see what's the matter. What've you got the guards here for?'

Eileen divided the question between Mrs Barrett and Philomena. 'You looked a bit upset, like, when you opened the door just now,' she added for good measure.

'Oh Jaysus, Eileen, come here till I tell you, girl!' Philomena sat down limply at the kitchen table while Mrs Barrett poured out three cups of tea, added a few extra scones to the plate already on the table and pulled out a chair for herself. Eileen resisted an impulse to take out her journalist notebook. She always kept it in her mind that as well as being a typist at a publishing firm and a university student, she also had to find odd moments of the day to work as part-time reporter for the *Cork Examiner* newspaper – and that this was the most exciting and most interesting part of her daily life. Any opportunity that came up she had to seize it and turn a story into a 'must-read' newspaper article. Now, with the presence of the inspector and the words of the maidservant, she knew immediately that something had happened. It was an opportunity not to be missed.

'It's the missus,' said the cook and she mopped her eyes with a handkerchief. 'Poor, poor lady,' she added.

This began to sound interesting. Someone must have been injured or robbed or something. Otherwise Patrick wouldn't be calling to the house, thought Eileen.

'Don't tell me,' she said. 'Your missus never went out last night. Not out on to the quays. Not with all the rioting about landlords going on! And she with all the property that she has!'

'It's worse than that,' said the cook with bated breath. 'Much worser. Go on, girl, you tell her. You was the one that found her.'

'Found her!' breathed Eileen. Her heart was beginning to beat with excitement and apprehension. Had something else happened last night during the riot?

'The missus. Mrs Hendrick. Murdered in her own bedroom! Lying on the floor. Her throat was slit.' Philomena made a gesture across her own throat. 'Blood everywhere. You should have heard me scream! Made me sick to my stomach!' she continued a little indistinctly as her mouth was full of half-chewed scone.

Eileen widened her eyes. 'Never!' she said mechanically.

'Cross my heart and hope to die! There she was. Lying on the floor. Didn't see her at first. The bedclothes were heaped up in a sort of ridge, half covering the pillow. Just like she was still in bed and still asleep. I went right up to it. Was going to tell her that her tea was there and then I saw it.'

'Saw it? The knife?' Eileen's mind was making frantic notes, sentences were forming themselves and slotting into place.

'Nah, the body on the floor. The blood. Everywhere! The rug was soaked with it. Didn't see no knife.'

'Lying on her side, was she?' Eileen's mind went on drafting a dramatic article. 'God, missus, my mam would kill for a scone like that; don't know how you do it and you all upset this morning, all the same,' she said to the cook in a quick aside, before going back to Philomena. 'Do you think she saw who killed her then, did she?'

'Why was she out of bed, otherwise? Must have heard a sound. Must have been a man hiding behind the curtains, mustn't there?'

'Behind the curtains? How did he get there?' This was beginning to sound interesting. *Send a shiver down their backs*, an elderly reporter had once advised Eileen, *they love to have their blood run cold while they are eating their morning toast.*

'The window was open, Eileen,' explained Philomena. 'The rope from the wheel had been let down. First thing I noticed when I went out to do the steps. Undid itself perhaps, that's what I thought then. Thought it might have been the wind in the night. Sets the wheel spinning. Sometimes if it's strong enough it can unwind the rope. That happened once or twice. Hanging right down the front of the house. Someone must have come up it, climbed up, come in the window.'

'A man! Hiding behind the curtains,' said Eileen, mechanically echoing the words. Her mind was in a turmoil, filled with visions of the rioting last night. Nothing to do with me, she said to herself, nothing to do with me. It can't be! Nothing to do with that loudhailer business. Nothing to do with the demonstration against the landlords. This place is a good ten minutes' walk away from Merchant's Quay. Just a burglary gone wrong. She hoped that was true. Her mind had gone to that terribly injured landlord with the shard of glass sticking out from his stomach and blood pouring from his head.

'What happened?' she asked quickly trying to blot out the image.

'Cut her throat, didn't he? Killed her dead before she could scream for help.'

The cook crossed herself rapidly. 'Pray God she had time for a quick act of contrition before she went to meet her maker,' she said piously while Eileen drafted a series of dramatic questions for her article in the *Cork Examiner*. Already she had decided on the headline – very much in the *Cork Examiner* style, but nevertheless intriguing. *Death of a Prominent Citizen*. That would give a good start.

'Terrible shock, it must have been for you two. Did she live alone except for you all?'

'Nah, house full of visitors, her nephew, Professor Hendrick, cousins. Even the Reverend Mother from St Mary's of the Isle. She was the one that phoned up for the guards.'

'Didn't touch their breakfast, none of them. Not a thing. Drank the tea and coffee. Didn't even have a scone. Nothing wrong with them scones,' said the cook complacently as she took another bite.

'All of them in a state,' said Philomena. 'Upset, like.'

'Won't stay in a state too long. They'll cheer up. There'll be plenty of money to be handed out. Rich as anything she was. And them all her relations.' To Eileen's inner amusement the cook smacked her lips. She was beginning to feel relieved, herself. Yes, it must have been a burglar or even a relation. She relaxed a little and took another bite from the scone. Didn't seem as though there was a connection with that riot on Merchant's Quay or with that other business.

'Wish she'd leave us some of her money.' Philomena, also, took another bite from her scone.

'Well, you can go on wishing. She's got enough relations with their tongues hanging out.' The cook swallowed the rest of the scone, wiped her mouth, and went across to the cooker.

'All of them staying in the house,' hinted Eileen.

'That's right. You've said it. All of them there last night at dinner. Sitting around the table. All sucking up to her.'

'You'd think that one of them might have murdered her?'

'Not a bit of it! Where did you get that idea?' Suddenly the cook sounded very shocked. 'Respectable people all of them. You don't catch me saying a thing like that. Terrible riot last night, down Merchant's Quay. The milkman was telling us about it before we ever found out about the missus.' She closed her lips firmly and started to pile the cups and plates.

'I'd better be off,' said Eileen, getting to her feet. This was a story and she couldn't waste any more time before she got to the *Cork Examiner* offices and claimed it for her own. 'You have enough on your hands with a dead body in the house,' she added, suppressing a giggle at the thought that this was rather a good phrase. 'Thanks for the tea and the scones, missus. I'll see you, Phil.'

She had a good look around when she reached the gate to the kitchen yard. A couple of cars there in the stable yard and yes, there was Professor Hendrick's Model T Ford. Good! No point in her going in early to the university to talk to him about the pictures in his book before her first lecture of the day. She'd have time to get the article done and to hand in the ones which she had written last night. Professor Hendrick would be kept busy. Lucky for him if he got a legacy from the rich old lady. Those pictures were going to add to the cost of the whole project, and she had been prepared for him to change his mind once he heard the final estimate. She was not due at the Lee Printing Works until early in the afternoon so, now she had some time on her hands, she would pop into the *Cork Examiner* newspaper offices. Just go back down Grattan Street and then up the Grand Parade and into Patrick's Street, she told herself. No need to go down to Merchant's Quay. After what had happened last night she never wanted to see the place again. She swallowed hastily and tried to divert her mind from that terrible picture of the bleeding man. She needed to concentrate instead on planning the article that she was going to write and which, hopefully, might be published in tonight's *Evening Echo* and perhaps even reprinted in the *Cork Examiner* on the following morning.

And then she stopped. To the back of the stable yard and beside the big house there was a small lodge. It would, she reckoned, have been the place where the man and boys who looked after the horses would have lived in the past and nowadays it probably housed the chauffeur, the fellow she had met last night, the one who drove that shining Rolls-Royce. She had no interest in seeing him again, but something else stopped her. A voice had sounded from within, and not a man's voice. A girl's voice came from the building, high-pitched and excitable.

'I can't wait,' said the voice. 'I just can't wait! Just think about it, Tony!'

Eileen stopped. It wasn't the words that interested her, but the voice itself. The accent. Not a servant. Definitely not. This was a posh accent, almost an English upper-class accent, the way that people like the Reverend Mother might speak, but more exaggeratedly posh. A girl's voice. Young, by the sound of it. What was a posh, young girl doing in the chauffeur's lodge?

Eileen cast a look back at the kitchen door. Still

closed. No sound from within. Probably the kitchen staff would still be recovering their nerves and very likely have gone back to eating the leftover scones. As silently as she could, she moved a little nearer to the lodge. Despite the fog a window was wide open, thrown open, perhaps by the posh young lady from inside. So the chauffeur, Anthony Buckley, had not been boasting last night when he said that he had a girlfriend from the house. She remembered his words: *A real gorgeous girl there, a young cousin of my mistress. Got hair like a film star, real blonde and all them marcel waves.*

Eileen was tempted to steal a little closer and examine the hair, when the girl's voice stopped her.

'The *Orient Express*!' she said with a ripple of excitement in her voice. 'We can travel by the *Orient Express*!'

The *Orient Express*! The words sent a shiver down Eileen's spine. They had a magical sound. Like something out of *Arabian Nights*. She was in a hurry, but now she could not move. Had to find out more. It was a train, she gathered. The chauffeur was saying that he would prefer to travel by car and the girl was laughing at him, telling him about a book that she had read about the *Orient Express* and about the fantastic luxury on the train and what they would see when they got to Russia, talking about going to St Petersburg, visiting the Winter Palace, travelling by boat down the river, going into museums, looking at some wonderful jewelled eggs . . . The girl's voice was hoarse with passion and desire and Eileen felt the palms of her hands grow damp as she listened, consumed with envy. Imagine having the money to see all of these wonderful places!

And then there was a sudden interruption. The man's voice. Harsh. A note of fear. 'You'd better be getting back. Don't come here again. Don't go on about spending money. Dangerous talk. There's going to be trouble. Get back as quick as you can. Don't let anyone see you. Wait a minute and I'll make sure that the coast is clear.'

Quickly and silently, Eileen slid back inside the gate to the kitchen yard. There was a collection of large rubbish bins there and she crouched down behind them. He wouldn't look in there, she thought. She had noticed a small passageway at the side of the lodge. That would lead out to Bachelor's Quay. This Grattan Street side was the back entrance, the kitchen side of the mansion. The owner of the house and the guests would not be coming around there. A moment later, she heard the chauffeur's voice, low and cautious.

'All clear. Get back now.'

'When will I see you again?' This time the girl's voice was low, not much above a whisper. Slightly frightened, also. She had been suddenly pulled from her dreams of *Orient Express* trains, Winter Palaces and fabulously bejewelled eggs.

'Not for a few days. Let the fuss die down. Wait until I get a note to you. I'll put it in your room.

158

Find an excuse. Fix a window, something like that.'

His voice had a frightened note to it, also. Eileen wondered about it. A woman had been killed, a rich woman.

Eileen cranked up her bike, once they had gone, and went off, sloshing through the water on the still-wet quays and riding slowly and carefully until she found herself going down Patrick Street in a happy dream. Already she had written her article about the riots and another about the attack on the landlord and now she would have a third article to write. The death, murder, she corrected herself, of a rich old lady would be great news and she had an inside contact, not just a few cautious words from the *Garda Síochána*. If all three articles were accepted that would be three fees. By the time that she had parked her bike by the premises of the *Cork Examiner* and the *Evening Echo*, the headline and first paragraph were in her mind and as soon as she found a vacant typewriter she pressed the caps lock and hammered on the keys.

DEATH OF A PROMINENT CITIZEN

And then she sat back, looked around at the roomful of reporters, typing boring news about the flood, eyewitness accounts of damage to various shops, long lists of those who attended funerals, the opening of a new shed in Ford's factory by the Lord Mayor of Cork. All routine

159

stuff. Though Joe Campbell was typing below a headline that said: 'Disgraceful Riot on the Quays'. Nothing new about that, she thought with scorn, though for a moment she was sorry that she had not been allocated that story to write as well. Still, there was a certain amount of trouble on the quays every time a crew was paid off after unloading a ship. But her story of the terrible event outside the public house would be one of two stories that sold the newspaper this evening. The other, of course, was the murder of a rich woman in her own bedroom. She knew Cork people and knew that what happened to one of the wealthy who dwelt in big houses would be of the utmost interest and concern to the newspaper-buying population.

'Hold the front page of the *Evening Echo*; I've got a scoop!' she called out.

CHAPTER 9

Dr Scher, was, thought the Reverend Mother, used to death. There was remarkably little emotion on his face when he came into the room, acknowledged her presence with a slight bow of the head and then took a seat on an upright chair quite close to the window.

Patrick remained standing. It was only now that the Reverend Mother realized that he was without a sergeant. Joe was not present. There had been trouble on the quays last night, Patrick had mentioned that. No doubt Joe was dealing with that. There may have been casualties, prisoners, statements to take, court cases to prepare. She sighed at the thought. She had begun to hope that all this had ceased. Her heart hardened against those thoughtless, so-called patriots who were trying to stir up trouble again. It had almost been easier when English rule could be blamed for all the social problems. Too many lives had already been lost. Was Charlotte Hendrick to be numbered among the murders triggered by this fight for justice? Her mind went to the banging of a window in the night-time. And the woman's bedroom locked securely against interference. Had there been collusion with anyone in the house?

Charlotte, she feared, would not perhaps be deeply mourned. She had not been a pleasant person. She had made the poor pay for her luxurious way of life, but that was beside the point. She should not have been murdered. Human life should be sacred, no matter what the cause.

The Reverend Mother looked around the room as one by one the seven relatives of the dead woman came into the library and took their place. The solicitor, she noticed, had taken what looked like a list of names from his attaché case. Unashamedly she leaned slightly back and looked over his shoulder. The first name was Miss Clancy, Julie Clancy; she saw that he checked the name from his list; the name and the words, housekeeper/companion by her name. She had come hurrying in, her face blotched and swollen with weeping. The solicitor looked across at her in a puzzled fashion, noticed the Reverend Mother. Poor Julie was never memorable, but once recollection dawned, the tear-stained face was ignored and he went back to a mental check-list, exchanging a cordial nod of recognition with Professor Nicholas Hendrick and a somewhat less friendly one with Claude Clancy, and then, after a quick stare, ticking off Brenda O'Mahony and her niece Florence. So, despite the absence of his client, Mrs Hendrick, he was making sure that all the relatives were present.

The Reverend Mother settled herself to listen to Patrick.

'I'm afraid that I have some bad news for you.' He looked keenly around the room. 'It will, I know, come as a shock to you to hear that your hostess, Mrs Hendrick, is dead.' He stopped then, his eyes travelling over the audience. No great surprise visible on their faces, thought the Reverend Mother. Of course, she knew, and her cousin Lucy knew and Julie Clancy knew. The housemaid knew – and no doubt had shared the news with the rest of the kitchen staff. It would be surprising if the rest of the relatives did not know already. Whatever the reason, there was no shock, no visible reaction. Mrs Hendrick's seven closest relations sat quietly and waited for what was to come next.

'I would, of course, in any case, have called you all in here to announce the sad news,' went on Patrick, 'but, as it happens, Mr O'Brien, solicitor to the late Mrs Hendrick, also has been instructed to make an announcement to all present.'

'Instructed?' Claude took up the word and repeated it with a note of interrogation in his voice. He looked across at the solicitor with an air of curiosity. 'Who instructed you, Mr O'Brien?'

'Both I and Miss Julie Clancy were instructed by Mrs Hendrick, prior to her unfortunate demise, as to the procedure of events on this morning. We were given very clear instructions and I feel that it is best if I carry them through.' The solicitor

163

looked across at Julie, but she wept even more into her soaked handkerchief and shook her head at him. He hesitated for a moment, but then seemed to make up his mind to continue. 'I understand that Miss Clancy was told to gather everyone here in the library and to say that when I have finished my statements all were to leave the house without seeking an audience with their hostess.'

'She told me that she intended to be ill. I was to tell everyone that she was ill,' Julie sobbed hysterically. 'But someone killed her before she could finish her plans.' She gulped hard, dried her eyes and then with a valiant effort calmed herself enough to say, 'She told me to make sure that you were all in the library so that Mr O'Brien could talk to you and then I was to tell you to go without saying goodbye as she was too ill for visitors.' Julie looked around at the amazed faces and then huddled back into her chair as though disowning her instructions.

'You came here to make her will, to draft a new will, is that right, Mr O'Brien.' Claude seemed to have seized the leadership of the group in the library. Nicholas Hendrick continued to sit in silence, Julie still sobbed and all the others looked somewhat bewildered by this latest development.

'No, Mr Clancy, that was not quite the way of it,' said the solicitor to Claude's question. He bent down, opened his briefcase and took from it a scrolled document, tied with a pink linen ribbon. He undid the knot on the ribbon and flattened the document on the table in front of him. One page only, noted the Reverend Mother. It was all rather strange, these instructions given to Julie. All were to listen to the will and then were to depart. No one was to be admitted to the hostess who was keeping to her bed on the pretext of ill-health. And, so according to instructions and dominated by that strong voice from the dead woman, all had taken their places in the library. The Reverend Mother sat next to her cousin Lucy on one of the sofas and opposite to them were Brenda and her adopted daughter, now no longer a sophisticated young woman but a slightly scared and worried girl. Florence and Brenda held hands, noted the Reverend Mother, and she felt touched and slightly worried by the gesture. Brenda, she thought, would do anything for that girl. Claude placed himself by the window, tense and fidgety, shredding a small piece of paper into minute pieces. Julie sat nervously in her chair by the door and kept her eyes fixed attentively upon the solicitor. Nicholas, Professor Hendrick, was the most at ease, sitting in a relaxed fashion, legs crossed and one hand resting lightly upon the small table beside him.

'The will is a very simple one,' said the solicitor. 'To cut matters short, it summarizes the entire estate of the deceased, money in the bank, property owned in the city of Cork, including, of course, this house and shares in two gold mines in South Africa. The value of the estate will be calculated when probate is given, but very roughly

I think that one could put an estimate of forty-five thousand pounds upon it.' The solicitor paused and looked as though he were inviting questions, but no one moved and no one spoke.

The Reverend Mother did her best to conceal a sudden start of surprise. That was an enormous sum, far more than she had dreamed. Her mind refused to do the simple sum of dividing this into seven equal parts, but it would be, she was ashamed to acknowledge, an absolute god-sent boost to the work that she planned in her most fanciful moments. Looking around the room she could see how the gloom had lifted and the pleasure of money to be acquired had cheered everyone. To have all would have been very pleasant, but six thousand pounds would meet most needs. After all a house could be bought for just five or six hundred pounds. She took her mind away from the dazzling prospect of money like that to be available to spend on facilities for the poor.

The solicitor cleared his throat in a meaningful way. 'Mrs Hendrick, at the same time as she made her will, also made provision for her funeral arrangements. A bit premature, perhaps, but it has turned out to be, sadly, most apposite.' The solicitor shook his head, sighed heavily and quoted with relish, 'Man knoweth not the hour', before saying in a more normal tone, 'Since everyone is here, perhaps it would be appropriate now for me to read out the arrangements for her funeral,' he said and looked around at his audience.

'"One: I, Charlotte Louise Hendrick, having donated a suitable sum to the Bishop of Cork to spend as is deemed appropriate by him, wish that my body will lie in the cathedral for the space of two days so that all relations, friends, business acquaintances and tenants may have the opportunity of viewing my body and praying for my soul.

'"Two: I desire that a requiem mass will be sung by the cathedral choir and prayers said by my lord, the bishop, for the repose of my soul.

'"Three: I desire that all of my living relations will attend my funeral and that the cars will follow the funeral hearse in order of seniority and I instruct my heir to ensure this proceeds in an orderly fashion.

'"Four: I wish to be buried in St Finbar's Cemetery and have purchased a plot in that place and have made arrangements for a stone to be engraved.

'"Five: I instruct my solicitor to ensure that a detailed account of the proceedings be sent to the *Cork Examiner* and *Irish Times* newspapers."

'And now to the will,' said the solicitor hurriedly and he avoided looking at anyone. 'It is a very simple one.' He paused and then he did look at the faces assembled around him before saying with due solemnity, '"I leave all that I possess to my nephew by marriage, Professor Nicholas Hendrick."'

Only one person in the room did not look surprised and that was Nicholas. Had he known? the Reverend Mother wondered as she processed the meaning of the solicitor's

167

pronouncement. But how could he have known? That presentation of his hopes and dreams, of his plans and his detailed accounts of how money could be spent, including an ambitious Viking festival in the heart of Cork city with invited guests from Norway, Sweden and Denmark, had been delivered with such passion, such very obvious yearning to convince, that she wondered whether the will had been made late last night. The Reverend Mother pondered over the matter and thought that it was time that a question was asked, but she did not want to be the one who asked it. She looked across at Patrick and saw him frown. The expressions of utter amazement on the faces of all the relatives, except one, had not escaped him.

'But she was going to make it this morning,' said Claude eventually. 'That was what she told everyone. She said that she was going to draw up her will this morning. We all had to make a case last night for how we would use her money if we inherited and then she would decide. We all sat there, like a crowd of fools. We sat around and put hours of work and of hard thinking into it and then we made fools of ourselves there in front of her. And all the time . . .' His voice had started off plaintive, but now it rose to an angry pitch. 'We were lied to!' he thundered and then turned to Nicholas. 'Did you know of this?'

'Don't be such an idiot. How could I know?' said Nicholas roughly. 'You heard Mrs Hendrick, herself. She told us all that she was going to reflect on what was said and then to change her will. I know no more than you. You were there last night. Why should I have gone to the trouble of making a presentation if I had known that I was to inherit, in any case?'

It might be true, though it did not explain the signed will turning up this morning. Once again all eyes went to the solicitor. The same question was in all of these eyes, but no one spoke and even Patrick did not ask it. He waited politely to see if there were further questions for the solicitor, but then got to his feet. Not a tall man, Patrick, but he held himself very straight and appeared, every inch of him, the competent police inspector. He glanced around the room and said with great formality. 'I would be very sorry to inconvenience anyone, and I realize that you will all want to get back to your homes and places of business as soon as possible, but it would be helpful, for the record, to have a brief statement from everybody, so I would ask you not to leave this house until I authorize it. Would it be possible, Miss Clancy, for the police to retain the use of this room for the moment?'

'I don't know why you are asking me, inspector. It's nothing to do with me. Whether you go or you stay, whether you take over the whole house or occupy any room that you take a fancy to; it's not for me to say yea or nay. I'm of no importance in this house. Ask Nicholas Hendrick. I'm out on the street now and I'd better go and find a corner for myself and my begging bowl.' With that Julie burst into a hysterical bout of laughter that ended up in a flood of tears.

The Reverend Mother got to her feet. 'Come, Julie,' she said authoritatively. 'I think we should all go into the drawing room, don't you? We can wait there for the inspector's summons.'

Lucy immediately came to her rescue. 'I'm dying for a cup of tea,' she announced blandly. 'Come on, Julie, let's go to the kitchen and see what they can do for us. I'm sure that provision will be made for you, Julie, so stop worrying.'

Lucy, before standing up, gave a very straight and very direct look at Nicholas and he in turn looked helplessly at the solicitor. The solicitor looked at Lucy and knew her to be the wife of the foremost solicitor in the city of Cork. It was interesting to watch the different emotions play across his face. They graded from indifference, to awareness and then to an expression of concern and a false energy that suddenly seemed to galvanize the man as he glanced quickly from Lucy to the tear-stained face of Julie Clancy.

'I suppose that it will be a matter for the executor of the will,' said the Reverend Mother and she also looked at the solicitor, with a very penetrating stare. His long-dead father, the first O'Brien in O'Brien, Dunne & O'Brien, as far as the Reverend Mother could remember, had been a kind man, but this one had a sharp look about him. Nevertheless, he would not want any scandal about an elderly lady who had given years of faithful and unpaid service. And he would know that the Reverend Mother, also, had great influence in the city of Cork. 'No doubt,' she continued, 'the executors will have to ensure that the house is maintained in good condition until probate is granted; in other words that it is cared for by one who has devoted herself to that purpose for many years,' she said with a meaningful glance at him and he bowed his head in reply. It was a long minute before he spoke again, and the Reverend Mother was inwardly amused to imagine what was flashing through that good brain. She would be astonished if he did not find a way to solve the problem of Julie and was not surprised when he came up with a solution.

'Probate should be granted within a few months, though it could be six months, or even longer. Perhaps, in view of the widespread properties of the deceased, it may indeed take even a year,' said Mr O'Brien. 'And until then it is for the executors of the will, that is the firm of O'Brien, Dunne & O'Brien, to look after the property and I would suggest to my partners,' he said with the air of one who has suddenly thought of a brilliant suggestion, 'that Miss Julie Clancy is employed, at a suitable stipend, to care for the house and to supervise the servants.'

'What a very good idea,' said the Reverend Mother sedately. That would mean that Nicholas would get less as the estate would be charged with a salary for Julie and for the servants until probate was granted, but that was a price worth paying. After all he was going to be an immensely rich man once he did inherit. The Reverend Mother cast a quick glance at him from the corner of her eye and saw a certain range of emotions pass over his face. Not relief that a difficult situation had been solved, more a certain aspect of disappointment, and perhaps of apprehension. But why apprehension? Did Nicholas fear that some matter, better concealed, might be uncovered during that lengthy time?

'I was thinking of moving in here instantly,' he said with a certain hesitation, and the Reverend Mother noticed the use of the past tense. He spoke, despite his denials, as though he had known of this legacy and had, already, decided what to do. She observed with approval the quick glance that Patrick gave the man. She looked across at the solicitor. His father, she remembered, had been a decisive and quick-thinking man and the son did not disappoint her.

'Not possible,' said Mr O'Brien firmly. 'The property is not yours to move into until probate is granted. In the meantime, it is for our firm, as executors, to care for the estate as well as any owner could do and that includes, in my judgement, keeping this house in good order. I feel sure that Miss Clancy will, as she has always done, give it her full attention and keep the domestic wheels well-oiled. I'm certain that the estate will bear the relatively small wage of ten shillings a week.'

Julie's face lit up so much that the Reverend Mother forgave young O'Brien his pomposity.

'Oh, thank you,' she said. 'It's very kind of you and talking about wheels, the wheel outside Mrs Hendrick's window will need attention. Somehow, perhaps it was the storm, but the wheel seems to have stopped turning. It must be jammed. I noticed it when I went out to pay the milkman. And, of course, the inspector has locked Mrs Hendrick's room, otherwise I'd have sent the chauffeur in immediately once I had noticed that the rope had come loose in the night and was hanging right down to the pavement.' Julie sat back with an air of one who has justified the proposed wage, which, to someone who had worked for years for nothing but her keep, was probably quite munificent.

The Reverend Mother looked across at her with pleasure, and then began to think about the significance of the rope hanging to pavement level. Of course, Patrick was dealing with more than one crime. There had been trouble on the quays; a man had died, he had said. Was the rope connected with it in any way? And the open window in the room above it – could that have significance? It would be a shamefully easy solution to pin this murder on the rioters of last night, but she could see a look of interest on the faces of the dead woman's relatives. The solicitor, however, wasted no time on this matter.

'Yes, yes. Well, Miss Clancy, I'm sure that you know of a handyman. I'll leave you to deal with that, in due course, once the inspector gives the word. Tell him to submit his bill to my office.' Mr O'Brien was on his feet, wisely making the decision to leave Julie to her task before he got involved in any more household matters. 'Well, thank you all for attending, but now I must get back to work. Don't stir, Miss Clancy, don't stir. I'll let myself out. You'll be in touch with me, inspector, won't you?' He shook hands with all present, rapidly and decisively, and conveyed an unmistakable air of being unavailable for any questions or complaints and his authority was such that Julie, who had got up, sat down again and looked helplessly around the room.

It was Patrick who followed the man to the door, took the knob into his own hand, opened the door for both and then closed it firmly behind him in the hallway.

Gone to find out when the will was made. The Reverend Mother thought that there was a general curiosity about that. No one spoke, but all strained their ears. The firm of O'Brien, Dunne & O'Brien did a lot of court work and this O'Brien certainly had a carrying voice. The question was unheard, but everyone in the room could hear the answer.

'No, certainly, not. No, not last night. The will was made exactly one month ago. Mrs Hendrick came to my office and she made it then. She told me that she felt that she would do more good with her money and would be acting in a way that would follow the wishes of her deceased husband by leaving everything to her nephew. I did suggest that it might be wise to avoid trouble by informing her other relatives of . . .' And then Mr O'Brien, as though conscious of an unseen audience, lowered his voice. Everyone within the library remained tense, and in a listening position until the front door slammed shut a few minutes later.

And then all eyes went to Nicholas.

'So, old son, when did our late lamented relative tell you that she was going to leave her every penny to you?'

Claude had an unpleasant note in his voice and the Reverend Mother regretted that both Patrick and the lawyer had left the room. Too late to suggest saying the rosary for the repose of the soul of the dead woman, she thought regretfully. She might have got away with that suggestion before the reading of the will, but not now when all, except one, were hurt, disappointed and angry. They had, in fact, been treated with cruelty and derision. What on earth had been Charlotte Hendrick's motive in allowing all to go through the charade last night and then to leave it to the lawyer to make the announcement while she hid behind an imaginary illness? She fingered her rosary beads, bowed her head, but was aware that all eyes in the room had turned towards Nicholas.

'I don't know what you are implying, Claude, but I've told you already that I knew nothing of a new will.' The professor's voice was taut with anger and the two men glared at each other. There was a cold silence for a moment while the women in the room looked from one to the other of the cousins.

Nicholas finally broke the silence. 'Though I don't mind telling you that I was fairly convinced that Mrs Hendrick would leave the money to me. She was genuinely interested in the Viking history and since her own family had been unpleasant about her marrying a Protestant, she had regarded her husband's family as her own. And I was the only Hendrick left in this city.' Nicholas sat back and looked belligerently around the room.

That was probably true, thought the Reverend Mother, but if Charlotte had arranged with the bishop that she was to lie in state in the cathedral and be buried in St Finbar's Cemetery, then she must have reneged on the Protestant faith which she seemed to have adopted after her marriage. It was somehow odd, though certainly not unknown, for an elderly person to return to the faith of their childhood and make their peace with God before death arrived. That, at least, would be the charitable view. Though the elaborate funeral arrangements, perhaps, told another story. The Church of Ireland were fairly austere in their funeral arrangements.

'She told you.' Claude had an angry flush on his face.

Nicholas gave him a contemptuous glance. 'No, she didn't tell me, but I guessed,' he said cuttingly.

'And, yes, I suppose that I did almost know. She told me that she was writing to everyone to ask them to come and put forward their ideas, but she did say that they had to be worthwhile ideas and that she wasn't going to squander Uncle James's money on some ridiculous schemes, or' – Nicholas looked meaningfully at Claude – 'to send good money after bad. I knew then that it was almost a certainty that I would inherit the whole sum because she was so interested in my research.'

It was an explanation, of kinds, and was possibly true. And yet, could a man have been as certain as Nicholas had appeared to be unless he had actually known that the will had been signed and sealed. The Reverend Mother had grave doubts about the matter. Her mind went to the picture of the dead woman lying on the floor before the window. There had been a mass of clotted blood around the neck and under the ear. And the carpet on the floor beside her had been soaked in blood. A very savage murder, she thought. Harder, she would imagine, to cut someone's throat than even to hit them on the head, and far harder than firing a shot. Nicholas, she would have thought, would have found it relatively easy to lay his hands on a gun. And Claude, also. He, she seemed to remember, was part of the hunting and shooting crowd. On the other hand, to bring a gun would have meant prior knowledge of the will.

She looked around the room, thinking about her disappointed relatives.

Last night had been a disaster. Charlotte had very clearly shown that she disdained all ideas except the one put forward by her husband's nephew, Nicholas Hendrick. The rest were left under no illusion. And yet, up until recently all of the seven nearest relations had been left in the expectation that they would inherit a substantial sum on the death of Charlotte Hendrick. None, save perhaps Nicholas, knew that the will had been already changed. Faced with the merciless verdicts from the wealthy widow, could one of the six persons, sitting here in the library, have been desperate enough to put an end to the life that stood between them and the money that they had perhaps counted on?

A ridiculous waste of time, Lucy had character-ized the evening, but Lucy was the wife of a rich man who was becoming richer all the time. Claude, on the other hand, if faced with a possible bankruptcy, may well have been desperate enough to put an end to Charlotte's life before she could change her will. A knife, she thought, was messy, but it was quick; it made no sound; it was easily available from the cutlery drawers of every house-hold and most people possessed one in any case. Even she, herself, had a small, sharp knife attached to her bunch of keys and found it useful for cutting string and such tasks. The Reverend Mother scanned the faces and weighed up the odds.

Florence, she considered to be a high-minded, imaginative girl. Yes, she was keen on the idea of

178

studying abroad, but was it such a passion with her that she would have slit the throat of an elderly woman? The same applied to Brenda. Yes, her husband's business was failing, but would she have been driven to murder? When it came down to it, she supposed that the most likely candidate was Claude, but was he ruthless enough? He was in money trouble, according to Lucy. And yet, money troubles were suffered by many people and could perhaps be solved with the aid of a sympathetic bank manager. After all, if it came to it, Claude was a widower with just one son with whom he had frequently quarrelled and whom he could have refused to maintain if his affairs became worse.

And, last of all, there was Julie. Now leaning back in an armchair, white-faced, drained by emotion. What was it that Lucy had said about the relationship between Julie and her wealthy cousin?

'They hate each other!' These had been Lucy's words. The ill-use of Julie would have been seen by all those relatives gathered here. They would have been used to it, but it would come into all minds once the questioning began.

Quietly the Reverend Mother got to her feet and left the room. Let them think that she had gone in search of the bathroom. She needed to see Patrick urgently and to tell him of the thought that had come to her. There was, she thought, a grave danger that one tragedy might be followed by another.

CHAPTER 10

The Reverend Mother climbed the circular staircase with difficulty. She was well used to stairs, but there was something about the circular form of this particular staircase and perhaps the polished marble rather than wood on the stair treads themselves that made it an exhausting journey. Or perhaps it was the events of the morning which had drained her energy. Nevertheless, she was determined to see the body once more before it was enclosed within a coffin.

And so, when she reached Charlotte's room, she turned the doorknob and went straight inside, closing the door behind her as she went.

As she had expected, Patrick and Dr Scher were in the room. It was warmer in there now as the window had been closed, but otherwise it was as it had been when she had seen it this morning.

'I do apologize,' she said, but without any real feeling of contrition. The thought that had come to her had been a valuable one and it was one that might not occur to either of the men in front of her. She looked from one to the other. 'I wondered whether Dr Scher knows an approximate time of death,' she said.

Neither looked surprised and Dr Scher answered immediately. 'I'd put it, taking into account how cold the room is, at about midnight to half-past midnight,' he said. 'Has to be always a bit of an approximation, but should be correct within a half hour or so, I should imagine.'

The Reverend Mother nodded with satisfaction. 'I would say that you are right, Dr Scher. The noise that woke me occurred at twelve thirty, and I did check my watch when I went back to my own bedroom after finding the door to this room locked and receiving no answer to a gentle knock.'

'Good,' said Dr Scher, and he looked at her enquiringly.

'Have you thought of something else that happened in the middle of the night, Reverend Mother?' asked Patrick.

The Reverend Mother shook her head. 'I wanted to see Charlotte again and to check my memory,' she said. She looked down at the body. She should, she thought, say another prayer, but then told herself that the living were more important than the dead. 'I wanted,' she repeated, 'to check my memory and I find that it is correct. Charlotte is dressed, she is still wearing the same clothes as she wore last evening when she entertained all of us, all of her near relatives to dinner. The odd thing is, though, that we all, including Charlotte, retired to bed about half past eleven o'clock. Why was Charlotte still wearing her dinner dress an hour later?'

'And corsets,' put in Dr Scher while Patrick looked slightly embarrassed.

The Reverend Mother discreetly repressed a smile. 'Exactly,' she said. 'I don't, myself, wear corsets, but from memory they were most uncomfortable garments. So why was she fully dressed? Although she seemed to have changed her shoes for slippers.'

'So she wasn't thinking of going out again,' said Dr Scher and then quickly apologized. 'Sorry, of course she wouldn't, not a woman of her age and type, not go out on the streets at midnight. I'm thinking of myself. As soon as I take my shoes off, I am bound to get a night call and so I wait until half past twelve when my calls are answered by a young colleague from the Mercy Hospital.'

'Perhaps she was reading and so didn't bother getting undressed,' suggested Patrick, probably thinking of the long hours that he spent studying in the evening.

The Reverend Mother hastened to disabuse him. 'Not a reader in the evening,' she said briskly. 'Look around you, Patrick. No bookshelves, no sign of any books. Nothing on the bedside table, or anywhere else in the room. In any case, if she did want to read, one would imagine she would go to bed and read in comfort, or at least slip into a dressing gown. No, all of the books that Charlotte read are in the library downstairs.'

'Had too much to drink and fell asleep, still in her clothes,' suggested Dr Scher. 'What do you think, Patrick?'

'From my observation, my cousin, Mrs Hendrick, like myself, just drank water,' said the Reverend Mother. 'No, I would imagine that the only reason why she was still in her evening dress almost an hour after retiring to bed would be because she had a visitor, or even, that she expected a visitor. This seems to be more likely and might account for the sound that I heard which could have been a door clicking shut and a key being turned in it, perhaps.'

'And the open window?' queried Patrick.

The Reverend Mother thought about the open window. She had an uneasy intuition that it might possibly be the key to the strange events of the night before.

'Could it have been someone came, invited or uninvited, and that person smoked a cigar or even one of those Turkish cigarettes which were served after dinner? Personally I disliked the smell and I would find it feasible that Charlotte might have thrown her window open once her visitor had left. That's if the visitor had smoked a cigarette.'

'So the visitor would have been one of the men,' said Patrick thoughtfully.

'Possibly,' said the Reverend Mother, although an image of young Florence had come to her mind. Was it possible that the girl had asked for another interview? Had pleaded that she had been caught unawares by being chosen to be the first to give a presentation. Possible, she told herself. And it did seem to fit with the girl's forcible personality. And Charlotte, to give the woman her due, seemed to have a strong sense of fair play. That whole charade they had taken part in last night was an example of how the dead woman felt under a moral obligation to be fair to all.

'Perhaps there had been no appointment, just a tap on the door five or ten minutes after she had retired to her bedroom,' she said aloud. 'My cousin and I were next door, but we were talking over old times, reliving some of our girlhood social occasions. I doubt that we would have heard anything or even taken any notice. This is an old house and with people running baths, cleaning teeth and washing, the plumbing clanked from time to time. I remember noticing this. A tap on a door would not have attracted my attention, in any case. It would be natural, for instance, if Florence had gone to borrow something from her aunt, or if Nicholas had sought some cigarettes or matches from Claude, or if a maid was bringing hot milk to someone. One would have expected a certain amount of coming and going as people settled in for the night in a strange house. For myself, I am sure that I would have noticed nothing.'

At that moment there was a sharp knock on the door. Patrick went to it instantly, opening it a fraction, and placing his body firmly in the space.

'Oh, Inspector! I was looking for the Reverend Mother.' Brenda pushed her way resolutely past Patrick's effort at blocking the doorway. 'Oh, there you are, Reverend Mother. I was sure that I heard your voice. I thought that you might be organizing prayers for the departed soul of our dear cousin.'

Now she was in the room, looking shrewdly around and then walking up to place herself at the Reverend Mother's side.

'I heard your voice,' she repeated. 'I said to myself "prayers for the dead" and so I came to join you.' She looked from Inspector Cashman to Dr Scher and then back again to the Reverend Mother. 'Oh, dear,' she said, looking down at the body. 'How terribly sad! Poor, poor Charlotte! I was so close to dear cousin Charlotte and so very fond of her,' she added and then waited.

Always was someone who liked to know what was going on, thought the Reverend Mother resignedly. Not any exaggerated gasps of horror at the sight of the clotted blood, though and for that the Reverend Mother accorded her some respect. A practical woman.

'I'm sure that Inspector Cashman will welcome your help, Brenda,' she said aloud.

'We were wondering whether Mrs Hendrick had been talking to someone after you had all retired to your bedrooms. Perhaps it was you, Mrs O'Mahony, was it?' Patrick had seized on an opportunity and it was possible that this bold stroke might just work.

Brenda, however, looked most taken aback, quite genuinely so, thought the Reverend Mother. 'Come here, into her bedroom, so late at night, well, of course I wouldn't do that, Inspector.'

'But you were very good friends, weren't you?' Dr Scher took up the attack. 'You've just said so, haven't you?'

Brenda preened herself a little. 'Well, of course, she did like to ask my advice and of course I could see that she was very, very worried, poor, poor cousin Charlotte.' Now Brenda touched her eyes with a neatly laundered handkerchief and looked over the top of it at Inspector Cashman.

'She had worries, then.' Patrick produced his notebook and the Reverend Mother stepped back and wondered whether she should leave and began to move softly towards the door. But the next words stopped her in the process of a discreet withdrawal. 'Of course, she had, poor thing. It is always a problem when a near relative is involved. I felt sorry for Cousin Charlotte. And dear Julie, of course! So, so hard-working. And so talented too. I wish I could sew like she does. But, you know, inspector, it doesn't always work out to employ a member of the family.'

'So Mrs Hendrick was worried about something to do with Miss Julie Clancy.' Patrick said the words bluntly, but held his indelible pencil poised in the air.

'Well, you're a young man, so you wouldn't understand how complicated family relationships can be; men don't anyway, no matter what age they are,' said Brenda with an indulgent air. 'My husband, Tom, now, when Florence was getting such high marks in school from her French teacher, well Tom got the idea that she could come into business with him and she would manage all the French side, buying all the wine and French cheeses. He had a notion that it would go wonderfully well, despite the fact that the two of them were always quarrelling. I must say I put my foot down. It never works to employ a member of your own family, I told him that and I stuck to it. And that's what I said to poor, dear cousin Charlotte. Find her some other post, that's what I said to her.'

Patrick wrote on impassively while Brenda went through another few anecdotes from the families of friends and acquaintances.

'How long ago did this conversation take place?' he asked and the Reverend Mother applauded his discretion in not mentioning any names at this stage. Brenda, she guessed, would prefer to hint rather than to speak out. It was interesting though, that the conversation had taken place at all. Brenda, after all, lived in Fermoy, a town that must be a good twenty or twenty-five miles away from the centre of Cork city.

'Let me see . . .' Brenda was deep in thought. 'It was on the train coming back from Dublin. I had been up for the sales. I just spotted her in a carriage and got straight in. I thought she looked tired. Of course, these sales are exhausting. I was most surprised at Cousin Charlotte to bother about sales, not with her money. Didn't find a thing, not a shopping bag with her. But it was nice to meet her. We had a good chat together. I could see that she had something on her mind and of course, when it comes to it, a relation is always closer and more worthy of confidence than a friend; Cousin Charlotte had, of course, plenty of friends, but I don't suppose that she could confide in them in the way that she could do in me.'

Patrick should now say 'just so' and try to keep the conversation going, thought the Reverend Mother but these small phrases that oil the everyday conversation were not yet on the tip of his tongue. They would come, but in the meantime she would lend a hand.

'Too true, too true,' she murmured with an absent-minded air.

Brenda brightened. 'Of course, she knew it was safe to confide in me and I didn't need too many explanations to understand how she and dear, dear Julie might well get on each other's nerves. She was, of course, thinking of Julie as much as herself. Cousin Charlotte was always so self-sacrificing.'

The Reverend Mother abruptly lost all faith in the veracity of Brenda's memories at that summing-up of Charlotte Hendrick's character. She even began to doubt that any such conversation had ever taken place. But why pretend? From beneath the starched hood of her veil, she eyed Brenda carefully. Worried, she decided, but why? Lucy had some story about a failure of Brenda's husband's business in Fermoy. But he could have nothing to do with the murder of Charlotte Hendrick. After all the man was back in Fermoy and nowhere near Bachelor's Quay last night. And then another name came to her. Florence – not a daughter of her own, just her brother's daughter, but immensely dear to her. Brenda had brought the girl up, had, she seemed to remember, taken her on in babyhood. Was Brenda worried that Florence might have had something to do with last night's violent attack on the woman who had openly sneered at her some hours earlier? The Reverend Mother thought about Florence, recalling the flushed and mortified face as the girl realized that she had not done herself justice and had made a spectacular mess of trying to explain how she would use Charlotte's money if she were to inherit it. There was an intensity and a single-mindedness about teenage girls. She had often had hopes of a girl whom she had persuaded to stay on in school, had hoped that with a school certificate she might get a job in an office, a shop, only to be confronted by a sudden and emotional determination to leave school for a job in a pub or to join a friend in taking the boat for Liverpool. In her experience, teenage girls were fatally inclined to take quick, impulsive decisions. Brenda, she guessed, would know this.

Yes, Brenda had a look of anxiety behind the flow of conversation in which hints about the bad feeling between Charlotte and poor Julie abounded.

Julie, thought the Reverend Mother, when Brenda had eventually departed, might be in grave danger if some or many of her relatives decided that she was an ideal scapegoat. She took leave of Patrick and Dr Scher and went downstairs, thinking hard about the murder of Charlotte Hendrick.

It was only when she had reached the bottom of the stairs that it occurred to her that Charlotte was unlikely to remain fully dressed for the sake of an interview with Julie whom she regarded as almost a servant in the house. If, however, the expected guest was Nicholas, then that would be an entirely different matter.

And, whereas it was impossible to imagine Julie smoking one of those Turkish cigarettes, and even more impossible to imagine her having the temerity to do so in Charlotte's bedroom, it was perfectly feasible that Nicholas would have been persuaded to indulge himself by an adoring and admiring aunt.

CHAPTER 11

'And so, because dear, dear Mrs Hendrick so loves, so loved, I mean, her cup of tea first thing in the morning, well, I went back up with the girl to look at the door.' Julie took a long breath and Patrick resisted the impulse to pencil in a question mark on top of one of the oft-repeated 'dear'. There was, despite the woman's obvious distress, such an acid, insincere and totally unaffectionate emphasis on that word. He did not, though. Such a piece of indiscretion, though tempting, would do nothing for his career. He knew well that his notes might have to be produced at court and so he contented himself with waiting patiently for the end of the story. It was odd, he thought briefly, that there was none of the usual pious wishes, such as 'God have mercy on her' or 'God grant her peace'. Perhaps the enormity of the murder wiped out the conventions.

'And when I came to the door,' continued Julie, 'well, I found that Ann was right after all and that the door was locked. I took out my own set of keys and I put the key into the lock. It wasn't

jammed, inspector, not in any way. Just locked –
no key left in the lock, either. So once I put in
my own key it turned instantly and I went in.'
Julie stopped and fished out a handkerchief from
her handbag and mopped her eyes. The Reverend
Mother, Patrick saw with a tinge of amusement,
had suppressed her impatience to know the rest
of the story and patted the flaccid hand in a
comforting fashion. He, though too experienced
to give open expression to his impatience, swore
beneath his breath. The woman's story was of
the utmost importance and the sooner it could be
extracted from her, the better for his investigation.
He looked across at Joe. His assistant who had
arrived at the house just a short while ago still
wore a bandage around his head, was still pale
after the previous night's events. But he, also, was
eagerly awaiting the evidence from this relation of
the dead woman.

'So when you found that the door was locked,
you opened it with your own key and then . . .
who went in first? You, or the maid?'

'Me,' said Julie after a moment's thought.

'And what did you see next? Take your time, you
are being of great help,' said Patrick with a
conscious effort to be kind to the woman. It was,
he knew, a fault in him that he found it hard to
be compassionate to the rich and the powerful of
the city. And yet, this poor woman was in a terrible
state. He was glad that he had the presence of
mind to invite the Reverend Mother to come along

with her and to hold her hand as though she were a child who had involved herself in some dangerous event. 'Tell us all about it, Miss Clancy,' he said gently.

She responded to his tone. Looked up from the handkerchief with which she had been mopping her eyes. 'I opened the door and I said to Ann – the maid is called Ann, Inspector, you see we had to change—'

'Go on with the story, Julie,' said the Reverend Mother. Her voice, thought Patrick, was just right. Gentle, but very firm and the woman responded with an obedient nod.

'And I said to her, "Oh, the window, Ann!" You see, Inspector, the room was stone cold. Quite freezing. And I could see why. The window was wide open.'

'You are being most helpful,' put in Patrick, noting uneasily that the woman was working herself up to bursting into tears again.

It succeeded. She gulped, but that was all.

'And then I screamed. Mrs Hendrick was lying in a pool of blood on the floor. I told the girl to go away. I wanted to lift her and put her on the bed, but I was trembling too much. I think I was going to faint. I kept screaming. I think Ann helped me out of the room. Said we'd get the Reverend Mother. She was the one that thought of doing that. I was beyond thinking, Inspector.'

'Well,' said Patrick firmly. 'I'm not going to trouble you anymore, Miss Clancy. I can see how upset you are. What you should do now is to have a nice cup of tea and try to forget things for the moment.' He should, he knew, tell her to have a lie down on her bed, but at this very moment, a pair of young constables were searching the bedrooms and the dead woman's relations were all confined to the library, next door to this small office. He rose to his feet and went across to open the door for her. In the early days of his career, he had felt a fool doing things like that, but now he was used to it and stood gravely holding the doorknob before she sidled out. He shut the door with a certain feeling of relief and went back to the table, sitting on the edge of it, looking gratefully at the Reverend Mother.

'Thanks for staying with her,' he said and then, somewhat more hesitantly, 'Is she really very upset. Were they close?'

The Reverend Mother thought about that. He could see her turning the matter over in her mind and he waited for her verdict. When she spoke, he listened with a small shock of surprise, initially, but then with a conviction that she was, as always, correct and shrewd in her judgement.

'My dear Patrick,' she said, 'I may be wrong, but my experience is that a wholly dependent relationship where one partner has all of the wealth, and all of the power, really only works with small children or with dogs. Julie Clancy and Charlotte Hendrick had that sort of relation-ship. Charlotte had the wealth and the power and

Julie had nothing and so was dependent upon her. You yourself can guess what their relationship was.' She stopped with a slight nod of the head and he knew that she had answered his question in her own inimitable fashion. He remembered that about her from his school days as a child. Other nuns, other teachers, snapped out an answer, but the Reverend Mother always made you think through the matter for yourself. He began to imagine the life of that poor woman who had just left the room, a life where she was at the beck and call of her rich relative.

'The key is missing, you know,' he said. 'The girl, Ann, told us about the key and Joe here got his constables to search for it. Not a sign of it. And it wouldn't be something that you would overlook. It was the same as the one that Miss Clancy produced and that must weigh about half a pound. One of those old-fashioned keys. And it's well over six inches long. So it's a mystery about what happened to that key. The murderer must have locked the door, but why?'

The Reverend Mother thought about that, but then, as she so often did, answered one question with another. 'Why do you think that the window was opened and left open, Patrick?' she enquired.

'I've been thinking about that,' said Patrick slowly. 'The obvious solution is that someone escaped that way, but it could have been left open to lead us along the wrong path. There was all that trouble about landlords on the quays last night. And, of course, the rope was unlooped from the bracket and left dangling down to pavement level.'

'So it could be that one of those wild fellas climbed in the window and murdered Mrs Hendrick,' said Joe eagerly. 'And then he climbed out again. Excuse me, Reverend Mother. She's a relation of yours, I know. But she was known as a very bad landlord. A moneylender, too. Of course, it was perhaps her agent . . .' His voice tailed away with a dubious sound to it and he blushed a little at his own temerity.

'Yes, she would, deservedly, be most unpopular among the poor of the city,' said the Reverend Mother, briskly sweeping aside the poor excuse about it being the agent's fault, 'but how could anyone have got in? The house would, I'm sure, have been securely locked up at night. I'm sure that you have checked on that?' She looked from one to the other.

'Yes, it must have been someone in the house who opened the window and let the rope down to pavement level,' said Patrick thoughtfully. 'Apparently the long end is normally coiled around two brackets above the window of Mrs Hendrick's room. It does seem to point at collusion from someone within the house. Once that rope was down to pavement level a strong and active person could easily climb up to the window of the main bedroom in the house.'

'But the window would have had to be left

unlatched,' said the Reverend Mother. 'Mrs Hendrick would not have gone to bed with the bottom half of the window left open. Apart from security, it was a very wet night with a heavy mist and rain. But left unlatched is a possibility, I imagine. I don't think that she was a particularly nervous woman. Apparently, according to the maid, she never locked her own bedroom door, so it would be quite likely that she would not bother to latch her window. It is, after all, right up on the third storey of the house so an unlatched window is certainly a possibility,' she repeated, thinking back on the nature of her cousin.

'Yes, it is. But the unlooped rope points to collusion. So Professor Hendrick pointed out. One of the servants, he thought.' Patrick's tone was dry. 'I'm keeping all options open,' he added as she got to her feet.

'So I would expect,' she said, but said it with a smile of approval. He felt a certain warmth as he turned to Joe.

'Ask Mr Claude Clancy if he could spare me a word,' he said and then as Joe slipped out, he said to the Reverend Mother, 'Mr Clancy's son is a wild lad. His name is Michael Joseph, commonly known as Mickey Joe. He was in the forefront of that business last night on the quays. I think that he was one of the organizers of the building of the Viking house business – a bit of a cover-up for an onslaught against the landlords. The event looked innocent and shed an interesting light on the history of our city, but, of course, that was just a front. As soon as they had the house built the rioting started.' Patrick stopped, hesitated for a moment and then said, 'Eileen is going out with him, Reverend Mother. She's going out with Mickey Joe, not really *doing a line* with him, but seeing a lot of him.'

'Oh, dear,' said the Reverend Mother.

Patrick watched her reaction to this piece of news and knew what was going through her mind. Eileen had extricated herself a few years ago from the illegal Irish Republican Army and he hoped that she was not about to be sucked back into unlawful company again. The trouble with Eileen was that she was easily taken in, he thought with exasperation. Aloud, he said in neutral tones, 'These things, these protests, you'd want to be very careful about these people. Some of them have their own axes to grind. Eileen should keep away from them.'

'Perhaps she should try to become a member of parliament,' said the Reverend Mother.

He didn't like to contradict her and tell her that in Ireland, nowadays, it was called the *Dáil*. And although Countess Markievicz had been in the first *Dáil*, they were unlikely to elect a girl from the slums of Cork city. In any case what was the point of this *Dáil*? Nothing but a talking shop, he thought impatiently and then did his best to dismiss the matter from his mind. Not his affair. And he had always tried to steer clear of politics,

Now he had a murder to solve and he had to make a good job of it. Anything could be solved by hard work; that was the motto that he worked under. Once the Reverend Mother had left the room, he went back to his notes. Somehow or other he was going to solve this murder.

Claude Clancy: first cousin, once removed of the victim; had hoped to get one seventh of her estate at her death. A widower with one son, Michael Joseph Clancy, known as Mickey Joe, student of history at University College, Cork. Claude Clancy was the owner of Clancy's Bar, a money-making concern in the past – more of a club than a bar – but probably only up to the last year or so. Now the recession, the loss of wealthy people from the city, the trouble caused by the so-called 'Free-staters' – all of these things had considerably reduced the takings at his club, while the running costs, with the economic war with England, were mounting steadily over the years.

Patrick opened a fresh page in his notebook and then sat back. Yesterday evening all seven relatives of the dead woman would have confidently expected to inherit a seventh of her income – a very considerable sum, when one took into account the bank balance, the shares, the rents, the moneylending business and, of course, the considerable income from the gold mine shares. A wonderful windfall to a man in financial trouble. The bank manager, initially reluctant when he phoned, but realizing his duty to the safety of the realm as represented by Inspector Cashman, had been eventually very open about Mr Claude Clancy's financial problems. The man was on the knife-edge of bankruptcy. His elderly cousin's legacy would have been a lifeline.

'Come in,' he called as Joe, in his polite and well-trained way, knocked on the door in order to give his superior a moment in which to prepare for the interview. It never hurt – both Patrick and Joe had agreed upon this – to allow a witness a few minutes of apprehension before an interview designed to elicit the truth. Not too tough a character, Claude Clancy, he thought, though he would probably try to sound aristocratic and disdainful of an ordinary policeman.

'Well, well, well, Inspector, we do seem to keep bumping into each other this morning, do we not?'

Patrick, recognizing the edge of dislike and disdain under the words, did not reply to them. Time, he thought, for him, as inspector in charge of a murder case, to take control. Of course, Claude Clancy was in a bad mood. He had been hauled to the police station by Joe first thing that morning to confront an unrepentant son, who had spent the night behind bars, and had felt obliged to write a substantial cheque in order that Mickey Joe could be released from prison on bail. This had been a humiliating business and Claude Clancy was determined to show his superior status.

'Do sit down, Mr Clancy,' he said. 'I'm interviewing all who were in the house last night just to see whether anyone heard or saw anything that might lead us to the person who committed this deed.' Patrick was glad to hear how steady and clear his voice sounded.

'Well, I can't help you,' said Claude Clancy. 'I know nothing.' He had a pettish note in his voice, just as though he had been wrongfully accused of something.

Patrick forced himself to sound authoritative. 'It does sometimes happen, Mr Clancy, that a witness will give us a small piece of information, something that seems of no significance to him or to her, but which turns out to be extremely helpful to the investigation, so, if you will be so kind, I'd like you to give me a brief description of all that happened in this house during yesterday evening and, indeed, if you heard anything during the night.'

Claude Clancy turned out to be one of those people who like the sound of their own voices. His description of the evening did not quite fit in with the description given by the Reverend Mother or by his sister Julie. Claude felt that the late Mrs Hendrick had been deeply interested in all that he had to say and had asked several pointed questions which showed what a very good businesswoman she was. He passed over Nicholas's contribution: impassioned, according to the Reverend Mother; dull and academic, according to Claude. His cousin Brenda wanted Mrs Hendrick to throw good money after bad into her husband's business and Florence was a silly girl who should be looking for a husband for herself. And Mrs Murphy, wife to a very rich solicitor, could surely purchase a few luxuries for her daughters, if they needed them. Patrick allowed him to run down to an inconclusive finish before he put his last question to the man.

'Several people noticed hearing heavy footsteps, a man's footsteps on the stairs. Did you notice that, Mr Clancy?'

No, Claude had not noticed that. There had been, surmised Patrick, too much of a link between the city manager and his protest about the conditions of Mrs Hendrick's tenants, and his own son who had been a ringleader in the affair on the quays last night.

That opened window, just above where the body lay. Was that a clue to the murderer? Or was it a false trail, designed to link the murder of this very wealthy property owner with last night's disturbances on the quays. No doubt many, many of Mrs Hendrick's unfortunate tenants from Devonshire Street or from the lanes that abutted North Main Street had been present last night. And the woman was also a moneylender. *Mrs Hundred Per Cent*, he had heard her called. A woman who would lend a shilling to a tenant in dire need and would then require two shillings in return. Pay up or be thrown out on the streets; that had been the reputation of the woman whose death he was now investigating.

'Thank you, Mr Clancy. Very good of you to spare us so much of your time.' Patrick had phrases like that off by heart now. He had practised them and had perfected a decisive getting-to-his-feet action along with a purposeful move to the door of the room. Cork people were great talkers and once the interview was over most wanted to embark upon a friendly conversation.

'And now for Mr . . . I mean Professor Nicholas Hendrick,' he said to Joe once he had shut the door.

'So he's the other side of the family, the husband's side. Odd that she should favour him, isn't it? They say blood is thicker than water, but that doesn't seem to be the case here,' said Joe.

'Perhaps she liked the idea of his being a professor,' said Patrick, but Joe in his efficient way had already departed and Patrick sat and thought about Mrs Charlotte Hendrick, landlord and moneylender. The professor, he thought, had certain questions to answer and he meant to make sure that the man responded adequately to them.

When Nicholas was ushered in by Joe, Patrick greeted him coldly. The man, he thought, was more at ease than he should have been considering that he was the sole heir of a woman who had been murdered while he stayed overnight in her house.

Deliberately therefore, and in order to lull him into a false sense of security, Patrick went step by step through the events of the day and of the evening before. When he had finished, he read aloud his notes and asked whether they seemed to be a fair account of the conversation.

'I think you are trying to make me nervous, Inspector.' Nicholas smiled across the desk, but Patrick did not return the smile. A cool customer, he thought and then fired his question.

'When were you made aware that you were to be the sole heir to the Hendrick fortune?' He barked the words out, omitting the courtesy title of professor. Nicholas, he noted, looked taken aback and somewhat alarmed.

'I'm not sure what you mean,' he said slowly. Playing for time, thought Patrick.

'Come now,' he said hardening his voice and staring across the desk. He picked up a pencil and deliberately broke it into halves. A Christian Brother, who had taught him when he was ten years old, had a trick of doing this and it had always alarmed the class more than any shout could do. It seemed somehow to indicate that the snapping of a pencil was the penultimate step to a complete loss of control. Patrick carefully arranged the two halves on the pen tray, placing them, as this sadistic man used to do, in the shape of the letter T – or if you were imaginative or guilty you could see the shape as that of a gallows, he thought and looked up to meet a pair of alarmed eyes.

'No,' said Nicholas hurriedly. 'No, I didn't know. But I suppose that I did guess. It was such a worthwhile way to spend money – and she did seem very friendly and encouraging to me. After all, rich people through the centuries have sponsored academic research. Though I warned myself to say nothing, I could see that she wanted to appear to be fair, she wanted to show her other relatives that mine was the greater claim; that I would use her money in a way that would ensure the name of Hendrick had great significance in the history of Cork city.'

'So when did you guess?' Patrick did his best to conceal his triumph.

'A couple of weeks ago she talked to me about a presentation,' said Nicholas. 'Everyone was to be told at the same time. She made sure to emphasize that. Only she talked to me about it face to face whereas the others had heard by letter. That was the only difference made. You see, Inspector . . .'

A fortnight, thought Patrick, hardly listening to Nicholas's self-righteous justifications. After all, if a wealthy widow wanted to leave a rising academic an enormous sum of money to fund his research – well there was no law about that. But when that widow is brutally murdered, then questions had to be asked and motives probed. And yet the man did not look guilt-ridden. He seemed, rather, to look like someone who is accused in the wrong.

Weren't my fault – one of the worst troublemakers in the city, Patsy MacConor, repeated these three words every time he started a fight going in Dennehy's Bar. Despite the fact that one was tall, handsome and well-groomed and the other was squat, unshaven and unwashed there was, at the moment, a resemblance between Patsy and Nicholas. Patrick sat back and looked severely at Professor Hendrick.

'Fourteen days,' he said slowly. 'Well, that was long enough to make arrangements, I suppose, wasn't it, Professor Hendrick?'

'I don't know what on earth you are talking about.' Now the professor was angry. 'What the hell are you insinuating? Are you saying that I killed my aunt?' He stood up. A very large man, he towered over Patrick but Patrick sat very still in the chair designated for the person in charge.

'Sit down, Professor,' he said quietly.

It took a long minute, but Patrick did not waver, did not move a muscle, nor did he even look towards the bell on his desk. But then Nicholas Hendrick seemed to crumple. He passed a hand over his forehead, sat back in his chair and looked across at the inspector.

'Sorry,' he muttered. 'Nerves not good. A bit upsetting all of this. She was always very good to me. And then finding out that she had left her entire fortune to me. Well, it's all been a bit of a shock.'

Patrick nodded politely, but inwardly he was cynical. He would wager that Nicholas had more or less known that the money was going to come to him and to him only. Somehow, he didn't look like a man to take a knife to the throat of an elderly aunt who had been good to him, but how about

206

if someone else did it and he could pretend, even to himself, that he had nothing whatsoever to do with the matter.

'Of course,' he said pensively, 'this Viking festival.' He stopped there and waited for a reaction and was rewarded by a leap of fear in the man's light-blue eyes. The festival, he thought, might have been mooted some time ago, but with a pile of hazel scrub trees already cut down in the lower grounds of the university and given the energy and muscle power of forty or fifty young men and given the fact that Cork, this city of rivers, had that handy route via the River Lee back from the university to the city quays, it could have been arranged at short notice . . .

'I wonder how long it took to organize?' he said aloud. 'The trees were cut a few weeks ago, weren't they? A nuisance, they were, too! The president of the university – your president, Professor Merriman – had been on to me to post a policeman to stop the wood from being stolen for firewood. I suppose that he was only too glad for you to use them.' He stopped and looked enquiringly at the professor. There was a sudden cessation of Joe's rather heavy breathing as he took down notes. Joe, thought Patrick, was a sharp lad and he had immediately understood the point.

'It would have been easy for you to make an arrangement with the rowing club to tow the saplings to Merchant's Quay, wouldn't it?' he continued.

'No problem,' said the professor briefly. 'But I'm not sure what you are driving at, Inspector.'

'And one of your students is Mickey Joe Clancy – that's right, is it?'

'Goodness, Inspector, you can't expect me to remember all of my students who are studying for a primary degree. I normally only know them apart when they start into a master's or a doctorate.' The words were said on a crest of confidence, but Patrick was not deceived. You made a mistake there, he thought. Impossible for anyone not to have noticed Mickey Joe. The lad was brimming with self-confidence and assurance. He'd stand out a mile in any gathering even without that head of bright orange hair.

'Mickey Joe Clancy was the student who organized the floating of the logs to Merchant's Quay,' he said mildly.

'Oh, yes, I think I know who you mean.' The words were uttered hurriedly and Patrick waited for a moment. 'A red-headed fellow, isn't he?' Nicholas added and Patrick could have sworn that there was a clear picture of the young man in the mind of the man sitting opposite to him.

'And he is the son of Mr Claude Clancy and a distant relation of Mrs Hendrick, a blood relation,' added Patrick and waited to see whether Nicholas Hendrick would respond to the hint that he himself was no blood relative and so, by law, would have got nothing if the wealthy Mrs Hendrick died intestate.

He didn't. Just gazed stonily ahead and so Patrick went on. 'Whosoever murdered Mrs Hendrick left the body lying on the floor beneath the window and the window itself was wide open. Something, I think you will agree, which seems unlikely on a foggy, wet February night.'

It was a trap and Nicholas fell into it instantly. 'You mean that it was one of the rioters who killed her,' he said, and Patrick could hear a note of hope in his voice.

'That is possible,' said Patrick and delayed for a few seconds before adding, 'And of course, it could form a diversion, or even a smokescreen if a murder was planned.'

'I'm not sure whether I understand your meaning, Inspector.'

'It's quite simple, Professor.'

'Not to me.'

'Surely it's obvious. If a murder was planned by a person living in this house, the fact that a riot was going on down the quays, might divert attention from the guilty person. And given that the building of the Viking house sparked off a comparison with the terrible lodgings that people in the neighbourhood had to put up with – given the fact that it was well known that a demonstration against landlords was also planned to take place – well, to my mind, Professor, all of these facts add up.'

'And what do they add up to, Inspector?'

'They add up,' said Patrick slowly and

209

deliberately, 'to the conclusion that there could be two reasons for last night's murder. One, the late Mrs Hendrick was murdered by one of the gang demonstrating against the landlords here around the quays of Cork . . .' Patrick stopped for a second, keeping his eyes fixed intently upon Nicholas Hendrick's face and then continued, 'Or two, Mrs Hendrick was murdered by someone who hoped to inherit her money.'

'I think you are probably right, Inspector.' With a great effort, Nicholas had forced his voice to sound casual. 'And as one of the possible seven suspects for your second reason for murder, I do hope that it turns out that one of those murderous crew last night climbed up by means of the rope and opened my aunt's window and killed the poor woman.'

Patrick nodded. He got to his feet. He did not offer to shake hands and neither did the other man. They eyed each other for a moment. Joe put down his notebook and moved across to hold the door invitingly open. It was only then that Nicholas went out and he did so after a long, level look at Patrick, a look that held a certain threat within it.

'Well, what do you make of him?' asked Joe, once the door had closed behind the man.

I don't like him. The words jumped into Patrick's brain but he suppressed them as being, even to Joe, too emotional, too lacking in impartiality. 'I think,' he said aloud, 'that it is possible he organized that event as a cover for Mickey Joe and his gang. I think it's almost certain he guessed what was going on – but I say "possible" and I do think that's a long way from killing the woman who had been kind to him. Yes, of course, she could have changed her mind again and divided it between the seven of them . . .'

'Might have ruined his plans,' said Joe.

'But could he have persuaded some of these poor fellows to break into the house and kill the woman?' Patrick brooded on the matter. It would be an easy solution, but he didn't feel that it was the true one. Even that killing last night on the quays was partly an accident and wouldn't have occurred if that landlord had stayed snug in his own house and had not come out and tried to throw his weight about and frighten his own tenants. 'I don't think so. There are, were, worse landlords in the city than Mrs Hendrick.'

'And, also, she was a woman,' pointed out Joe.

'That's right, one woman among a dozen or so men. They'd be squeamish about killing her. Even the British wouldn't hang Countess Constance Markievicz, when the rest of the 1916 crowd were executed. No, I'd be more for the notion that it was your man, himself. That he took advantage of all the wild boys in the street, thought that if he left a window open, and the rope hanging down to the pavement that the blame would be laid at the door of the rioters. But I'm not happy about it; it's not really such a good motive. One seventh of money like that would have been enough for him, I'd say. Although nobody turns down money, that doesn't mean that they would murder to get it,' added Patrick. 'Come in,' he called in response to a firm knock on the door.

'Just found this, Inspector,' said the cheerful-looking constable. 'Dr Scher was with us when we found it. He thinks that it might be what we are looking for, thinks they would do the business. It's got a bloodstain on it.' And, very gingerly, he took something from a small box. It was wrapped in a piece of cotton, but the light from the window struck a gleam of kaleidoscopic colour from it. 'I found it in a big vase of artificial flowers in the hallway.'

'A dagger,' said Joe.

'No,' said Patrick quietly as he bent his head over the box. 'Not a dagger, Joe. It's half a scissors, one half of a very large pair of extremely sharp, steel scissors. Let's hear what Dr Scher has to say about it.'

CHAPTER 12

'You'll never guess what that husband of mine wants to do.' Lucy burst into the drawing room where six people sat listlessly looking out of the window or pretending to read, or, in the Reverend Mother's case, passing her rosary beads through her fingers while praying for the repose of the soul of the dead woman. She put in a special prayer to Holy Mary, Mother of God, to free her mind from the sin of avarice and to take from her mind the thought of how the prospect of inherited money might have meant that she would not have to justify the quarterly expenses of the convent and its school to the bishop's secretary when he came along to do his four times a year audit. Brenda, she had just noticed, had put aside her book and was having a whispered conversation with Julie, which consisted mainly of Brenda repeating endlessly, 'Of course I won't say a word'. The Reverend Mother, looking at Julie's distressed face, had just decided to intervene when Lucy, who had been summoned to the kitchen telephone (as the only other telephone in the house was in the office where Inspector

Cashman and a constable were now in possession), came back into the library in a state of indignation.

'Wanted to pick me up after lunch, if you please! Did you ever hear of such a ridiculous idea? "My good man," I said to him, "you don't seem to realize that I am a suspect in a murder case. How on earth can I leave the scene of the crime?" I told him that he could call for me at five o'clock this evening and to bring plenty of law books with him so that he could bail me out, if that is the right expression.' Lucy took a seat by the fire, one that Claude had just vacated for her, and smiled sweetly up at him. Everyone brightened and books were cast aside. Even Julie managed a slight smile. There was, thought the Reverend Mother, very little genuine distress about the death of Charlotte Hendrick amongst her relatives. Lucy's robust attitude gave all liberty to be themselves.

'I say,' said Claude. 'This is a strange business, isn't it? It would be rather fun if we could work out what happened. Who does everyone think has done it?'

'You,' said Nicholas.

The word, thought the Reverend Mother, was delivered in a rather unnecessarily provocative tone. Claude, however, didn't take offence.

'No jumping to hasty conclusions, now,' he said merrily. 'Now let's put our brains together. Anyone read those Sherlock Holmes mysteries?' He looked around the room.

'Oh, Sherlock Holmes is very old hat. I much prefer Agatha Christie and Dorothy Sayers,' said Florence in her determined fashion. 'Aunt Charlotte has a collection of them, and lots of other murder mysteries, here in the library. I always snatched one to read when I came here to see her. She was always busy with rent collectors and boring people like that and I used to be sent into the library. I stole a book from her this summer. It's called *The Murder of Roger Ackroyd* and she missed it. Telephoned to tell me to bring it back immediately once I had finished it because it was one of her favourite books. I must say that she wasn't too bad when I brought it back. We had quite a chat about it.'

'I read that,' put in Lucy. 'I was going to give it to the Reverend Mother, but I gave her a Father Brown mystery instead, in case the bishop was looking through her bookshelves. I thought it would look better.'

The Reverend Mother smiled discreetly. She had persuaded a bookseller on the Grand Parade to donate his shop-soiled novels to her school so that the oldest girls in the school would have a chance to acquire reading habits and she herself guiltily dipped into them, salving her conscience with the thought that she had to make sure that they were suitable.

'I've read *The Murder of Roger Ackroyd*,' she confessed aloud. 'I thought it extremely clever. I don't suppose anyone could guess the murderer.'

'I was reading a book once where the person who found the body was the one who committed the murder. That was you, Lucy, wasn't it?' Claude was determined to keep the party atmosphere going.

'Don't be silly, Claude. You know it was one of the maids,' said Lucy with an air of unconcern, 'but, of course, I slept next door and so I must be a prime suspect. Just what I told Rupert when he phoned up.'

A laugh followed this and the atmosphere lightened. There had been, recognized the Reverend Mother, a feeling of tension in the room and though, in theory, opposed to untruths, she thought that Lucy's little white lie about the discovery of the body had been quite justified. Julie, who had been looking flustered and defensive, now relaxed into a smile, though she said, almost as though duty bound, 'Oh, dear, poor Cousin Charlotte.'

This produced a relapse into an uncomfortable silence and then a babble of inconsequential remarks. The Reverend Mother searched her mind for a comment on detective novels but at that moment the door opened and Inspector Cashman came in, accompanied by a young constable, carrying a box marked with the *Garda Síochána* emblem. All conversation stopped instantly and every eye went to the box.

'Sorry to interrupt you,' said Patrick. 'Constable Hayes found this in that vase of dried flowers on the hall table. I would be glad to know if anyone

216

recognizes it. Perhaps you could show it to the ladies and gentlemen, Constable. Please don't touch it, anyone, will you?'

There was a metal object lying within the box. The Reverend Mother felt a cold feeling within her as the young man came politely across and held it out in front of her. She bent over it and examined it carefully. Wickedly sharp and ominously stained. She sat back.

'It is not mine,' she said impassively.

Lucy took her cue from her cousin and repeated the same words. Florence took in a breath that sounded like a gasp, but on a look from Brenda, shook her head wordlessly. Brenda said loudly and clearly, 'This belongs to neither of us.' And Julie, from a distance, buried her face into her hands and refused to look.

Claude got to his feet, went across to stand beside the constable, staring with curiosity into the box and, after a slight hesitation, Nicholas joined him and they both looked at each other.

'It's a scissors, half a scissors,' said Claude. Then his eyes widened and he said, with a certain degree of theatrical emphasis, 'Oh, my God! Is that blood on it?'

And then came Nicholas's voice, cool, very calm, very self-possessed and very positive. 'Surely that is your scissors, Julie? Or at least half of your pair of scissors. I remember remarking upon them. Do you remember me saying to you when you were doing that patchwork quilt that they seemed lethally

217

sharp? I recall observing how they cut through two layers of corduroy—'

He was interrupted by a frantic scream from Julie. 'I knew it. I knew it. I knew that it would be pinned on me. Just because I'm poor and unimportant. And I don't have a solicitor for a husband. No, no one bothers about me.'

'Oh dear,' said Brenda. 'Poor, poor Julie.'

'Don't be ridiculous, Julie,' said the Reverend Mother sharply. 'Stop crying instantly. Would it be possible to get her a cup of tea,' she said in an undertone to her cousin, before putting her arm around the woman and escorting her from the room and into the small office next door. It was always her instinct with hysterical adolescent girls to get them away immediately from an interested audience and this seemed to work as well with Julie who was a good forty years older than the girls in her school. In any case, the loud sobbing turned into a subdued weeping.

The office was not empty though. Dr Scher was there, sitting at the desk and filling out a form in his sprawling handwriting. He assessed the situation instantly, without any show of surprise, and was on his feet in an instant.

'Come and sit down, Miss Clancy,' he said in a calm and assured manner. He took Julie by the arm and had her seated within seconds, and then stood before her, one finger on the pulse in her wrist and the other hand holding a large and rather battered watch. There was something rather mesmerizing about the sight of someone completely absorbed in counting out the seconds; it provides a moment of calm and of distraction. I must remember that for the future, thought the Reverend Mother as she sank into the one easy chair that the room provided. She waited quietly, thankful that Julie had stopped that terrible gasping.

I am feeling my age, she thought. The sight of that bloodstained half of a pair of scissors had made her feel slightly queasy. She had seen Charlotte Hendrick. Had seen the bloodstained neck and shoulder, had seen the pool of blood on the floor and one look at that lethally sharp instrument had told her that it was, in all probability, the weapon which had severed a vein in the throat of her elderly cousin. She hardly looked up when the door opened and Patrick came in, followed by Joe with his notebook at the ready. Dr Scher released Julie's hand, patted it gently as it fell upon the desk, pocketed his watch and then stepped back.

The law, thought the Reverend Mother, must now go through its due process. She looked enquiringly at Patrick but he did not look at her and so she decided to stay where she was. At least she would be able to help if Julie had another fit of hysterics and would be available to answer the door when Lucy arrived with the tea.

Patrick sat down at the desk, read through the form that Dr Scher had filled out and then looked across at Julie.

'Feeling somewhat better, Miss Clancy?' he enquired solicitously.

Julie stared ahead, soundless and dull-eyed.

'That's good,' he said as though she had answered the question. 'Now, would you like to have Dr Scher and the Reverend Mother stay in the room while I ask you a few questions?' His voice was gentle, but his manner was assured.

Julie nodded and Joe, in the background, made a note.

'Just a few questions, Miss Clancy. I understand that you are a great needlewoman, you embroider, stitch curtains, make rugs and cushion covers . . .' Patrick ran out of ideas, but the deadly piece of steel in front of him seemed to be telling another story. *They hate each other*. Lucy had said that of the relationship between Julie and her cousin, the wealthy Charlotte Hendrick. The Reverend Mother sat and thought. She was confident, from long experience in controlling her feelings, that nothing would be showing on that pale face and heavy-lidded, green eyes beneath the shadow of wimple and veil, but behind that façade her mind was working fast, remembering the past; sifting the present through her long experience of human nature.

'And this is a piece of your scissors?' Patrick's voice was very gentle, but Julie reacted with alarm.

'I don't know what you are talking about. One scissors looks the same as another scissors. How do you know that is mine?'

'There is a piece of sticking plaster wrapped around the handle. One of the maids identified the scissors, the part of the scissors, from that. She said that you had scratched your thumb last week and you put the sticking plaster on the scissors to cushion it. Is that true, Miss Clancy?'

Julie sobbed in reply.

'I'm afraid I must press you for a reply, Miss Clancy,' said Patrick. 'Does this belong to your scissors, do you think?' His voice had become more firm, more resolute and Julie responded obediently.

'I think it might.' Her voice trembled and the Reverend Mother felt very sorry for her. Could Julie have been driven by some piece of cruelty, some final and unforgiveable taunt into planning a murder? The woman was staring with horror at the weapon. There was no doubt about the blood and the piece of sticking plaster. 'I couldn't have broken that,' she said. 'I couldn't have broken a pair of scissors in half. My hands aren't strong enough. I could never have done that.' There was a note of terrible desperation in her voice.

'Don't you think it has been unscrewed,' said Patrick quietly. 'I suppose that it is made like that so that it can be easily sharpened. This has been sharpened on many occasions, I would imagine.' He left a silence for a few long moments before he asked another question.

'Who does the maintenance work in the house, Miss Clancy? For instance, who might have a box of tools, might be able to sharpen your pair of scissors?'

'The chauffeur,' she said dully. 'He does all the work around the house. Mrs Hendrick never liked me to call in a tradesman unless it was completely necessary. She was always on to me to find jobs for him. Said he didn't do enough. Sent him out with the rent collector to give him protection. Made him sweep the pavement in front of the house and clean the outside of the windows, too. He hated her,' said Julie with a sudden burst of aggression. 'Why aren't you questioning him? I wouldn't know how to break the scissors. He always does it.'

'Always does it . . .' prompted Patrick.

'Sharpens them. I like to have my scissors very sharp.' Julie wailed and buried her face in her hands. The Reverend Mother looked discreetly at the single half of a pair of scissors. Quite a big instrument. Must have come from a large pair. The blade looked very sharp, even from a distance it was noticeable that it had been sharpened to the extent that the edge of the metal was quite thin and that this was now quite a lethal weapon. Halfway down, between the blade and the handle, was a small, round hole. It was obvious how the scissors were made to be easily taken apart for sharpening and then the two halves could be screwed together again. It would not, she thought, need a workman to unscrew them. Given a screw-driver, she could have done so herself, though she, unlike Julie, was no needlewoman.

'We'll talk to everyone in the house,' said Patrick gently. 'In the meantime, perhaps you could tell me where you normally keep your scissors.'

'In my workbox,' said Julie.

'And you keep your workbox . . . where? In your bedroom, perhaps?' prompted Patrick after he received no answer to his initial question.

Julie shook her head. 'No, in the drawing room. Mrs Hendrick liked to have someone with her when she was talking.'

So anyone could have slipped them out of the workbox, thought the Reverend Mother and saw that the same thought was written on Patrick's face as he made another one of his rapid notes. It was, she thought, a very sad statement of Julie's position in the house. The rich widow talked and the poor, unmarried cousin listened while working. No doubt threw in a few words of admiration or interest from time to time. But that was not a conversation. If only Julie had been left her well-deserved one-seventh of Charlotte's estate – with a feeling of sadness the Reverend Mother had now worked out the sum – more than six thousand pounds, she repeated to herself, seeing the numbers written large in front of her. A fortune to be spent by her, she thought, though she was aware that it was a tiny drop in the ocean of need in the city of Cork. But for Julie, well it would have been more than adequate. Enough money to buy herself a nice small house, to afford a servant and to live in comfort, in comparative wealth, really, for the rest of her life. She looked with pity at the worn face of the woman beside her and patted the flaccid hand.

It was a mistake. Julie, sensing sympathy and reminded of her troubles, began to weep silently. There was a moment's silence in the room. Patrick shut his notebook and so did Joe and looked expectantly at his chief. Dr Scher got to his feet and then went quickly to the door.

'Ah,' he said genially. 'I thought I heard something. Fairy footsteps tripping down the hallway. It's Ann, with the tea.' He cast a rapid glance at Patrick, received an almost imperceptible nod in return and then continued, 'Now, Miss Clancy, you go with Ann and she'll take the tea up to your room and I'd advise you to have a little rest on your bed. Ann might bring you a hot water bottle, would you, Ann?'

A nice girl, thought the Reverend Mother, thinking back to the time when Ann/Philomena was at her school. Always cheerful despite total neglect from a scatty mother who took little care of her fancifully named daughters, but spent most of her time in a public house in South Main Street. Her younger daughter, she hoped, as she watched the girl follow poor Julie up the stairs, might have a better future than either her mother or her sister.

'Nice girl that,' said Dr Scher. 'Should probably get the boat to England. Not much of a future for her here.'

A bleak summing up, but a true one, thought the Reverend Mother and was conscious of a wave of anger against those, like her deceased cousin Charlotte Hendrick, who exploited the poor, refused them the right to decent housing, protested against paying taxes that might be of help in building decent houses and setting up industries to pay them a living wage. And anger, also, against a government who, despite all of the fine promises, had done little to give the citizens a decent education, a means of earning their own living, and of providing food and clothing for the children that were brought into the world. Why should a bright, hardworking girl like Ann have that bleak future in front of her if she stayed in her native city? Her only chance of a decent life was to forego marriage and children and to remain as a servant in a wealthy household. Or else, as Dr Scher had suggested, get the boat to Liverpool.

'If only the wretched will had not been made,' she said. 'I suppose that Mrs Hendrick's money would have been divided equally amongst her relations.'

'Miss Clancy could buy herself a house and offer a good job to that girl,' said Dr Scher. 'And perhaps she might marry the chauffeur,' he added after a minute.

The Reverend Mother thought about this for a moment. It did seem like a good solution. It required a death, though. And deaths don't always come to order, she thought.

'He's a good-looking lad, that chauffeur,' said Dr Scher, going on with his idea. 'But then they tell me that these days girls like older men. You should see how the nurses flutter around me in the Mercy Hospital, Patrick.'

'And that brings up an interesting question,' said Patrick, ignoring the last statement to the Reverend Mother's secret amusement. 'I assume that last night all, except, perhaps, Professor Hendrick, believed that they would inherit virtually six thousand pounds if Mrs Hendrick did not change her will.'

'That is correct,' said the Reverend Mother. 'Let me explain to you what happened last night.'

As succinctly as she could she detailed the scene the evening before and finished by saying, 'I would think that no one there had any doubt that if my cousin Charlotte were to make a will the next day, then her entire fortune, all forty thousand and more of it, would be left to Nicholas. But, of course, my cousin Mrs Murphy has ascertained from her husband, Mr Rupert Murphy, the solicitor, that Nicholas would have received nothing if she had died leaving no will. He was, you see, not a blood relative.'

'Would he have known that?' asked Patrick.

The Reverend Mother thought about that for a moment. 'My cousin, Mrs Hendrick, was a woman who talked continuously about her will and how she had left her estate to be divided equally in seven parts, of which her husband's nephew,

Professor Hendrick, was one. I doubt that Nicholas feared that he would receive nothing, but then, according to Mr Rupert Murphy, people who talk a lot about their will often have been found, after their death, never to have made one. Still, Charlotte was a businesswoman, so I'd say that Nicholas would have relied upon getting at least a share of her wealth.'

'And, of course,' said Patrick, 'during the last few weeks, he would have been hoping, probably expecting, to receive more than forty thousand pounds. A very, very large sum of money.'

'I won't say, worth murdering for!' murmured Dr Scher.

The Reverend Mother, by habit, gave him a severe look but watched as Patrick opened his notebook again. Her mind was on Nicholas. If you were a brilliant academic and fiercely ambitious, and with the unifocal vision that such a combination could bring, well, yes, it might well have been worth a murder to pocket such a sum as over forty thousand pounds. She sat very straight and upright and waited for a question from Patrick.

It was, however, Dr Scher who asked the question. 'But why murder the woman if he was fairly sure that he would inherit the lot?'

'You forget that Charlotte Hendrick was almost ten years younger than myself,' said the Reverend Mother, allowing a slightly tart note to come into her voice. 'Professor Hendrick is a youngish man, presently at the top of his tree in a small provincial university. I would say that he has more heights to scale and mountains to conquer. And this book might have been his first step.' And after that fanciful image, she sat back, placed her hands within her long loose sleeves and allowed them to debate the age-old question of a bird in the hand or a pair of birds in the bush. She esteemed herself as a fair judge of character and thought that Nicholas was a man who would be impatient for action, for immediate progress and that for someone like him the bird in the hand would matter.

'Ten, fifteen, twenty years more of life would be nothing for a well-fed woman who took good care of herself and had the best of everything,' mused Dr Scher. 'Not that I know anything much about her, but that would be my surmise. I find that a lot of my wealthy clients are in their eighties or even their nineties. Nothing like good feeding, plenty of money to call a doctor when needed, to stay in bed when ill with an infection – even pop up to Dublin to see a specialist if necessary. People with money tend to go on living for a long time as long as they are moderate with food and with drink. Mrs Hendrick was a slim woman and, I'd guess, would probably have lived a long life and no one would be surprised if she did. But, of course, someone slit her throat,' said Dr Scher. 'A very quick way of ending a life. One cut and that would be that. Two arteries in the throat, Reverend

Mother. She wouldn't have had much chance of surviving. Probably died within minutes. Nice, quick way to go.'

It occurred to the Reverend Mother to wonder whether her cousin Charlotte saw the face of the assassin before her life ebbed away, saw whether it was a stranger who had come through the open window, or else a member of her own family. She seemed to remember a Sherlock Holmes book where the dying man had tried to write a name in blood. She said a quick prayer that Charlotte had passed away peacefully.

'Will you do an autopsy, Dr Scher?' queried Patrick.

'Not unless I am authorized, and I can't see the superintendent wanting to pay for one. After all, it's completely obvious that she died because her throat was cut. There's evidence of massive bleeding up there in that bedroom. No one could have lived for more than a couple of minutes after that. No point in me examining her liver or her spleen or anything else. I know how she died, so no point, I'd say, unless you want me to do one.'

'Odd weapon to choose, wasn't it?' mused Patrick. 'One would have expected a knife.'

'That scissors was as sharp as any knife, sharper than most. According to the maid, Ann, the chauffeur used to sharpen the scissors every week for Miss Clancy. That's right, isn't it, Joe?'

'Yes, sir, and I checked on that. He said that she liked them as sharp as possible. He put them to the grinding wheel every week, said that he had done them three days ago. Unscrews them in the centre and then sharpens each side. Always has done so. He told me,' said Joe, opening his notebook, and finding the page that he sought, 'yes, here it is. When Mr Nicholas's youngest was playing in the drawing room he found the scissors and cut himself badly. Mr Nicholas was furious with Miss Clancy for leaving them where a child could find them. There was a big row, according to the chauffeur. Mrs Hendrick blamed him for sharpening the scissors too much, which was probably a bit unfair. And, of course, Miss Clancy always kept her workbox in the drawing room.'

'So the chances are that most people knew about Miss Clancy having a pair of scissors in her workbox and also that these scissors were kept lethally sharp,' said Patrick and he, too, made a note and then nodded at Joe, giving his sergeant, thought the Reverend Mother, the permission to speak his mind.

'It just crossed my mind that the use of the scissors rules out the possibility that it was an outsider, one of the rioters on the quays,' said Joe and Patrick nodded, but waited.

'But, of course, it might have been a collusion job,' said Joe. 'Someone in the house had taken the scissors apart and had them ready. What do you think, sir?'

'Not happy with it,' said Patrick with a grimace. 'Why bother? If someone came in from that crowd in the quay, you'd expect them to come in armed. Didn't even need a knife. Plenty of broken bottles around on the quays that night. We saw ourselves what could be done with them. Dr Scher will tell you that man died of wounds, not of strangulation. I think the rope around his neck was there to frighten him. I don't suppose they meant to kill him. But someone will hang for it, be that as it may,' he finished bleakly. He left a moment's silence while he looked around the room.

'Be more of a woman's weapon, this half a pair of scissors,' said Joe tentatively.

'Or perhaps that is what the murderer wants us to think,' said Patrick.

There was a silence after that. The Reverend Mother's mind touched on those relatives of hers, on the small girls playing in the sun, on the baby in the pram, on the butterflies and, last of all, on the driving force of ambition when coupled with an academically gifted mind. There were so many more possibilities, but the lure of easy money was a very potent motive. There was, she thought, a huge danger that this murder was carefully planned with two victims in mind – the first, of course, was the wealthy Charlotte Hendrick, but the second could be the scapegoat. She shuddered slightly. She had always been sickened and horrified by that biblical story of the goat, in Leviticus, she seemed to remember, suddenly picturing the words on a page, about the unfortunate goat, burdened with the sins of the community and driven out into the desert to die of heat and thirst. She looked across at Patrick and saw from the thoughtful look on his face that he was meditating upon what he had just said.

'Just so,' she said crisply and was glad to see him nod and half-smile. She could leave it to Patrick, she thought. He was not someone to jump to any hasty conclusion. The use of the blade from half a pair of scissors would be borne in mind and assessed for various possibilities. She would, she thought, do her best to assist him by filling in the background to that strange dinner party last night. Later on she would meditate again upon the reasons for that open window and the rope hanging down to pavement level. When she spoke, her voice was brisk and vigorous.

'I'm glad that Dr Scher made that remark about Mrs Hendrick's age, and about the longevity of many of his patients. It did occur to me,' said the Reverend Mother, 'that a lot of the plans, including my own plans, I have to admit, were founded on the prospect of getting the money quite quickly. In fact, it now seems that for me to make those plans, considering I am a good ten years older than the late Charlotte Hendrick, was the height of folly.'

'So all those people, not just Nicholas – all of those who spoke last night, as you described, Reverend Mother, were urging their claims, but probably feeling that they made a poor impression. All of them, when they thought about the matter in the privacy of their own bedroom, might well have decided that they wanted the money immediately. And we come back again to the bird in the hand, don't we, Patrick,' said Dr Scher. 'And I wouldn't make an exception for Nicholas. In the first place he may well have known that a new will had been drawn up, giving him everything, but in the second case, even if he didn't, he might have decided, with a young man's impatience, that he wanted money now, not in twenty years' time. Twenty years,' said Dr Scher solemnly, 'is a lifetime to a young man like Nicholas Hendrick.'

'Yes, indeed,' said Patrick energetically. 'If I think over the list of relatives – obviously we can rule out Mrs Murphy from the suspect list as she shared a bedroom with the Reverend Mother, but of the other five – Professor Hendrick, Mr Claude Clancy, Miss Julie Clancy, Mrs Brenda O'Mahony and Miss Florence Clancy, all of these had a strong motive to hasten the death of their wealthy relative and all of these would have known about, would have seen the fatal scissors. And, of course, in all probability would have heard the story of how sharp they were, might even have tested them for themselves.'

He stayed very still for a moment, staring down at the well-polished desk in front of him. And then, quickly and decisively, he made a note. 'But, of course,' he said, after replacing his pencil, 'this murder may not, after all, have been committed by anyone in the house. I can't rule that out. After all, a window was found open and the Reverend Mother did hear a noise in the night as if from a window or from a door. Her own relatives are not the only people in this city who might have wanted to get rid of Mrs Hendrick. As we know there was a lot of violence and a lot of ill-will – hatred, in fact – stirred up last night against the landlords who treated their tenants so badly. There might,' said Patrick, 'have been collusion with someone in the house, someone who provided the half a scissors, let down the rope and then went off to bed. One of the servants. They share rooms, by the way. Or there is the chauffeur? He is by himself in the lodge. Could he have a motive as Miss Julie Clancy suggested?'

'Easy enough to get up that rope from the wheel. That's if someone let it down first,' said Joe.

'That's what I was thinking,' said Patrick. He looked down at his notes, turning back the pages until he reached the first page. The Reverend Mother could see that a long list of names, long enough to fill a page, were written there. Not just the names of the relatives, but also those of the servants, and perhaps tenants, she surmised.

Patrick turned to Joe. 'Would you just pop into the kitchen, Joe, and get hold of that girl who showed out Mr Monahan when he came round last night to deliver the notes from the meeting of the Housing Committee.'

There was a silence after Joe had left the room. Dr Scher looked uncomfortable. The Reverend

Mother thought about the sound of heavy footsteps on the stairs a while after she'd assumed Philip Monahan had left the house. She said nothing, however, and awaited the arrival of Ann. It had been Ann, she remembered, who had shown him out. Ann, whom he had addressed by her real name of Philomena.

'This is Ann, sir. She showed Mr Monahan out.' Joe was back so quickly that he must have met the girl in the hallway, perhaps coming back from Julie's bedroom.

Not looking guilty or even worried, thought the Reverend Mother. She always had a protective feeling towards her past pupils and she was glad to see Ann looking so self-possessed.

'Did Mr Monahan go straight out?' enquired Patrick. He showed no sign of remembering the girl, though she must have lived quite near to him when he was young.

'No, sir.' Ann was still polite and unconcerned. 'No, he went upstairs because he wanted to see if the flood was lower from the other side of the house. He thought he might go out by the Grattan Street entrance, through the kitchens, sir.'

'And so he went up the stairs to have a look. Did you go with him?'

'No, I didn't, sir. He said to wait. That he'd just be a minute. He knew the house, you see. He'd been here a few times to see Mrs Hendrick. The first time he came she showed him all around.'

'Including up into the three bedrooms at the

top of the Bachelor's Quay side of the house, including the room that has the wheel beneath the windowsill?' Patrick kept his voice very even, almost casual, but the Reverend Mother sensed a certain excitement emanating from him as the girl nodded. This was, she thought, with a certain sinking of the heart, very significant news. Philip Monahan, unaccompanied, had gone upstairs, could possibly have gone into that room, knowing that Mrs Hendrick was downstairs. And if he had done so, could he, perhaps, have opened the window and dropped the coiled rope down to near pavement level. And by doing that, had he left the way open for an assassin to climb up through the window and then into the bedroom of the woman who was landlord of a large amount of slum property in Cork. A woman, moreover, who had threatened to wreck his scheme by campaigning for landlord rights and landlord compensation. She turned the matter over in her mind while Patrick was thanking and dismissing Ann and then she followed the girl from the room and up the stairs towards the drawing room.

They had reached the landing when there was a loud crash from the hallway. Ann sped on down to the stairs at lightning speed and the Reverend Mother followed, holding tightly to the rail of the balusters. Oh dear, she thought, when she reached the safety of the hall.

The magnificent Japanese antique vase was lying, broken into fragments, on the hall floor. The elaborate fronds of dried flowers were strewn all over the floor and Julie stood amongst them, her cheeks flaming in contrast to her white face.

'Oh dear,' said the Reverend Mother calmly. 'Never mind, Julie. Accidents will happen. Come with me, dear.'

She managed to get the woman through the dining-room door before the outburst. The Reverend Mother moved her as far from the door as possible and then settled down to listen to what Julie had to say. It was interesting, she thought as she absorbed the flood of complaints and deciphered the words from amidst the sobs, that Julie blamed Charlotte for everything, including her obvious dislike of her cousin, thereby allowing the police to accuse her of murder.

'Don't worry, Julie, I don't think that Inspector Cashman has ever met our Cousin Charlotte,' she said eventually as Lucy, followed by the girl, Ann, came to her rescue. One gulped phrase, repeated again and again, stayed in her mind after Julie had been taken off to bed.

'She made jokes about Julie's Dead Garden, about my dried flowers to everyone who came into the house.'

CHAPTER 13

Even after almost three months, Eileen still got a thrill when she walked into the college, University College Cork. It was, she thought, a most beautiful place. It had been built over seventy years ago from the white limestone, excavated from Little Island in Cork Harbour and then brought up the river on barges to this site on the western road leading out of the city and towards west Cork. The university was designed in the shape of a quadrangle around a green lawn. She had been told that it was a copy of an Oxford college and many of the professors held doctorates from that university. Eileen resolved that one day she, too, would go to Oxford, but in the meantime she luxuriated in the thought that, thanks to a Honan scholarship, she had a place in these hallowed surroundings. She too had the right to wear a gown over her shabby coat; a right to go through the heavy wooden doors into lecture halls, offices, and the magnificent *Aula Maxima*, which housed a library that held more books than Eileen had ever imagined. And the opportunity to stretch her brain more than she had ever believed possible.

And she might be about to lose it all this very morning.

She was no sooner through the entrance beneath the tower when the porter poked his head out. 'The president wants to see you, Miss MacSweeney. Not been parking your bike on the green, again, have you?'

Eileen was aghast. The president. She had only once seen Professor Merriman in his office and that was when she had first won her scholarship and he had given her a little talk, telling her how much was expected of her. The bike business had been just a joke and had been dealt with by the porter. Perhaps he was going to congratulate her on an essay, she tried to tell herself as she walked primly around the quad, keeping well clear of the sacred, emerald green grass in the centre. But she knew in her heart that this was unlikely. She had kept up with the work, but that was about all, and even that had been at the expense of a night's sleep and had resulted in her dozing off during a class and amusing all the time wasters who sat up high in the back rows of the tiered lecture halls and passed their time in writing limericks.

She should, and she knew it, give up the job at the printers. But if she did that her mother would have to work even harder at scrubbing out the public house in South Main Street. At least now, with Eileen's earnings, she was able to finish work early in the afternoon, able to come home, rest her aching legs and look after her swollen hands. And there was never a shortage of food in the house anymore. Eileen saw to that. She needed to keep her job going. The scholarship funds soon got eaten up with meals at the university and the huge cost of books. And petrol for her bike, of course. And clothes. And that new dress for the college dance. Eileen guiltily examined her conscience and wondered where money disappeared.

The president, according to his secretary, had one of the professors with him so Eileen prepared for a long wait. All of those professors, in her experience, were great talkers and when two of them got together it was unlikely that they would finish up quickly because a student was waiting outside to speak to the president. They were in the middle of an argument, she thought, but the heavy wooden door, lined on both sides with green baize, shut off the sound and prevented her from hearing any words – just raised voices.

She was wrong, though. In a few moments, Professor Hendrick came through the door. He frowned when he saw her and swept past with his gown flying. Eileen looked after him. It would be nice, she thought, to have a full gown like that, not the skimpy little sleeveless gown that under-graduates had to wear. Then she thought of the huge cost of that gown and mortarboard if she ever attained even a bachelor's degree and knew that, come what may, she would have to try to keep her job going in the printers and somehow fit it in around the study time that was necessary for her to gain a first class honours. As she got to her feet and followed the secretary, she resolved, virtuously, that she would give up most of the social life and, if necessary, writing articles for the *Cork Examiner* and devote every spare minute to writing outstanding essays in the five subjects in her curriculum.

Filled with this new resolution she sat down on the chair opposite the president's desk and demurely adjusted her skirt to approach a little nearer to her knees. The president was known for disliking these 1920 fashions and she should avoid putting him in a worse humour. He was not looking too well pleased, she thought.

'That was a disgraceful affair last night,' he began abruptly.

She didn't pretend to ignorance. That would never work with him.

'It was horrible,' she said and allowed a small catch to come into her voice.

'And you were there, in the thick of it! You, a scholarship girl. I thought I told you at the beginning of the term that this scholarship was dependent upon good behaviour and hard work.'

This annoyed her. Why was there one rule for students whose parents were rich enough to pay their fees and another rule for a 'scholarship girl'?

'There were lots of students there, sir. All of Professor Hendrick's class,' she pointed out.

'But you are not in Professor Hendrick's class. You are studying a different period completely.

You are studying nineteenth-century history, not early medieval. You are in Dr McGraith's class for history.'

Eileen lifted her chin. 'I'm interested in everything, Professor. I'd like to study everything.'

It wasn't a bad remark. It took him rather aback and he passed a hand over his clean-shaven face. 'But that's ridiculous, you know,' he said, 'no one could do that.' Nevertheless, he half-smiled as he said, 'Well, you're young! But, now tell me, what's your explanation about getting involved with these propaganda speeches? Men down from Dublin, too, I understand.'

There was nothing for it. If necessary, Mickey Joe had to be sacrificed. 'That was an accident,' she said and tried to inject a note of sincerity into her voice. 'One of Professor Hendrick's students asked me to help with the loudhailer and I agreed. I didn't really know what it was all about. And then when I saw that there was trouble coming from it, I just went away. I went home to my mother,' she ended humbly.

'His name?' He had his pen in his hand and his eyes were still cold. She hesitated, but not for long. She had to safeguard her own career.

'Mr Clancy,' she said. Lots of that name in Cork.

'Mr Michael Joseph Clancy,' he said, and there was a grim note in his voice.

She nodded.

'I understand that the police have interviewed that young man. According to my enquiries, he

242

doesn't seem to be in college today,' he said and looked at her keenly.

'I hardly know him, Professor,' she said. Essential to stand up for herself now. She was in danger. In danger from the university and in danger from the police. With her background – and that was something that the university knew nothing about as it had been the very highly respected Reverend Mother Aquinas who had written her references – if the police got involved she would be in danger of losing that scholarship for which she had worked so hard. Inwardly she vowed to keep well away from Mickey Joe in the future, but now she had to think of a way of getting herself out of this mess. She silently took in a deep breath and proceeded to lie her way out of trouble.

'Mr Clancy is a friend of a friend and I was interested in that idea of building a Viking house. It was amazing how quickly they did it.' And before he could say anything, Eileen embarked on a detailed account of just how it had been put together. It was easy for her as she had just written an article for the *Cork Examiner* and her own words, full of enthusiasm, still rang in her head. She could see that he was interested and impressed by her. He had a look of attentiveness in his eyes and she blessed the gift of storytelling that her own mother had handed down to her. She dismissed the handing over of the loudhailer in a couple of short sentences, and inserted a quick comment, 'I just got tired of looking after the

243

thing.' Then she went on to the atrocity and there, once again, she could give vent to her genuine feelings of horror and helplessness when she first saw the bleeding man, feelings that had already been probed for sincerity and were already written out and ready to be handed into the *Cork Examiner* office.

When she had finished, he gave her a long look. 'Well, I think that perhaps you were not so much to blame as I thought. Professor Hendrick seemed to think that you were perhaps a trouble-maker and had been involved in the move to invite those abominable men who came to stir up the feelings of those unfortunates.'

'I had nothing whatsoever to do with that.' She heard her voice and knew that it struck the right note. 'And all that Mickey Joe – Mr Clancy, I mean – told me was that they were going to build a Viking house on the quay. I thought that it would be fun to help.' And then she took a chance. 'I don't know why Professor Hendrick would think that of me,' she said in a tone of injured inno-cence. 'He knows how interested I am in his book.'

Why had Professor Hendrick tried to involve her in trouble? And then she remembered that he was some sort of distant relation of Mickey Joe. Well, tough luck. She had to safeguard her own future. Mickey Joe was the son of a rich man. Aloud she said, 'He knows Mickey Joe, of course, as well. He's a cousin of Professor Hendrick's.'

That worked well. She could see him look slightly

embarrassed and when he spoke, his voice was apologetic. 'Professor Hendrick is, naturally, most upset about the death of his aunt, Mrs Hendrick, possibly at the hands of those ruffians,' he said, and she did not contradict him. She thought it was unlikely that the police, that Patrick, thought that one of the rioters was responsible, or he would not be spending time searching the house and interviewing the people in it – as, according to Philomena, he was doing. She just bowed her head and stood silently waiting for her dismissal.

She saw the secretary give her a sympathetic look on her way out and knew that she was skating on extremely thin ice at the moment, so when she came out and saw a shock of red hair appearing over the hedge she deliberately turned her back and strode away towards the library.

He followed her, though, right up the steps and into the *Aula Max*. And once she had scribbled her order for books, she knew he was beside her, standing there, pretending not to see her while he too filled up his order. They waited in silence, side by side, until the trolley arrived but then, although she had not looked at him, she realized that he was following her down the room and that he had taken a seat at the bottom of the same table. A couple of physics students were whispering together over a mould-stained volume and he said nothing while they were there. But as soon as they had taken the book back, he changed his seat so that now he sat beside her.

'Go away,' she said, without looking at him.

'No, but Eileen, I'm in bad trouble. Really, Eileen. I really need help.'

'Shut up. I'm working,' she said. The library was very quiet this morning and in a minute the librarian would probably notice and ask him to be quiet. In the meantime, she buried her head in Madame de Sévigné's letters, making diligent notes and trying to shut her ears to the voice beside her. The library trolley was trundling around the room, now dropping off books and picking up books and making enough noise to cloak his voice, but she did not look at him.

'The police have got it into their heads that I set up that business last night to help my father. I think they believe that I climbed up and murdered the old bag. You see she was his cousin and he hoped to get a legacy.'

'Nothing to do with me,' she said, making another note. What a tedious old woman this famous Madame de Sévigné was! *Trés beau dans sa simplicité,* she wrote after one pompous statement.

'Yes, but it is. You can help me. Something very simple.'

'I'm not listening,' she said and turned over another page. Painstakingly she copied out a sentence: "'*Si vous demeurez sur la frontière, l'amitié solide y trouvera son compte; si vous revenez, l'amitié tendre sera satisfaite.*" *Un exemple . . .*' she began to write and then threw down her pen in exasperation. 'Go away. I'm working.'

'You're great friends with that inspector. I've seen you talking and laughing with him. Just tell him I was with you all night. You could do this for me. Would cost you nothing.' His voice was angry and it rose to an unacceptable degree. The librarian replaced her pen in its tray and strode over.

'Now, then, you two, go and have your quarrel outside in the quad. Or in the restaurant. Anywhere you like, but not in here.'

White with anger, Eileen slipped her book and her notebook into her bag and strode off. Now she was in trouble all around. And the librarian had been very good to her, had recognized that she was very short of money and had given her special privileges, allowing her to keep books out on longer loans than usual, something that meant she had not had to buy as many books as the others in her class had been forced to do.

'Get away from me,' she hissed. Now she would have to go and find a corner where she could work, shutting her ears against disturbances.

He didn't move, though. He stood very still and looked intently at her.

'You don't care, do you?' Now his face had turned white and he looked angrily at her. 'You don't care whether I am arrested or whether I am hanged. It wouldn't matter to you, would it? Oh, no. As long as Eileen can be a good little girl and hand in her essays on time, the rest of the world can go to pot. Just a few words from you to that inspector friend of yours. Just a few words, just telling him that you were with me all of the night. All of the night,' he repeated, looking at her with narrowed eyes. 'He'll believe it. You've quite a reputation, you know. The girl who lived in a house with a gang of IRA men; that was the first thing that I ever heard about you. One of the fellows in the law department told me that about you. Well, have it your own way. And don't be surprised if you have an accident on that bike of yours. A guilty conscience is a great distracter. Heard of a fellow who was knocked down by a tram. Said that he was worrying about something and didn't notice the tram coming along. Same thing could happen to you, you know!'

Eileen did not answer. She walked ahead of him down to the bicycle shed. It took an effort not to turn her head as she knew that he was following her. But when she was near to it, she stopped and hesitated for a moment. What if he meant what he had said? He might stop short of wrecking her bike, but he might damage it and she had already spent good money on it. She could not afford new repairs. She pulled the bike out from its place in the stand and wheeled it decorously across to the porter's lodge. Propping it against the wall, she went in. The porter was busy with a delivery man and so she waited patiently until he had finished.

'Now, then, Miss Trouble,' he said amiably, 'what's the matter with you now?'

'Someone has threatened to damage my bike,' she said baldly.

'Well, don't come to me. Go and tell the president.'

'I'm in trouble with him already,' she said. 'All I want is to leave my bike here for ten minutes while I go and talk with a professor.'

'So, why have you been threatened then?'

'Someone wants me to do something that I don't want to do.' She looked him straight in the face and was glad to note that he looked embarrassed.

'Never should have admitted women to the college; the English have the right idea,' he muttered as he turned towards a shelf. 'Here. There's a padlock and key. Picked it up in the quad the other day. No one has claimed it. You can borrow it for half an hour, but don't leave that thing there any longer. Yes, yes, I'll keep an eye on it. Now off with you before I change my mind.'

Eileen went quickly. She knew what she wanted to say and she knew how to do it. It had been, she had thought at the time, quite strange that Professor Hendrick left the quays so early yesterday evening and had allowed matters to get so out of control.

He was in his office, she was relieved to find; she didn't want to go on a hunt for him around the university. He didn't seem to be doing too much work, just sitting and dreaming. There was an elaborate doodle on the top page of the writing pad in front of him. Nothing else on the desk. No books, no other notes.

'Eileen! What brings you here? Anything wrong? Any problems about the book?' He was always very informal. All of her other professors and lecturers addressed her as Miss MacSweeney.

'Oh, no, Professor, nothing like that,' she reassured him. 'The book is all right. Mr Lee is happy about the pictures. Everything is going fine with your book. But everything is going wrong with me, Professor. The president has been on to me. I'm in trouble. And it's all because of one of your students,' she added and watched his eyes narrow. He didn't ask which student, but she told him anyway.

'It's Mickey Joe Clancy,' she said. She was fairly sure that someone had told her that they were cousins, but Mickey Joe himself had never mentioned this. Cork people were great at tracing out relationships, but it might not be true. The professor's lips, though, had tightened when she mentioned the name. She would leave it and move on to other matters.

'The president thinks that I went there to make trouble,' she said. 'He thinks that it was deliberate. He thinks that the riot was something to do with the students, but I'm the one who is being blamed, just because I have a scholarship and—'

'And because you are a woman so it's easy to pick you out from all those young men.' He was making his voice sound very sympathetic now and so she nodded and tried to look grateful.

'So why did you go?' he asked. And he sounded genuinely interested.

'Mickey Joe Clancy persuaded me into it,' she explained. 'And, of course, I've read all of your book and I was just so interested in the Vikings,' she added. She kept her face as blank as she could, but she had noticed that the repetition of the name of Mickey Joe seemed to bother him a little. He fiddled with his doodle again, drawing an elaborate set of interlacing spirals – Viking, perhaps. And then he put down the pen with an air of decision.

'No need to bring anyone else's name into this matter,' he said. 'I'll have a word with the president and tell him how interested you are and how many good suggestions you have made about my book. It was perfectly understandable that you should wish to see the house being built. No need to mention anyone else,' he repeated. 'The president will accept my word for it. I don't suppose that you saw anything that night which might be of interest to the police, did you?'

She thought about that for the moment. There was an odd note in his voice, perhaps a slight sound of anxiety. And the last sentence sounded more like an instruction than a genuine question.

'I'm not sure what you mean, Professor,' she said. And she watched him carefully. Yes, he did look somewhat worried. Then she said, and hoped that it sounded innocent, 'You mean about the riot, do you? You wouldn't have seen that, of course, as you went off early, didn't you?'

'Yes, I did.' He, too, watched her. 'As far as I was concerned, the business of the evening was over. I was due to have dinner with an elderly relative and so I left.' He had the air of one who is rehearsing an explanation and she wondered whether Patrick had talked with him yet. After all a woman was murdered in the house where he had gone to have his dinner, leaving his students in the midst of a riot on the quays. She nodded gravely with as good an air of understanding as she could produce.

And it worked.

He put his hand in his pocket and pulled out a ten-shilling note.

'You've been so very useful to me in the production of this book, Eileen,' he said in a gracious way, smiling kindly at her. 'I'm most grateful and have been meaning to give you a little present to compensate you for all of the trouble that you have taken.'

She pocketed it instantly. She was paid by the printing works to liaise with Cork University Press, this new publishing company that had been set up at the university by Professor O'Rahilly, but that did not deter her from accepting his money – or was it a bribe? She didn't care. He could well afford it, she reckoned, and it would come in useful to her.

'Thank you, Professor,' she said demurely. 'And thank you for sparing the time to see me. I feel so relieved now that you have promised to have a word with the president. I wouldn't like anything to get in the way of my studies.'

'That's all right, Eileen. Your bike back in action again?' He was determined to be pleasant and he smiled at her benignly.

It was only after she had left the room that it occurred to her to wonder how he had known that her bike had been out of action for a few days.

Interesting, she thought, as she went back to retrieve her bike. More of a link between him and Micky Joe than he would want to admit. Some strange goings on that Monday night on the quays in Cork. Two landlords murdered. One on Merchant's Quay, right out in the open, and the other, tucked up in her bed, a mile away, down on Bachelor's Quay.

And Professor Hendrick seemed to have been on the scene in both cases. She stood for a few moments thinking hard. What had been going on last night on the quays? She had an odd feeling that Mickey Joe knew more than he was pretending to know. It was, she thought, rather strange that Mrs Hendrick had been murdered. The other landlord was different. You could even have said that he went looking for trouble. And it was an accident, really. Drunk men, wound up to a pitch of terrible anger by those abusive words. That was it. Violence that went too far.

But Mrs Hendrick didn't go looking for trouble. Never showed her face. Employed a rent collector who took all of the abuse. And somehow, even if she had come out there on the quays and shouted to the men to get out of the pub, she would, thought Eileen, have been treated differently. Somehow she could not see those big hefty dock workers attacking a woman.

Nevertheless, the picture of that rope came to her mind. Why had the window in the centre of the house been left open on a foggy wet night? And why was the rope, that should have been wound around the bracket, left dangling down the wall to just above the pavement? No wonder there was a question over whether Mrs Hendrick had been murdered by a tenant.

CHAPTER 14

'What utter nonsense men do talk!' Lucy, once a couple of dreary hours had passed after lunch, had managed to inveigle the obliging Ann, or Philomena, into kindling a magnificent fire in the bedroom and, on the spurious grounds of the Reverend Mother's fatigue, to serve them with a mid-afternoon snack of tea and fat slices of homemade white bread that could be toasted in front of the flames. On the table was a huge teapot swathed in a hand-knitted cosy, probably the work of the industrious Julie. And beside it was a plate bearing a substantial, raisin-studded barm brack, just in case they were still hungry after the toast – this, Lucy declared, would keep them going until her husband arrived to collect them at the end of the day. The Reverend Mother would have liked to get back to the convent earlier, but a sense of obligation towards Julie and a slightly guilty enjoyment of Lucy's company made her decide to stay and to accept the proffered lift back to the door of the convent. Brenda was chatting with Julie, and Claude was busy with the police, but they, too, planned to leave at the end of the day.

'Nonsense?' queried the Reverend Mother. Her enunciation was not as clear as usual as her mouth was full of crisp, hot toast. She was slightly ashamed of herself but she had found a huge enjoyment in toasting her own bread and spreading it liberally with unsalted butter. It was as if her cousin and she were back in their girlhoods again and Lucy was declaring her opinion of their music master. 'Why nonsense?' she queried as she handed the toasting fork to her cousin and bit through the crisp, butter-soaked toast. 'I wonder, did Cousin Charlotte get that unsalted butter from the English Market?' she said when she had swallowed it.

'Probably. But don't get too fond of it. You can't afford it in your convent. It's twice the price of the ordinary salted butter. But to go back to the point. It's utter nonsense of Inspector Cashman to say that Julie would be better off living with Charlotte Hendrick than she would be in a little house of her own. I'm surprised that Dr Scher said nothing. I would have thought that any doctor would recognize that the poor woman is on the verge of a complete breakdown and has been so for years. You know, she led a terrible life here, Dottie. That woman! Yes, yes, one should not speak ill of the dead, but she was like a medieval torturer. She amused herself with little digs at Julie all day long. Talking about sharp scissors! Charlotte stuck a pin into Julie forty times a day. She used her and abused her. Surely that can be seen by anyone who meets Julie. She's a bag of nerves. I wouldn't be surprised if she did slash Charlotte's throat with the sharp edge of the scissor blade. She might have been thinking . . . I can just imagine her thinking: "*At least this will shut her up.*" And she might well have thought no further. Not seen the consequences, the police, the investigation and—' Lucy stopped suddenly, shook her head with a slight shudder and then examined her piece of toast carefully. She judged it to be perfect and went across to the table to lavish plenty of the expensive unsalted butter upon it.

'You see,' she said, coming back to her seat by the fire. 'Men, even men with a nagging wife, can get away from a woman. They go out to work, go to the pub or to their club or something like that in the evening. They don't think about how unpleasant a nagging, taunting woman can be if you have to be with her day after day, from morning to night. That young inspector probably has no notion of how much Julie had to put up with. I told you, didn't I? They hated each other. Charlotte and Julie just hated each other.'

'That puzzled me, though. I've been wondering what you meant.' The Reverend Mother had a great respect for her cousin's sharp brain and now she looked at her enquiringly. 'I can see why Julie should hate Charlotte. She was the one with the power and she abused that power. But why should Charlotte hate Julie? I'd have thought – if I ever did think about it – that she just despised her.'

Lucy frowned a little. 'Hard to say exactly. She

257

did hate her, though. I've seen her glare at Julie, some occasions when she didn't know that anyone was looking. I think myself that Brenda started it all – yes, I know, Brenda always seems very sweet-natured and motherly, but believe me, she gets a lot of fun out of setting people at odds with each other. She's one of these women that will repeat a piece of gossip and then clap her hand over her mouth and say, "Oh, I didn't mean to tell you that. Please forget it." And you see Brenda, despite her dowdy appearance, is very much "old Cork" – very "in" with all the Fermoy crowd and those sort and she would drop hints, tell someone in confidence, and she spread it all around that lot that Charlotte was very nasty to Julie – all meant to be a great secret – you know the sort of thing, but Charlotte found herself left off the list when parties were held by the Cootes and the Olivers and all of that crowd. She was no fool, was Charlotte. She soon got to hear the rumours that were circulating about her, but she blamed Julie for it.'

'In any case,' said the Reverend Mother, 'I suppose it's human nature to dislike someone who elicits bad behaviour from you. I see it often in the playground. That's often the way that bullying escalates. In fact,' she said thoughtfully, 'a school playground can be a microcosm of behaviour that will be hidden under the surface when the children become adults. But why do you think that Brenda did it? Why did she want to make trouble for Charlotte?'

Lucy shrugged. 'Who knows? She's such a bore, Brenda. She could spend half an hour telling you how she tidied out her store cupboard. And, of course, when she talked like that, people sidled away, but when she started telling gossipy stories of how vicious Charlotte was to poor old inoffensive Julie – the things that she said and did to the poor thing – well, she found people were listening to her and passing on the titbits to others. So, the result in the end was Charlotte heard from someone that people were talking about how unpleasant she was to Julie and that was why invitations began to dwindle.'

'I didn't know that Brenda was in with that crowd; surely they are all very monied, the Fermoy, Mitchelstown crowd,' said the Reverend Mother thoughtfully. 'It must have been a bit of a shock when her husband's business went downhill so rapidly. I suppose times have changed, but I remember them as being a very high-spending crowd.'

'Still are,' said Lucy briefly, 'but Brenda's husband is Church of Ireland, you know, and Protestants stick together. Like Charlotte. Her husband, James Hendrick, was also Church of Ireland and was always one of that crowd. Had pots of money, too, of course and that always helps. Yes, I think it must have been a bit of a shock to Charlotte when that lot began to drop her, you know, little by little, fewer and fewer invitations coming, excuses not to come to Bachelor's Quay. In fact,

I heard that the house was half-empty last June for the Cork Regatta and that had always been a big event, in the past. We didn't go because Rupert can't stand that boating crowd, and he makes me come up with an excuse every second year, but I did hear that hardly anyone came, except relations. Charlotte was furious and she accused Julie of gossiping about her. Brenda, of course, went. She never passed up on an opportunity to ingratiate herself with Charlotte and I'd guess that she memorized a few more spiteful stories. Of course, her husband's business failed at that time so that probably made Brenda desperate to ensure her legacy from Charlotte.'

The Reverend Mother sighed impatiently. She had begun to wish that she had not eaten that slice of barm brack. Her stomach was not used to such an abundance of rich food. It had given her a slightly sick feeling, a feeling of disgust. 'It's not a nice thought, is it, Lucy? There are all of these people, all of us. All wanting money, but all wanting it sooner rather than later. That's what bothers me.'

'That's right,' said Lucy placidly. 'Makes you think, doesn't it? You start to wonder why someone didn't murder her earlier than this. Perhaps Brenda and Florence are in it together. She's good with her hands, young Florence. Someone told me that she makes ornamental jewellery in her spare time. She could easily have a tool that would take the scissors apart. In fact, I seem to remember her showing one of Nicholas's boys how to make a leather boy scout badge. She had a very professional little set of tools. All sorts of things for making holes and screwing bits on and off – I didn't take much notice, but I thought that she was very good with her hands and had made some lovely and unusual jewellery. Come to think of it, she's a very likely suspect. She's fanatical about going abroad, going to places like Paris and St Petersburg, and these fanatics never let things get in their way.'

'And young,' said the Reverend Mother thoughtfully. She was very fond of the young, but she had long recognized that girls on the threshold of womanhood could have a very egocentric view of life.

'And she'd certainly know how to take a pair of scissors apart,' added Lucy. 'You know she's a funny girl. I've heard a few rumours about her. Just gossip, I suppose, but I know there was a bit of talk when Brenda took her over. The father died and the mother apparently took against the girl for some reason and went back to her own family. Brenda had no children. I suppose in the beginning it was supposed to be while the father was so ill. Apparently he couldn't stand the child. Odd family, the Clancys.'

'But not Brenda,' said the Reverend Mother gently. 'Brenda is a Clancy and you must admit that it was kind of her to keep Florence.'

'True. But, you know, now that I come to think

of it, there is something odd about that girl. No smoke without fire and I'm sure that Maureen Clayton told me that there was some scandal attached to her, some problem that Brenda was having with her, perhaps. The trouble was that she was whispering in my ear when we were having lunch at the Oyster Tavern and you know how noisy that place is at lunch time and all I could think of was that I was going to be late for my hairdresser. You know how irritable these people get when you are late. They pretend they are not, but then they give you a bad hairdo.'

The Reverend Mother, who had not been to a hairdresser for over fifty years and had never lunched at the Oyster Tavern, turned these pieces of information about Florence over in her mind. Aloud, she said, '"The world's a city of straying streets/ And death is the marketplace where all do meet."

'Shakespeare,' she added, as her cousin looked puzzled.

'What's Shakespeare got to do with it?' said Lucy with a tart note in her voice as she cut another slice of barm brack.

'Just thinking of those streets of Cork straying back into rivers, and rivers of gossip at the market-place,' said the Reverend Mother vaguely. She rather discounted the gossip about Florence. After all the child must have been only about ten when her father died. It was unlikely that any serious offence could be laid at her door at that age. But now she must be about eighteen years old. Could a desire to see Paris and to see Russian icons at first hand, she wondered, be enough to prompt a young girl to take the life of an elderly woman? Hard to know. It did seem a trivial reason. But an intense longing might have triggered, first a desire that Charlotte Hendrick would die quickly, and then the thought might come that it would be easy to get rid of her. The young, she knew from experience, could be very self-centred and determined that their own desires and needs would come first. All this talk about a will and all this encouraging of speculation about an inheritance might well have triggered a fatal desire.

'I wonder whether this was planned or whether someone took advantage of the riot going on in the quays,' she said aloud. 'That open window did seem to point to the fact that it might have a connection with that affair. But, of course, that could have been arranged to look like that. Very easy, Lucy, for someone to open the window, and uncoil the rope, wouldn't it be? We all popped out to the bathroom from time to time during the evening. So very easily done. May not have even been noticed as people passing by would be used to the rope being tested. We saw the chauffeur do it when we arrived. Remember?'

'And of course the wall is very dark, isn't it? Rupert was remarking on that one day when we drove down Bachelor's Quay. He was saying that he didn't know why she didn't get the bricks scrubbed. You have to do that in Cork with all the smoky fogs we get here. A dark wall and a rope hanging down – no one would notice it much, would they?'

The Reverend Mother was considering this when a soft knock came to the door. Lucy finished her barm brack in a couple of rapid mouthfuls and then went to the door.

'Just in time, Ann,' she said. 'The Reverend Mother and I have had a delicious afternoon tea and you had better take everything away now before I am tempted into eating more than is good for me. Do tell cook that it was the best barm brack I've ever tasted,' said Lucy graciously.

'Thank you, ma'am. I'll tell her. She'll be that pleased. And, I just came to say that someone is looking for the Reverend Mother. It's Eileen, Reverend Mother; Eileen MacSweeney from Barrack Street. Shall I bring her up? Or ask her to wait?'

'Ask her to wait in the library, please,' said the Reverend Mother. Lucy, she knew, liked a little nap in the afternoon and Eileen would be free to speak openly if they were alone. 'Don't worry, though,' she said aloud. 'I'll make my own way to the library. Eileen will be in the hall, won't she?' She noticed that Lucy had taken up her handbag and guessed that she wanted to give Ann a tip and so left the room straight away and was through the door as soon as she finished speaking. The girl had been very polite and most helpful and Lucy, she knew, was generous with her money. They would both be best without her presence.

She made her way thoughtfully down to the hall, thinking less of Eileen than of Florence Clancy. The girl had a strange background. She was beginning to remember some details now. Lucy was right. Some old story about the child and her grandmother, or was it the mother? It would come back to her. She dismissed a vain effort to retrieve it from memories of the past and concentrated on descending the stairs carefully. They were steeper than she was used to and once again reminded her of the antiquity of the house and the story of its original building.

She had reached the hallway when the door to the basement door opened, quite suddenly, quite abruptly. A figure shot out and then stopped and averted her head. The Reverend Mother gave her a keen glance. Florence had hidden her face, but not before the traces of tears and a flush of tempestuous rage had been noted. She stopped abruptly at the sight of the Reverend Mother and stood quivering. The girl, thought the Reverend Mother, looked very upset. For a moment she was sorry that Eileen was there, sitting primly on a hall chair, but then she decided that Florence needed five minutes to recover.

'My dear child,' she said gently. 'I was looking for you. Something I wanted to ask you about. Now come in here and I will be with you in a moment.' She opened the door to the library and ushered the girl in there. The room, she saw at a glance, was empty, but, in accordance with the high standards of the house, it was warm and comfortable with a fire burning brightly and the curtains drawn to shut out the miserable wet and the icy cold of outside. 'Stay there, Florence,' she said and allowed a note of command to steal into her voice. There were several decanters on a large cherry wood sideboard, crafted in the time of Queen Anne, she guessed by the tasteful ornate style, but she reckoned that Florence had probably downed enough alcohol during the morning. There was a strong smell of brandy emanating from her. 'Sit down by the fire, Florence, and I will be with you as soon as possible.'

And with that she closed the door gently and went out into the hall. Eileen was resourceful and intelligent. The two of them could perfectly well carry on a conversation here in the hallway with a good view of the stairs, the drawing room, dining room and library doors and the staircase, several yards away.

And so she sat on the chair next to Eileen and asked in a soft voice, which she knew would not carry, 'God bless you, my child. What is troubling you?'

Eileen smiled a little, probably at the word 'child', but soon grew serious. 'I'm in a bit of a quandary, Reverend Mother,' she said, also speaking in a soft, quiet voice. 'I don't really rightfully know what to do.'

266

The Reverend Mother waited. Eileen was decisive and articulate. She would sort her thoughts and then explain her meaning.

'You see, someone is putting a lot of pressure on me. They want me to say something, something that I know isn't true. There may be no harm in it, Reverend Mother . . .' She stopped there and then said abruptly, with the air of one who had resolved to be completely open and honest, 'The thing is, Reverend Mother, last night I was on the quays on Merchant's Quay for that Viking show. I thought it was just a bit of a laugh, though I have to admit that I knew that there were going to be speeches about the bad housing in Cork. But then it all went wrong.' Eileen stopped and bit her lip.

'One of the landlords decided to challenge the speechmakers – and his own tenants, also, was that it?' The Reverend Mother had heard the whole story from Patrick but she was interested to hear Eileen's version.

'It was my fault, in a way. You see Mickey Joe, the lad that I went with, asked me to show the speakers how to work the loudhailer. He showed me how to use it, but there wasn't much to it, really. Any old *amadán* could work it. It was more that he wanted an eye kept on it as he had borrowed it from the rowing club. Anyway, they all got on like a house on fire with it – the lads had gathered up a load of men who were willing to talk into it. Just grabbed it and yelled. Talked about the rent they had to pay and what their accommodation was like, they did well, all of them, but then this landlord came along and started shouting at his tenants . . .' Eileen stopped and a look of distress came over her face.

'I've heard about that. You heard him, of course. Was it very inflammatory?'

'Very! Called the tenants pigs. Said that they lived like pigs, but it was an insult to pigs to call them by that name. I didn't take too much notice. He was yelling his head off, telling them that if they spent the money they had earned from unloading the coal ship from Wales, that he would throw them, their wife and their children out on the street. Usual sort of stuff. These fellows are always sounding off like that. No one takes too much notice.'

None of the young students or young revolutionaries, thought the Reverend Mother. But she imagined the response of the men and women who were living in these conditions would have been sheer fury. Shame, even in the midst of some terrible household crisis, even when dealing with death itself, was strong within most. She had found that. Even faced with a dead child, her first task often was to reassure these poor unfortunate women that she wasn't shocked by what she saw of the conditions in which they lived. Humiliation and anger were a noxious combination. She said nothing, however. Eileen needed help and reassurance. She had not been responsible for the terrible events that had followed that inflammatory speech.

'What is it, Eileen?' she asked gently.

Eileen gave a half shiver, and shook her head violently as if to erase the images of the night before. 'It's Mickey Joe,' she said. 'He wants me to tell a lie for him. He knows that I am quite friendly with Patrick and he wants me to say something to him, casual-like. Patrick is here, I know, but I can't make up my mind . . .'

'That's Michael Joseph Clancy, the son of Mr Claude Clancy,' said the Reverend Mother. It wasn't a question. Most of the city knew who the flamboyant young Mickey Joe was. Always up to something, organizing something, getting into trouble, writing inflammatory letters to the *Cork Examiner*, getting his photo in that paper on at least a weekly basis.

'That's right.' Eileen now sounded more assured. 'That's the point, really. Patrick's sergeant went to see Mickey Joe and he more or less accused him of murdering the old woman, I mean murdering Mrs Hendrick so that his father would inherit some money.'

The Reverend Mother thought about that. It sounded rather far-fetched to her. Joe was an astute and reserved young man. She doubted very much that he was throwing an accusation like that around with no evidence to back it. 'Did the sergeant say how he could have done that?' she enquired.

'He said that a window had been left unfastened and that a rope had been left hanging down almost to the pavement and that Mickey Joe could have shinned up it and . . . and killed her then. He said that the whole business was planned to make a cover-up for the murder.'

Not a word of it sounded like Patrick's silent and conscientious sergeant, thought the Reverend Mother. Nevertheless, those thoughts may well have been in his mind. Aloud, she said, 'Do you think that he did that? That this Mickey Joe organized the whole affair to make a screen for the murder of Mrs Hendrick?'

Eileen shook her head. 'No, that's not like Mickey Joe. That's what bothers me. He's really not like that, Reverend Mother. He'd be more one to take advantage of an opportunity. And, why should he, anyway? He's not that fond of his father. Always complaining about him. Anyway, he wasn't one of the organizers, not that I know of, anyway.'

'So where do you come in, Eileen?'

'Mickey Joe wants me to say we were together all of the night, right up to this morning. He wants me to tell Patrick that.' Eileen avoided the Reverend Mother's eye, blushed scarlet and bent down to pick up an imaginary something from the carpet.

'But you weren't?'

'No, I got sickened by the whole thing and I just went off. I walked home. To be honest, I got a bit scared when I heard the police car siren. Didn't want to get involved.'

270

'So that is what you will tell Patrick if he asks you. I am,' said the Reverend Mother, thoughtfully, 'somewhat opposed to telling lies, unless the cause is a very good one, but, in any case, I seldom think that it is wise to tell lies on behalf of someone else. And, I am quite certain that, in this case, I think you should leave Mickey Joe to tell his own lies when and if his conscience allows him.'

Eileen's lips twitched, but she bit the giggle back with an adroitness that showed her one-time teacher that the girl was growing up fast.

'I think that you are right, Reverend Mother. Though I might tell Patrick that I don't suppose that he did do it, that he's not like that – works through other people. Gets people worked up and then, sort-of, melts away. Anyway,' she repeated with an air of relief, 'you've cleared my mind. I'll go off to work now, Reverend Mother. Professor Hendrick has suddenly decided to have lots of illustrations for his book on Viking Cork. It's doubling the cost and doubling our work at the printers, but still, if he wants to pay for it, who are we to say no?'

She got to her feet but then lowered her voice and said with a nod towards the library. 'That girl, Reverend Mother . . .'

The Reverend Mother had begun to move away, but then she turned back. 'Yes, Eileen.'

Eileen hesitated. 'Can I tell you something in confidence, Reverend Mother? I mean, *may I?*'

The Reverend Mother nodded approval at the

memory of grammar lessons, but took a moment of serious consideration before she answered the question. 'I think I'll have to remind you of what I always said when you were in school, Eileen. I will do my best to keep your words confidential, but you have to trust my judgement to do the best for everyone.'

'Yes, I see,' said Eileen. 'And I suppose that you are right. And I do trust you. It's a bit childish to worry about telling on someone when you should be thinking about keeping them safe, isn't it? Well, I just wanted to say that someone should keep an eye on that girl. How old is she, anyway?'

'About the same age as yourself,' said the Reverend Mother.

Eileen waved that aside with a quick gesture of her hand. 'Age doesn't come into it, really, though, does it. I can look after myself, but I'd say that she wouldn't be too streetwise. She's hanging around with that chap that works here, that chauffeur, and she was out on the quays with him last night. Ever so late, too.'

'Are you sure?' The Reverend Mother felt her heart sink a little.

'Yeah, quite sure. I noticed the marcel wave – not that I like them much, myself,' said Eileen with a toss of her head, 'but I do know that you have to have money to get your hair done like that – costs about a hundred pounds a year to keep it looking stylish, someone told me. This fellow, the chauffeur, Anthony Buckley is his name, well, he was boasting to me about her being his girlfriend and her being a lady with blond hair and a marcel wave.'

The Reverend Mother wasn't too sure about what was a marcel wave, but she presumed that it was Florence's hairstyle and trusted to Eileen to assess the expense of its upkeep. Brenda was fond of the girl and gave her everything, but this was serious.

'What time was she out on the quays?'

Eileen looked solemn. 'Must have been coming up to midnight, Reverend Mother. Stupid of her really. I wouldn't trust that chauffeur fellow, myself. Got a very nasty temper. Stupid of me, too, of course. I should have cleared off when I saw that chauffeur throw a rope at Mickey Joe. Should have guessed that there was going to be trouble.' And with a carefree wave of her hand, Eileen went off and left the Reverend Mother to her worries.

There was no doubt in her mind, though. She could not ignore that clear warning from Eileen. And, despite the similarities in age, she did appreciate that there was a huge difference between the two girls. It was injudicious of Eileen to be out on the quays at midnight, but Eileen could look after herself and would have had several friends in the vicinity. Florence, newly emerged from boarding school, would have a very different background. Brenda, she thought, would have to be told. She could not run the risk of keeping

Florence's guardian in the dark over the behaviour of her niece, her adopted daughter. But first of all she would have to see what Florence had to say for herself. With a sigh she went across the hallway and opened the door into the library.

Not a pretty hairstyle, this marcel wave, she thought, trying to be dispassionate about those tight waves and trying not to think about what one hundred pounds a year could purchase if the money wasn't squandered on that unbecomingly crimped hair. Still that was none of her business and she sat quietly down beside the girl on the sofa.

'Feeling any better, Florence?' she asked quietly.

Florence shot her an angry look. She must have noticed Eileen and suspected that she had been betrayed. Eileen would have been prominent last night if she had been dealing with the loudhailer.

'I wish people would mind their own business,' Florence's voice was aggressive. 'The world would be a better place if they did,' she added.

'Very true,' said the Reverend Mother. 'Only children and senile old ladies should be looked after. Everyone else should take responsibility for their own actions. Just as a matter of curiosity and since I am a very old lady, you might like to tell me whether you mean to marry this young man?'

'I don't know what you're talking about,' said Florence.

'He's got a job, of course,' continued the Reverend

Mother. 'He would be paid about thirty shillings a week, I suppose. That would be about seventy-five pounds in the year. Do you think that you could manage on that? Rent, food, clothing, hairdressers . . .' Her eyes strayed over the crimped blond waves and wandered down over the silk dress and cashmere cardigan. 'I fear, though, that you might have to give up the thought of going to Paris and to St Petersburg. That would be completely out of the question. And studies, also, might be out of the question, too. After all,' she said airily, 'a husband is usually followed by a baby, or two or three – one a year, quite often. Not too easy to study if you have a few howling babies around. And they do need a lot of feeding. And washing of their soiled napkins,' she continued, remembering rooms that she had visited.

A look of distaste came over Florence's face. 'I'm not thinking of getting married, Reverend Mother,' she said. 'And certainly not to a chauffeur!'

'I see,' said the Reverend Mother and she was conscious that her sympathy had begun to ebb away. Silliness she could put up with, but this girl had a calculating look about her. Was this midnight escapade with the chauffeur a means to an end?

'Why were you crying just now?' she asked. There had been a row, she guessed, and remembered Eileen's words about this chauffeur having a very bad temper. Eileen was shrewd and

275

streetwise and her judgement of people was usually fairly sound.

Florence looked at her, assessing her, thought the Reverend Mother. Wondering how soft she was, wondering whether she could fool this elderly nun. Brenda had been a loving mother to her orphaned niece, but had she been a sensible one?

'I'm just so upset about dear cousin Charlotte's death,' replied the girl. Her voice was vague, slightly apologetic, but her eyes were sharp.

'I suppose a lot of people in this house were upset when the will was read.' The Reverend Mother watched the girl's face. A heavy swathe of colour went across it. For a moment there was a look of fury in her eyes and then she swung around, went through the door and slammed it with unnecessary force behind her.

A pity really that she hadn't got more out of her, but perhaps she could guess what the row between the chauffeur and Florence had been. Perhaps a step had been taken that did not have the promised outcome. The rich widow was dead, but her demise had not profited Florence. With the exception of Nicholas Hendrick, all of Charlotte's relatives had been disappointed of a legacy. Disappointment, in the Reverend Mother's experience, mostly vented itself in recriminations. Perhaps the chauffeur was not prepared for a penniless wife. That would be another possibility.

She hesitated about going back to her bedroom. Lucy, she guessed, would by now be having her little nap from which she would emerge full of life and fun and brimming over with ideas. In any case, Eileen's last words had sparked an idea and so she went in search of Patrick.

CHAPTER 15

Patrick was with Dr Scher in the small estate office on the ground floor of the house. It was a comfortless but neat and orderly room, the walls lined with shelves supporting a series of upright box files. Each was labelled with the name of a street or a lane and each had a date below it. Some were out of date, had been sold, or the tenancy had terminated in the early years of the century, but all, including the modern files, were kept well dusted and were neatly arranged in alphabetical order on the shelves. There was a large desk with a well-cushioned chair behind it and a couple of uncomfortable-looking bentwood chairs in front of it.

A pair of easy chairs, taken in from the library, thought the Reverend Mother, identifying their patterned red-and-green upholstery, had been placed on either side of the stove that heated the room. Dr Scher sprawled in one and Patrick sat bolt upright in the other, while his sergeant, Joe, sat by the desk with a notebook open in front of him.

"'I should have cleared off when I saw that

chauffeur throw a rope at Mickey Joe. Should have guessed that there was going to be trouble." That is a quote from an informant and I felt that you should hear it,' said the Reverend Mother as Patrick got up from his chair and offered it to her.

'Thank you, Patrick,' she said, and looked at him to see his reaction to her words.

He perched on the side of the desk and gave a grin. 'Eileen told you that, I bet,' he said. 'Sounds like her. And she was there, right in the middle of the trouble as usual. I know that. Joe spotted her disappearing into a lane.' He thought about it for a moment and the smile disappeared. 'The chauffeur, the chauffeur from here,' he said with a frown. 'What was he doing there, out on the quays? He's not a tenant with a grievance. And he's not likely, with his job, to be a member of the IRA. You interviewed him, didn't you? What do we know about him?' He looked across at Joe.

'Anthony Buckley, age twenty-three. Has worked for the late Mrs Hendrick for nine years. Started off in the kitchen when he was fourteen and helped with the horse and then later with the car when Mrs Hendrick bought it five years ago. Took over from the previous man four years ago. Does odd jobs, general handyman as well as chauffeur. Never been in trouble.' Joe read aloud from his notes.

'And the rope?' asked Dr Scher.

'One of his duties is to attend to the old wheel and to keep it in working order. He may have a spare rope.' Joe turned over a page and then turned it back again.

'I can help you there,' said the Reverend Mother. 'When my cousin and I arrived at this house, the chauffeur had just replaced the old rope. He was testing the new one by sliding down it. A young cousin of mine had just arrived with her aunt and it may have been that he was keen to demonstrate his muscles to her, or, in fairness to him, it may be that he always tests the rope in that fashion. Though personally,' said the Reverend Mother, 'I saw no necessity for the display.' She searched through her memory. Yes, the young man had picked up a rope, coiled it and went off with it towards the back entrance in Grattan Street.

'So he had a spare rope and decided to donate it to the rioters. I think we'll pull him in on this, Joe, don't you?'

'As long as Eileen will give evidence.' Joe sounded doubtful.

'Plenty of people with hangovers littering our cells, and dying to get out of them by being helpful to the guards. You'll have a pain in your arm from writing, Joe, once you start to interview them.' Patrick's voice changed and became nonchalant as he said, 'I'll have a word with Eileen myself, though I doubt we'll need her in court.'

The Reverend Mother looked at him with interest, turning over in her mind an idea that had come to her some time ago. Both mothers would be delighted, of course. But would it work out?

Their personalities were so very different. Patrick, she thought, had seen her expression, perhaps guessed at her thoughts. He had a little extra colour in his cheeks and immediately changed the subject.

'I'm a bit worried about Miss Julie Clancy, Reverend Mother,' he said. 'She doesn't seem to realize that we have to check on details. She is reacting very badly to our questioning. She seems defensive and resents any questions. You would know her better than we, of course.'

With an effort the Reverend Mother switched her attention. This murder was an unpleasant affair. The death of a relation, a woman whom she had known since her childhood and the possibility that death had been caused by another relation. It was imperative that it be solved as soon as was possible.

'Do you suspect her?' she asked bluntly.

'Don't bully the boy,' said Dr Scher. 'At this stage everyone in the house that night has to be under suspicion.'

'Including me,' said the Reverend Mother. 'And there is no doubt that I would have liked to have some of that fortune which my cousin left.'

'Oh, you and Mrs Murphy give each other an alibi,' said Patrick hurriedly.

The Reverend Mother smiled indulgently at him. 'My dear Patrick, you must know that to be nonsense. Have you seen the size of that room? My cousin and I slept at least twenty, no . . . more like thirty feet apart, each in our own little curtained-off space. I would have no idea whether she got up in the night or not. I know that I did get up in the night when I heard a noise and thought the bathroom window had been left open. When that wasn't the case, I checked Mrs Hendrick's door and, as I told you, found it locked and convinced myself that I must have dreamt the sound of a bang and so went back to bed. My cousin, Mrs Murphy, had not heard me. She said so when I told her that I was disturbed in the middle of the night.' She stopped and thought about it for a moment.

'I suppose that what I heard might have been a window being pushed up in my cousin's room, or it may have been the wheel,' she said quietly when Patrick closed his notebook again. The sound still puzzled her. A window being opened did not make a sudden bang such as the one she thought had awoken her.

'Sounds as though it was an outside job, as Patrick here might say,' said Dr Scher.

Patrick pursed his lips and slightly shook his head with a half-smile. The Reverend Mother looked at him with interest. She had often wondered about the human brain and how long it goes on developing and expanding. Patrick, she was sure, was not only far more astute and intelligent than when he had first emerged from her school at the age of seven, but also, than when he had emerged from his primary education with the Christian

Brothers at the age of fourteen. The extra years of secondary education and then the years of study to become a policeman and to gain promotion had all added to his original potential. A feeling of anger rose within her at the thought that the Irish government, who had promised that all children would be equal, denied secondary education to all but the children of the rich and the very few who managed to get scholarships from the religious orders.

'I would imagine that Patrick thinks that the open window and the rope hanging down to pavement level might well be an effort to lay a false trail,' she said.

'Do you, indeed,' said Dr Scher looking across at Patrick. 'Well, if we are going to get these complications, I think I'll ring for some tea. I'm sure that Ann would oblige and I think better when I am fed and watered.'

'I wouldn't rule out an outsider,' said Patrick, as they waited for the bell to be answered. 'Or a pact between someone in the house and someone outside . . .' He hesitated and looked across at the Reverend Mother.

'You are thinking of my cousin Claude Clancy and his son, Michael Joseph,' she said and wondered whether he had yet questioned Eileen. Best if the story came from Eileen, she thought. Was Claude that desperate for money that he would involve his son in a murderous attack on an elderly relative? She thought not.

'I don't like this rope business,' said Patrick with a frown. 'I know that the rioting was half a mile away, at Merchant's Quay, but Cork is a city where people go to bed late. And out there on Bachelor's Quay! Even if there was no one on the quay itself at the time, a car or a bike could come along any minute. And what about people from across the river, walking along Pope's Quay? What do you think, Dr Scher? Could someone on Pope's Quay see a man coming down a rope from the top storey of the house?'

'Might have binoculars, or opera glasses, but then I'm an old man. I'm sure a youngster like yourself could see a man on a wall on Bachelor's Quay,' said Dr Scher as he went to the door.

The Reverend Mother looked across at Patrick's thoughtful face but said nothing for a few moments. He was, she thought, dismissing from his mind the idea of someone coming from outside and she believed that he was right to do so. With luck and audacity, or even if egged on by despair, it might have been done, but it was a less likely possibility. And what about the weapon? That lethally sharp piece of bloodstained steel was undoubtedly part of Julie's scissors. She turned the scissors over in her mind and then thought of something else.

'My cousin, Mrs Hendrick, never locked her door, Patrick,' she said. 'I'm not sure whether anyone has told you that, but I do remember in the morning that the maid, Ann, came up with the morning tea, as usual, but was unable to

284

get in and then had to go to fetch Miss Julie Clancy who, of course, as the person in charge of all household affairs, held a second set of keys to everything.'

'Yes, I know that,' he said slowly and there was a worried note in his voice. 'We picked that up, didn't we, Joe?'

'Was in the maid's evidence,' said Joe with a nod in the direction of the door where, though it was now closed, the voice of Dr Scher and the light, young laugh of Ann could be heard.

'Made us think,' said Patrick. 'A woman with her throat cut wouldn't – couldn't – walk the length of that huge room, lock the door – not cry for help, or anything, but lock the door – and then well, what next? We haven't found the key, have we, Joe?'

'Mrs Hendrick's key was always kept in the drawer by her bed, but the maid, Ann, said that she never locked the room. She has been working in the house for a few years and she said that the bedrooms were never locked normally. The only room that is often locked is the estate office and that is because there is pots of money there, sometimes, or so she said. She cleans the rooms, so she should know.'

'Do the kitchen staff hold a set of keys?' asked the Reverend Mother, but she guessed the answer before he shook his head. 'No,' she said in reply to her own question. 'I don't suppose so. But I suppose Mrs Hendrick had a spare set somewhere . . .'

'Locked in the safe and the key to the safe was in the poor lady's handbag,' said Joe. 'But, of course . . .'

Both he and Patrick were looking at her rather uneasily and the Reverend Mother understood. The name of Julie hung in the air between them but she was reluctant to utter it, or to say much more about keys. She waited until Dr Scher finished negotiating the matter of the mid-afternoon snack and returned to the room, but then it could not be put off any longer, and so she said, 'So perhaps the key to the bedroom door that is normally kept in the drawer by her bed may have been taken by the murderer if he had escaped by the window. He or she,' added the Reverend Mother, feeling that she could not be unfair to the male sex. After all, many women now wore some form of knickerbockers for cycling and horse riding. And Eileen, copying her idol, the rebellious republican, Countess Markievicz, wore a practical pair of tweed breeches when riding her motorcycle.

'There is another alternative, an alternative, I mean.' Patrick corrected himself. 'I think, don't you, Joe,' he said, 'that if the murderer did possess a key, then she, or he, could have merely locked the door on the way out, perhaps in an effort to avoid premature discovery of the body, before the murderer reached his or her bedroom,' he finished. 'The key might have ended up in the river.' He had addressed his remark to Joe, but the Reverend Mother knew that he wished her to hear it.

'And apart from the key in the bedside table and the spare set kept locked up by Mrs Hendrick, there was just the set that Miss Julie Clancy possessed.' Joe looked from his superior over to the Reverend Mother and then cast his eyes back down again to his notes. 'The kitchen staff didn't have any keys. The doors in the house were kept unlocked normally. If there was any reason to lock a door they had to ask Miss Julie Clancy to do it.'

'I see,' said the Reverend Mother. And she did, indeed, see. Poor Julie, everything always went wrong for her. Somehow, though, she did not see her as a murderess. It was time that she lent a hand.

'My late cousin, Mrs Charlotte Hendrick,' she said, 'was a great reader of detective novels, especially of the Agatha Christie novels. According to my cousin, Mrs Murphy, she was wont to say: "I usually guess the murderer because I always follow the money. I look to see who is going to inherit."'

'So in this case we look at Professor Nicholas Hendrick,' said Dr Scher.

The Reverend Mother bowed her head. 'He gets the entire fortune now as it stands, but who is to say that Charlotte Hendrick would not change her mind next week or next month. She was a woman very easily offended.'

'So, the good lady sends for Nicholas, tells him that she's made a will leaving everything to him,' said Dr Scher. 'But . . .'

'But she wants to appear fair and so she had decided to stage this elaborate charade where everyone had a chance to lay claim to her fortune if they could be persuasive enough,' said the Reverend Mother. 'Knowing her, she would not be able to resist putting in a slight threat that she might possibly change her mind.'

'Sounds like her, not that I ever met Mrs Hendrick, but I know what elderly ladies are like, and it fits in with what I've heard of her,' said Dr Scher with an air of self-satisfaction which made the Reverend Mother raise a sceptical eyebrow at him, though her mind was busy with thoughts of the unfortunate Julie Clancy who was almost bound to say or do the wrong thing.

She would, she decided, encourage this talk of Nicholas for the moment. Nicholas could look after himself. He was quick-thinking, articulate and would have plenty of money to finance the best possible legal advice. Julie, she thought with pity, would always say the wrong thing, would be her own worst enemy. And Florence, a girl barely past childhood, could she have been involved or perhaps just dropped a hint to the chauffeur? Brenda, she thought, was an unlikely suspect, despite her husband's need for money, but the police were bound to focus on Julie. Already Joe, at Patrick's request, was reading through her evidence from his notes. She only half-listened to the muddled, hysterical-sounding words. There was something at the back of her mind, some thread of thought that she needed to follow before everything became plain to her.

'She keeps correcting herself and saying she didn't mean what she said.' Even the discreet Joe sounded slightly exasperated.

'And we mustn't forget those scissors were hers,' said Patrick.

'That scissor blade was undoubtedly the weapon,' said Dr Scher. 'I would be pretty sure of that. Fits the wound exactly. Lethally sharp!'

He looked around the room, looked back at the Reverend Mother with an apologetic grimace and shrugged his shoulders. He had sensed her worries about Julie. She gave him a nod. Facts were facts and should not be changed because of individual sensibilities.

And then there was a silence for a moment or two. 'But would she have been able to take the scissors apart?' asked Dr Scher, with a note of hope in his voice. 'She seems a sort of incompetent . . . I just can't imagine her . . .' And then he, too, fell silent, his eyes upon Joe.

'We found the carpenter's tool, I'm afraid,' said Patrick. 'Joe found it. It would have done the job – a very well-made, small screwdriver. It was in Miss Julie Clancy's bedroom. Under her bed! The odd thing is, though,' said Joe looking around the room, 'it wasn't there earlier on. That room had been searched and I was there when that was done. I could swear that there had been nothing under the bed at that stage. I only found the screwdriver because Miss Julie Clancy asked me to search her room again, demanded that it be done and I only told the constable to do it just to calm her down – but then we found this screwdriver.' He waited for his words to take effect before he said, 'It's odd, really, but apparently young Miss Clancy, Miss Florence Clancy, had told her cousin, isn't it . . .? Anyway, she told Miss Julie Clancy that her aunt, Mrs Brenda O'Mahony, had told her that the screwdriver was probably hidden under Miss Julie's bed.' Joe took a deep breath.

Thereby hitting two nails with the one hammer. Getting both her aunt and her elderly cousin into trouble. The young have little mercy, thought the Reverend Mother, and not for the first time.

'One screwdriver must look like another screwdriver,' she said aloud.

'Not in this case, I'm afraid. The chauffeur has all of his tools marked with a blob of white paint and a number written in indelible ink on top of it. He's a very tidy man and has them all in their own place in a wooden box. He showed me his box. It definitely is a screwdriver belonging to the chauffeur.' Joe, once more, read from his notes.

Patrick raised his eyebrow at the Reverend Mother and then returned to Joe. There was an air, almost, as though this might have been a rehearsed performance. 'Very good, Joe,' he said. 'And has Mrs O'Mahony any explanation of how she knew that the screwdriver was under the bed of Miss Julie Clancy? You told her, did you not, that her niece had reported this piece of information?'

'When questioned, Mrs Brenda O'Mahony denied saying this to her niece, denied ever mentioning a screwdriver at all. Hadn't even thought about a screwdriver. She said that her adopted daughter was so upset by the murder of her father's cousin that she didn't know what she was saying.' Joe concluded his recital in a deadpan fashion.

Patrick gave an impatient sigh and spread his hands apart. 'It all sounds ridiculous to me. The screwdriver was, in all probability, used to separate the two halves of the scissors, turning one half into a lethal weapon – it's just the right size for the job, but why keep the screwdriver? Why not replace it in the box? Or throw it away? It could have been thrown into the river or left in the vase where the bloodstained scissor half was found.'

'I think,' said the Reverend Mother, 'that you should not spend too much time on this matter. I think it is highly likely that Florence, who, I understand, is friendly with the chauffeur to the extent of visiting his lodge, took his screwdriver, put it under Miss Julie Clancy's bed and then tried to cause some trouble. And if you ask me why,' she finished, 'I can only say that she may have felt herself, rightly or wrongly, to be under suspicion. That midnight escapade would have certainly not just caused her trouble with her aunt and guardian, but also have made her an object of suspicion to the police. Yes, I do think that it is possible that Florence put the screwdriver there.'

'And wanted to implicate her cousin, Miss Julie Clancy?' Dr Scher looked across at the Reverend Mother.

'Yes. They are first cousins, once removed. Florence's late father would have been a cousin to the late Charlotte Hendrick, to Julie and to her brother Claude,' said the Reverend Mother. She shut her eyes for the moment and thought about that summer weekend that Lucy had recalled to her memory. She could see clearly in her mind's eye that sunlit garden belonging to her grandparents. The house had been built in Blackrock, on the side of a steep hill overlooking the River Lee at a point shortly before it entered Cork harbour. She had almost forgotten the house, but she remembered the garden very clearly. She could picture the children. Herself and Lucy, older than the others and slightly bored. Julie about four, she thought, Claude in his pram, Brenda catching butterflies and dipping their heads into a killing jar filled with poison, Brenda's brother, Jack, Florence's father, practising his cricket skills and lobbing balls for the gardener's boy to retrieve. The boy should have been attending to the rose bushes, but Jack had persuaded his grandmother to sanction the boy's release. A very persuasive and manipulative boy. The Reverend Mother wondered whether Florence had taken after him. And Charlotte? Yes, Charlotte was there, too; would have been eight or nine, she thought, visualizing Charlotte trying by various means of threats and bribery to persuade all of her cousins to take part in one of the many plays which she had written that summer. She wasn't having much success. The older ones were bored by the idea, and the only enthusiastic one, Julie, wanted to be a princess and had been in floods of tears because Charlotte had told her that her hair was too short and she was too ugly to be a princess. Julie had been in a bad humour all of the afternoon, fits of bad temper alternating with hysterical sobs and saying that no one liked her and everyone preferred her baby brother. Was there, she wondered, any significance in Lucy's story. She remembered the incident clearly now. The low stone wall, the road just beyond it and the thick hedge of cotoneaster to one side. Neither pram nor baby had come to any harm, but it had been a frightening moment. Had it ever been brought up again to Julie as she grew older? Hopefully not. But if so it might account for the woman's perpetual sense of grievance, her dependency and her resentment, her fear that she was going to be blamed for anything that went wrong.

'"The child is father to the man",' she said aloud and then added, 'Wordsworth,' as she saw them look at her. She said no more. An idea had come to her, but she needed to think about it carefully.

There had been enough angry words, enough festering suspicion. Before she spoke out, she would have to be very certain. And she herself might have been guilty of an injustice.

CHAPTER 16

'I've just popped in to make a citizen's complaint, Patrick,' said Eileen brightly. She had walked past the sergeant in the outer office so quickly that he had not had time to put down his newspaper before she was through the door to the corridor and she had opened Inspector Cashman's door with a perfunctory knock.

She closed the door behind her firmly. Patrick, she thought, looked very weary and had black shadows under his eyes. If he wasn't careful he would be old before his time. The headlines on the *Cork Examiner*, pointing out that a week had elapsed and the police had still not solved the murder of such a prominent citizen, would have upset him badly. 'Well, go on,' she said, 'get your notebook out, Patrick.'

He gave her a tired smile. 'I don't normally deal with citizens' complaints. We've got a new constable who will write everything you say down in his brand-new notebook. Why don't you go and see him, Eileen; go on, make his day.'

Eileen picked up a chair from the side of the

room, carried it across and, once seated, put her
elbows on the desk.

'This is serious,' she said.

He sighed heavily. 'Well, come on, then, out with
it. I'll give you three minutes so don't make a long
story out of it. I'm busy.'

'I'm being harassed by Mickey Joe Clancy,' she
said.

'Well, harass him back,' he said impatiently.
'I'd say that you'd be a match for him. Or else
just say *no*.'

'I have, again and again. He wants me to give
false evidence. I'd have thought that you would
be interested in false evidence – about a murder.'

'That business on the quays?' he asked quickly
and she smiled a little. Witnesses who would talk
about that affair with the landlord, she guessed,
were almost impossible to find, although the quays
had been packed when the police had arrived.

'No,' she said, and for a moment her face
became very serious. 'No, not that. I could give
evidence, but it would be of no use to you as I
didn't know any of those people and don't think
that I would recognize any of them if I saw them
again, not with the river mist and the fog and
not much light. I don't think that I would give
evidence, anyway, so that is lucky, isn't it? You
won't have to torture me.'

'So what are you here for? Come on, Eileen, I'm
tired and I have a lot to do.' He did sound a bit
down, she thought and decided to come to the point.

'Well, you know the night when Mrs Hendrick was murdered. Mickey Joe wants me to tell you that he spent that Monday night, all night, with me.'

Very old fashioned, Patrick, she thought with amusement. He had gone very red and then a bit pale. Embarrassment, no doubt. Thought that she was still a little girl playing around Barrack Street. Joe mustn't have told him what Mickey Joe said. Very shy, some of these policemen types. She suppressed a smile.

'And did you? Are you making a statement?'

'No, of course I didn't. But I'm sick to death of being harassed by him. He tried to get me into trouble at the university, keeps threatening that he will swear that he saw me with a broken bottle in my hand attacking that man who died. Everywhere I go, he turns up and starts pestering me. Even got me thrown out of the library. He says that you all suspect him and his father so he needs an alibi.'

'Why doesn't he come and see us if he thinks he has been unfairly treated. Or ask his father to do so.' He had calmed down again now and was tidying the pencils, lining them up meticulously according to size, in his already tidy desk tray. 'Or does his father, also, think that he had something to do with the death of Mrs Charlotte Hendrick?'

'Well, the word on the town is that they were both in on it. That the father opened the window, dropped down the rope. Mickey Joe came swarming up it, killed the rich, old lady and went off down again, down the quays.'

'And did he?'

Patrick was in a strange mood, thought Eileen. This case was dragging on and getting him down. A week now since the old woman was murdered. He needed a bit of help. She shook her head.

'Mickey Joe says that everyone knows who's done it. Says that the family have been expecting this for years. They were all having a good laugh about it, he says, and they don't care that he's been questioned by the police. Mr Clancy, Mickey's father, says that it will keep the police busy for the moment, but that they are not really stupid enough to think that he and Mickey had anything to do with it. They know who cut the woman's throat.' Eileen tried a look of wide-eyed innocence at Patrick and was pleased to see how annoyed he looked as he rolled a pencil rapidly between his fingers.

'You wouldn't like to tell me who the guilty person is, would you, since no one else thinks it's their duty to inform the police. I'm sure that we'd be very grateful for some hints.'

'You know, Patrick, you're not the kind that sarcasm suits,' said Eileen. 'You're more of a Douglas Fairbanks, than a John Barrymore type, you know; more of the man-of-action than the suave, sarcastic type. But I don't mind passing on the hint. Apparently it's the woman who lives with her, one of the cousins, Miss Julie Clancy. Mickey Joe says that she stabbed the old woman with a pair of scissors – but you know that, I'm sure. It's just a bit awkward, isn't it?'

'I'm not sure why or how young Mr Michael Clancy thinks he knows all about how Mrs Hendrick was killed, but if he does have any information then he should bring it to the police,' said Patrick. He had a wooden-faced expression and did not look at her.

'Is he really under suspicion? Mickey Joe, I mean?' asked Eileen.

'I'm afraid that I can't discuss that matter with you.'

'You should do. I might give you some tips.' Patrick was irritating when he put on that stiff manner. 'For what it's worth,' she added, 'I wouldn't say that he has enough gumption, myself. It would be a bit stupid, anyway, to be climbing up a rope outside the house and in through a window. Anyone could see him. You can't think that he is that thick, can you? Wouldn't it make more sense if his father left a back door unlocked so that he could sneak in, cut the woman's throat and then sneak out again? Anyway, I can see that you don't want to discuss the matter so just you tell Mickey Joe to stop trying to harass me into telling lies.'

'On your way out, could you just pop in to see Joe – you could perhaps mention your problem with young Mr Clancy, and when you finish with him, ask him to come into my office,' said Patrick and Eileen gave him a grin.

299

'Cheer up, Patrick,' she said, standing up. 'You've a face as long as a fiddle. What's the matter?'

She didn't really expect to get an answer to that question and was surprised as she reached the door to hear him say, quite slowly, and almost as if it were despite himself, 'I think that I know the truth, Eileen, but I don't think that I will be allowed to go any further.' He had said it so quietly, almost under his breath, that she was unsure as to whether she had heard him correctly and after a moment's hesitation, she closed the door quietly behind her.

'You didn't tell him that Mickey Joe said that he had spent the night with me, did you?' she said when she barged into Joe's office. She sat on his desk and admired the shine on her boots.

'How's the old bike going?' asked Joe.

'Don't change the subject,' said Eileen severely. 'I bet you didn't. Tell him, I mean. Thought that it would bring a blush to his cheek, didn't you?'

'We don't talk about witness evidence or statements.'

'God, you're beginning to sound like him. I suppose that means that you didn't; that you have enough intelligence to know that Mickey Joe was lying, getting himself out of trouble by telling lies. Anyway, what's the matter with him?' She jerked her thumb towards Patrick's room.

'He's worried,' said Joe.

'Of course, if it was someone from off the streets

murdered *yer wan*, nobody would give a toss about slapping them in gaol, would they?' said Eileen getting to her feet. 'Oh, and himself, the high and mighty inspector, himself, wants to see you so you'd better hop in there like a good boy. He's in a very bad mood today.'

CHAPTER 17

'Thanks for coming over, Dr Scher.' Although the superintendent was present, and the meeting was taking place in the superintendent's office, Patrick was determined that he was going to be in control of the proceedings. It was his case. A woman had been murdered in her own bedroom and the matter could not be allowed to drop. After all, there was a man facing trial and probably the death penalty for that other death that night. Whatever about a possible argument between a verdict of murder, or a verdict of manslaughter for that death resulting from the riot on Merchant's Quay, the woman in the big house on Bachelor's Quay had undoubtedly had her throat slit, would have died almost instantly and that crime was definitely one of murder. It could not and should not be hushed up and a trial had to take place. Someone who has killed once will kill again, he told himself. He ignored the chair in the corner that had been allocated to him and took his place standing beside the superintendent's desk.

'Do sit down, Dr Scher,' he said. 'I've just got

a few questions for you.' And before the superintendent could take over the proceedings, he began
to tick off the items in his mind. He needed no
notes, he had been over and over this matter, had
debated them over and over again, night after
night, as he walked up to the top of Barrack Street
and gazed down upon the sleeping city while he
sought to find a different answer.

'On the night of Monday, the first of February,'
he began, 'the dinner party at Mrs Charlotte
Hendrick's house on Bachelor's Quay broke up
at half past eleven. The seven guests and their
hostess all went up the stairs together and retired
to their respective rooms. I am fairly firmly of
the opinion that one of these guests murdered
Mrs Hendrick. I think that the business of the
open window and the rope was meant to mislead
us. Cork is a city where people go late to bed. I
can't see any murderer climbing a rope out there
on the quay where he could be seen from across
the river even if there was no one on Bachelor's
Quay or on Grattan Street who could have seen
him. So we have to think about those seven
guests, all of whom expected to inherit money
from Mrs Hendrick. Now, why I asked you to
come here, Dr Scher, was that I wanted to ask
you whether you could be wrong about the time
of death?'

He stopped and waited. Dr Scher was looking
at him in a puzzled way.

'You said, you see, that you estimated the time

of death to be between twelve and twelve thirty p.m.,' Patrick went on. 'Now, Mrs Hendrick went into her room at eleven thirty and here is what the guests did. Mrs Rupert Murphy and the Reverend Mother shared a room. Each used the bathroom, chatted for a while, but both, according to the Reverend Mother's evidence, were asleep by twelve thirty. Mrs O'Mahony shared a room with her niece, or adopted daughter, Florence. They were, according to the evidence of both, probably still talking at about twelve thirty. In any case, Mrs O'Mahony was worried about her niece who was feeling upset and so she went down to the kitchen to get her some hot milk shortly before half-past twelve. One of the maids heard her in the kitchen so I think that story is correct. Now, the two gentlemen, Mr Claude Clancy and Mr Nicholas Hendrick, although they did not share a bedroom, occupied rooms on either side of the bathroom which they did share. It appears from the evidence that the doors to the bathroom were left open and they were smoking and talking until about half-past twelve when Mr Claude Clancy went to have a bath. Fifteen minutes later he ran the water out from his bath. Mr Nicholas Hendrick gave evidence that he distinctly heard the water gurgle and felt annoyed because he had just been dropping off to sleep. He said that he lit his bedside candle and he looked at the clock on the mantelpiece and saw it was a quarter to one on the dial. He called out something, some joke, and the other man replied . . .' Patrick stopped and looked across at the doctor.

'Go on,' said Dr Scher.

'There were seven relations of Mrs Hendrick present on that evening,' went on Patrick. 'I have named six, all of whom can vouch for another, probably to a degree of reasonable certainty, between twelve and twelve thirty that night. The seventh, Miss Julie Clancy, slept nowhere near to anyone else. Her bedroom is on the Grattan Street side of the property, up on the very top floor, which means, of course, that if you think about the way this house was built, it was not far from Mrs Hendrick's bedroom. A short walk around the passageway that connects the four gables would lead her to her employer's much more splendid bedroom. However, because she was not near to the other guests, nor to the servants, no one can vouch for her.'

'Go on,' said Dr Scher again.

'The case against Miss Julie Clancy, the evidence that she might have been the person who cut the throat of her cousin seems fairly strong,' Patrick continued. 'She, like the other members of the family present that night, was of the opinion that Mrs Hendrick was going to change her will, which had originally divided all of her estate evenly between her seven living relatives, and was going to leave everything to Nicholas Hendrick. This decision was a disappointment probably to the others, but to Miss Julie Clancy it was an outright disaster. During all the years when she worked for Mrs Hendrick she had received no salary, although of course she had been housed, fed and I understand was permitted to buy her clothes at Mrs Hendrick's expense and was given from time to time small sums of money to cover items like bus fares, presents, newspapers and such things. Not a very pleasant existence, I suppose, but a reasonably secure one. But if the entire fortune was left to Nicholas, then she might face being put out on the street. Unlikely, but I can understand her panicking at the idea. And panic,' said Patrick, 'can lead someone to an action which might seem quite extraordinary to anyone who knew them well.'

'Stuff and nonsense,' said the superintendent angrily. 'A lady like that to cut her cousin's throat. It's impossible.'

'The field is fairly narrow, unless, perhaps, Dr Scher feels that death could have taken place at about half past one in the morning, because that seems to be about the earliest time when the guests in the house ceased to be aware of each other and went off to sleep. In other words, if the murder took place from about half past one onwards then the field opens up,' said Patrick. 'Not only could it have been anyone within the house, but it seems more possible that someone from outside could have got into the house without being seen or heard. I understand that lights were being switched on and off and bathrooms being used until about

306

that time.' He looked hard at Dr Scher and watched the man shake his head.

'I would doubt that I would be that far out,' he said firmly.

'Half past twelve rules out the other six relations in the house and probably rules out anyone coming in from outside. The quays on either side of the river were still quite crowded at half past twelve. Anyone swarming up that rope would be bound to be seen. No, if you are fairly sure that it couldn't have been an hour or better still a couple of hours later then . . .'

'Then you feel that Julie Clancy is your suspect,' said Dr Scher. 'That would be a hard decision. Would you see her hanged?'

'Exactly,' said the superintendent.

'I am concerned with finding the truth,' said Patrick defensively. 'What happens next would be a matter for the court.' Stubbornly he said no more. Not a matter for me, he repeated to himself. Let the relatives, with the connivance of the super-intendent, fudge something. Mental illness, he supposed. Some sort of nursing home. Nicholas Hendrick would have enough to pay for it. The man would be one of the rich of Cork city. He wouldn't want a scandal like that either. He knew what the relatives would want to do, of course. Just blame it on one of the rioters. That would be the solution that the superintendent would like, also. He set his lips firmly and gazed above the top of the superintendent's head.

'Perhaps Dr Scher would have a word with the Reverend Mother,' said the superintendent, with a sudden sound of hope in his voice. 'Do that, Patrick. Take Dr Scher over to the convent. She's a cousin. She will know if there has been any hint of insanity in the family. She would be the person to talk to. Do that. No time like the present. Thank you, Dr Scher. What would we do without you?' And the superintendent turned back to his papers with an unmistakable air of dismissal.

CHAPTER 18

'Oh, my dear Patrick. Oh no! Oh, that's not right at all. You mustn't think that, Patrick.' The Reverend Mother was startled and overcome with remorse. She ignored a school bell which meant that she should be taking her regular Tuesday afternoon literature class with the older girls. Sister Mary Immaculate would have to cope. This was more important. She should have spoken before now.

He did not say anything for a moment. Did not ask her what she meant. There was a slightly stubborn expression on his face and she could see that there was a struggle going on between his trust in her and his feeling that he had to do his duty.

'I'm sorry, Reverend Mother,' he said. 'I know that she is your cousin, but you see I must do what I think is right and I have to be . . . I have to be impartial,' he finished and she hastened to reassure him.

'Of course,' she said vigorously. 'Yes, of course, Patrick. You must do what you feel is right. And, of course, I will accompany you to Bachelor's Quay . . .' She stopped for a few seconds and

309

appeared to be thinking hard. 'It's my fault,' said the Reverend Mother. 'I thought, you see, that I would wait until all the fuss about that grandiose funeral with the bishop and the clergy, all of that would be over and done with and then I would talk to you. I should have spoken earlier.'

'You wanted the good lady to be buried peacefully,' said Dr Scher. He spoke with an air of kindly understanding, but the Reverend Mother did not reply. She was thinking hard.

Patrick, she saw, waited and she knew that he did not want to make this too difficult for her, knew that he was sorry that she had to be involved. He had, moreover, she realized, no doubt in his mind of having found the right culprit and she would have to convince him of the true solution. She frowned slightly, passing her beads through her fingers in an absent-minded way. Then she raised her head decisively.

'I'm sorry to put you to this trouble, Patrick,' she said, 'and you, Dr Scher, but I think that in advance of any questioning of my cousin Julie, I would like you to listen to what I have to say. This matter should be dealt with immediately, but before I say any more I think that we should, all three of us, go over to Bachelor's Quay. I presume that the door to my cousin Charlotte's bedroom is still locked, Patrick, and that no one but the police have access to it, but . . .'

'I have the key to it,' said Patrick. She could see that he wondered what she wanted from the room, but he was in the habit of obeying her and he would not question her. He was, she thought, relieved that she had not refused to be present when he charged Julie Clancy with the murder, and no doubt he, always a sensitive boy, would think it was a good idea to carry out the arrest of an elderly lady within the house, rather than asking her to come down to the barracks.

'You'll come too, Dr Scher?' he asked with a certain note of anxiety in his voice. Presumably Patrick thought poor Julie would collapse into a fit of hysterics and Dr Scher should be on hand in order to administer a strong sedative and then there would be a nursing home. The Reverend Mother guessed that Patrick could go no further than an arrest in his thoughts. She had known him now for over twenty years, and knew how stubborn he was. He would, she knew, stick to the notion that justice would have to be seen to be done, that the law had to be impartial and she felt a certain pride in his righteousness in a city where money and position often took preference over simple justice.

'I'll go with Dr Scher,' she said firmly. 'We'll meet you there, Patrick. I have a few matters to see to and you will want to go over there straight away.'

'Very well,' he said, and she knew that now his mind was made up he would feel that the sooner the job was done, the better. He would want to ensure that Julie was not smuggled away by a relative or did not get any wind of what was in store for her. An arrest had to take place. That would be his duty.

Dr Scher did not speak on the five-minute journey from St Mary's of the Isle to Bachelor's Quay. He drove with more care than usual and without his normal cheerful abuse of other users of the road. Troubled about this business, thought the Reverend Mother, but she said nothing. She was too busy arranging her thoughts, too busy looking back into the past.

They were quicker than Patrick had expected. She saw him standing in Charlotte's room looking out of the window when Dr Scher's battered old car drew up beside the pavement. He did not come down to meet them, although he would have heard the doorbell and could hear their footsteps coming straight up the marble-tiled staircase. But when they were shown into the room, he came back from the window, pulled out an easy chair for the Reverend Mother and a pair of bedroom chairs for himself and Dr Scher. He said nothing. His face looked deeply troubled. And yet, she thought, he must have made hundreds of arrests during his years at the barracks.

The Reverend Mother, ignoring the chair, went straight across to the window. She opened the window and looked up, scrutinizing the wheel above.

'No one has touched it, not since that morning, have they, Patrick?' she asked.

'That's right. I myself just hauled up the rope,

looped it around the bracket and left it there.'
He looked at her enquiringly.

He would have done it with his usual efficiency, she thought. Would have held the rope firmly with one hand and looped it around the bracket with the other hand. If only he had been more slap-dash the truth may have been uncovered earlier.

'Of course,' she said, 'no one paid much attention to Julie when she told the solicitor that the pulley wheel was jammed. That is the problem, I often find, with people who talk quite a lot, as poor Julie certainly does. You cease to listen to them and then sometimes miss something of vital importance. Patrick,' she added, 'I wonder, could I trouble you to lean out here and pull out the object that is blocking the wheel from turning? You will need to unwind the other end of the rope from the bracket before you do so.'

She stood to one side while he followed her instructions obediently and then climbed on to the windowsill, holding on to the bracket with one hand and reaching with the other hand up to the wheel. He gave a slight exclamation almost immediately. She guessed that his fingers had felt something unexpected.

'A piece of string, no, a cord,' he said, correcting himself. He seemed to fumble with it, leaning over a little more until he found the knot. 'Something metal tied to it,' he said over his shoulder to Dr Scher, who had taken the Reverend Mother's place at the window.

'Need a knife? I have a good, little sharp one,' Dr Scher offered as he also leaned from the window.

'Got it, got it untied.' Patrick straightened, slipped back on to the floor and then looked at the object within his fingers. His eyes were wide with astonishment.

'It's the missing door key and . . . But that's the murder weap—' he started to say and then stopped. 'It's not; it's the other half,' he continued slowly. 'It's the other half of the scissors, of Miss Julie Clancy's dressmaking scissors,' he said then. 'No sticking plaster on the handle of this one.' He closed the window and came back into the room, looking from the objects in his hand to the Reverend Mother.

She leaned forward in her chair and nodded. 'The extraordinary thing, Patrick, is that once one half of a scissors was found in the vase of dried flowers on the hall table, none of us, certainly not I, even thought of asking where the other half had gone.' She looked at the piece of metal in his hand. 'I think that you'll find, Patrick, the two halves will screw together. There is, of course, no stain of blood on this half. It has, after all, remained for seven days and nights outside in the rain and the mist, but it is, I would venture to guess, the half which cut Charlotte Hendrick's throat. There was blood on the one found in the vase of dried flowers, but that was to lead the police astray. Blood is an easy commodity to find. I'm sure Dr Scher will inform you as to how many pints of blood there are in the human body – a scratch from a needle, a pinprick from an injection scab – it's very easy for a person to find some of their own blood without much trouble. The door key, I suggest, was necessary as a weight to help to hold the scissor blade in place.'

Patrick took a clean handkerchief from his pocket and carefully wrapped the sharp object, the cord and the key within its folds. Acting almost automatically, he took a large envelope from a cubby hole on Charlotte's desk, sealed the wrapped package within, wrote his name upon it and added date, time and location. Then, wordlessly, he passed it and the indelible pencil across to Dr Scher. The Reverend Mother looked at him with approval and waited until the doctor had signed his name and added a date and a time.

'My cousin, Mrs Murphy, is a very astute observer of people,' she said, 'and I think that a remark she made when we were talking over this wretched will stayed at the back of my mind. And I wish that I had realized its significance sooner, but I will tell you now what she said. I had suggested that the fairest legacy would have been for Charlotte Hendrick to leave her money to the woman who would be destitute otherwise. I pointed out that Julie Clancy had served Charlotte all of those years, almost as a slave serves her mistress, without salary or independence. But my cousin said immediately, and her words made such an impression on me that I will repeat them now:

315

"No, she'd probably love the idea of disappointing Julie. They hate each other, really." She was of the opinion that this dependent relationship had fostered a mutual hatred.'

'Giving Miss Julie Clancy an additional motive for murder,' said Patrick. He said it very quietly, but the Reverend Mother turned towards him instantly.

'Bear with me for a moment, Patrick,' she said. 'I need to go through this matter very carefully, because the conclusion that I have come to may appear quite fantastical to you both.' She stopped for a moment and thought back to that sunshine-filled garden of her grandparents and of the little girl, many years younger than she and Lucy, but strong-willed and determined, always writing plays and always wanting to direct everyone in their roles.

'Of course, the significance of the open window and the uncoiled rope escaped us all,' she said regretfully. 'Poor Julie could have escaped suspicion if I had thought about the significance of that. I should have done so. I knew that wheel; I had seen how it worked.'

'I am totally bemused,' announced Dr Scher. 'What are you saying, Reverend Mother? Why does this mean that Miss Julie Clancy did not commit the murder? Is this what you are saying?'

'That is what I am saying,' said the Reverend Mother. 'No, Julie did not commit the murder. She was the scapegoat. Somehow I always felt that she was a scapegoat, but I did not realize who actually did commit the murder until I was brooding over the past. The child, they say, is the father of the man. No, Julie did not commit a murder,' she repeated. 'The death of Charlotte Hendrick lies at a different door.'

'And if she didn't, well, who did? Who committed the murder?' Dr Scher, once again, was the one to ask the question. Patrick, noticed the Reverend Mother, sat very stiffly upright and the expression on his face was quite blank.

'There was no murder,' stated the Reverend Mother. 'But two crimes were committed. One against the laws of God, and the other against the laws of man. But no, no murder. What occurred here in this room on the night of the first of February was,' she said, speaking slowly and very distinctly, 'a suicide and also, more unforgivably, what I would term as an attempted murder.'

'A suicide,' exclaimed Dr Scher, but Patrick said nothing. His mind, thought the Reverend Mother, was working through the events of the last few days, sifting the evidence.

'Charlotte Hendrick,' said the Reverend Mother, 'committed suicide. I suspect that she may have had cancer. She was seen returning from Dublin on the train, seen coming out of the station in a taxi by Sister Mary Immaculate who thought she did not look well; another time met on the train by her cousin Brenda who was astonished to see her coming back from Dublin as it was well-known that Charlotte hated shopping trips. Brenda, Mrs

O'Mahony, also commented that Mrs Hendrick looked unwell. I, myself, did not think she looked well, and she had certainly lost a lot of weight. Her mother, I remember, died of cancer, as did one of her uncles and she may well have feared the worst for some time. She was, of course, an intensely private woman and, knowing the tendency to gossip in Cork, may have gone to a specialist in the city of Dublin to have her suspicions confirmed.'

'And so she took the easy way out.' Dr Scher knitted his brows. 'Understandable, sometimes,' he added, while Patrick looked at the Reverend Mother with an expression of total bewilderment.

'She was always someone who planned everything to the last detail,' said the Reverend Mother gravely. 'First she planned her funeral, eschewing the rather sober rites of her adopted Church of Ireland. She went to see the bishop, arranged all with his lordship, the lying-in-state at the cathedral, etc., and then, to make everything quite certain, she wrote down, almost as though it were a theatrical performance, the arrangements for her funeral. And then,' she continued gravely, 'she went a step further. She arranged a dramatic murder mystery as if she were in an Agatha Christie or a Dorothy Sayers mystery novel. She ensured that her relations would be in the house and would all have a motive to murder her.' The Reverend Mother stopped for a moment and then said, 'Although at the same time the arrangement of the bedrooms, the sharing of rooms and of bathrooms which she had decreed, ensured that most would have an alibi.'

'Suicide,' said Patrick almost to himself.

'As Dr Scher says, understandable. But what I think is not so understandable and is, to my mind, a very grave sin indeed, is that she tried to get her cousin, Julie, convicted of her murder,' said the Reverend Mother firmly. 'She worked it all out, you see – stage-managed it, you might say. As a child she was obsessed with writing plays for her cousins, wrote parts for all,' she said and stopped and thought for a moment about Charlotte. The child, she now recognized, thinking back, was probably quite gifted. She remembered how she and Lucy, almost ten years older, had laughed at the clever mimicry of family members, the sharp observation of characteristics and favourite sentences. Undoubtedly a clever child, she thought now. It may have been that early marriage, a childless marriage, had not provided any outlet for her gifts and they had festered within her and left nothing but bitterness and spite to take the place of all that bright promise. Charlotte, she thought, had planned out the ultimate stage piece, a deadly murder mystery. All the cousins, many of whom she disliked, thought the Reverend Mother, were gathered together beneath her roof, gathered on a strange pretext, so that they were all present on the night when her throat was cut. 'It may have been,' said the Reverend Mother, 'her original idea to set up her possible heirs as murder suspects, though at the same time arranging for shared and adjoining rooms, so that all might be exonerated eventually, but then perhaps it turned to a darker purpose when she decided that she would have a victim; that she would use half of Julie's scissors as a weapon with which to cut her throat. It was,' said the Reverend Mother, 'a particularly clever plan. Of course her arrangements for a grandiose funeral would have come to naught if there had been any suspicion of suicide, something that is deemed to be a mortal sin, a sin without forgiveness, in our church, Dr Scher, and condemns the body to a burial in unconsecrated ground. So it had to be deemed a murder. And why not settle a lifelong hatred of a cousin at the same time?' The Reverend Mother paused, looked from one man to the other and said in a low voice and rather sadly, 'Charlotte Hendrick planned Julie's ruin at the same moment as she planned her own death and the subsequent pomp and ceremony of her funeral.'

'I'm still bemused,' said Dr Scher. 'You wouldn't like to explain it a little more simply to an old man, Reverend Mother, would you? How on earth did she do it?'

The Reverend Mother looked kindly upon him. She was, she recognized, tense and worried and the sound of his matter-of-fact and humorous voice helped to firm her purpose.

'Yes, a strange matter, indeed,' she said. 'You see, you, Dr Scher, did not have the benefit of growing up in this city and looking up on the wheel during

Sunday morning walks as I did. It's just a simple pulley. If you pull down one side of the rope, the other side goes up. Charlotte knew that if she pulled down the knot, tied the scissor to it with the cord taken from her sponge bag, held the sharp-edged scissor blade and cut her throat – why, then as soon as her fingers opened and released her hold on the rope, this short end of the rope would fly up and the scissor would be hidden by the cover of the pulley while the other end fell down to ground level. The young chauffeur here compared it to a seesaw – when one side goes down, and in this case weighed by sixty feet or more of heavy rope, the other side flies up.' The Reverend Mother looked from one face to the other and nodded as she saw comprehension dawn.

'And, of course,' she continued, 'when the other half of the scissors was found in the vase of Julie's dried flowers on the table in the hall, stained with blood, but still very identifiable as Julie Clancy's scissors because of the piece of sticking plaster, well, then, suspicion was bound to fall upon poor Julie. Charlotte had, of course, prepared that false clue before going to bed. And once the police came to sift the evidence and it was discovered that the other people within the house, all of whom were sharing bedrooms or a bathroom, had believable alibis, why then the conclusion that Julie Clancy was the guilty person became unavoidable.' The Reverend Mother folded her hands within her sleeves, sat back and looked from one man's face to the other.

'I should have done an autopsy,' muttered Dr Scher. 'I'll remember this case. Always do an autopsy even if the cause of death is shouting aloud. I'd have discovered the cancer.'

The Reverend Mother said nothing. She, herself, felt quite shaken by the events which she had uncovered. Such malice, such hate, such demonical ingenuity.

Patrick was the first to recover. He gave a brisk nod, scribbled for a moment in his notebook and then looked across at her.

'And what comes next, Reverend Mother?' he asked with a simple faith which touched her.

She answered him instantly with no attempt to dodge the question or to pretend to false modesty. 'What needs to happen now, my dear Patrick, is for the law to take its usual course. There will be, I suppose, a coroner's inquest and I hope and should imagine that you will manage to convince the coroner that this was a case of suicide. It might be,' she suggested, instilling a note of diffidence into her voice, 'a useful thing to have photographs of the wheel, perhaps evidence about how it works from the chauffeur or some inhabitant of Bachelor's Quay. Some of these magistrates may not understand too readily. And, of course, Dr Scher's sworn witnessed account of how the instrument of death was found entangled within the wheel, will, I am sure, prove to be of great assistance.'

The Reverend Mother stopped and thought for a moment as Patrick wrote in his notebook.

Another idea had come to her and when she spoke again her voice noticeably lightened. 'I should imagine,' she said briskly, 'that here in Cork, where we don't like to confront unpleasant facts face to face, especially those connected with a well-off and prominent citizen such as Charlotte Hendrick, I should imagine that the verdict of the court will be: "suicide while the balance of her mind was disturbed". Which,' she added with an air of satisfaction, 'should be enough to ensure that the last will of Charlotte Hendrick, made only a few weeks before this suicide, could well be declared invalid and the earlier will, made several years ago, reinstated as a true testament to the real wishes of the deceased. That would seem to me to be the correct solution to this most unpleasant business,' finished the Reverend Mother.

It gave her immense pleasure to picture Julie's face when she realized that she would not be destitute, and to know that Florence could achieve her heart's desire and develop her brain and increase her learning in a way that surely God must approve; that Brenda would have a reward for her selfless devotion to her abandoned niece; that Claude would save his business; Lucy would have the pleasure of making extravagant presents to her daughters; and that the poor children of her own school would benefit from the money. She would reserve some, she decided, to sponsor secondary education for those who wished for it. She would not follow the Christian Brothers' model of offering schooling only to the clever and industrious, but would use the money to prepare girls of all abilities for adulthood and develop their minds so that they had the wisdom to make correct choices. Nicholas, she thought dismissively, would have enough to keep him happy.

Her patron saint, Thomas Aquinas, had spent a long time debating whether good could come from evil and had decided that it could not. '*Bonum ex integra causa, malum ex quocunque defectu*': that was his summing up. She was unable to remember all of his arguments just now, but she decided that if they met in an afterlife she would roundly tell him that he was wrong. His mentor, St Augustine, living hundreds of years earlier, had held a different view: from an evil plan, laid by an evil woman, good could come forth.

'My dear Patrick,' she said warmly, 'what a worthwhile vocation this is that you have chosen! The innocent to be protected and the guilty to be punished. And the troubled world to be set to rights. I'm sure that you will manage the coroner perfectly, but of course, if Mr Burke wants any background information I shall be more than happy to have a private word with him before the hearing takes place. I knew his father well and I'm sure that he is an intelligent man.'